W9-BDT-504

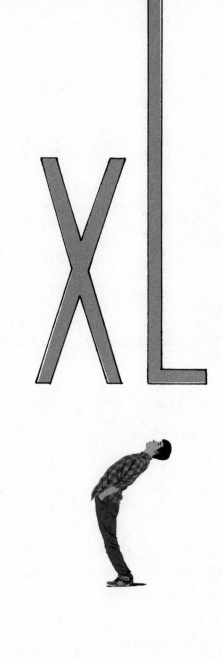

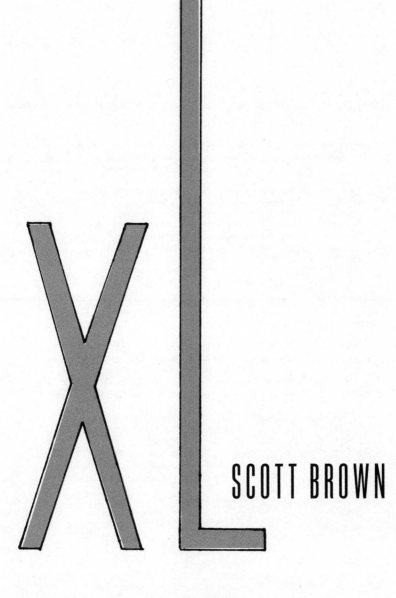

SCOTT BROWN

Alfred A. Knopf New York

THIS IS A BORZOI BOOK PUBLISHED BY ALFRED A. KNOPF

This is a work of fiction. Names, characters, places, and incidents either are the product of the author's imagination or are used fictitiously. Any resemblance to actual persons, living or dead, events, or locales is entirely coincidental.

Text copyright © 2019 by Scott Brown
Jacket art copyright © 2019 by Paul Blow

All rights reserved. Published in the United States by Alfred A. Knopf, an imprint of Random House Children's Books, a division of Penguin Random House LLC, New York.

Knopf, Borzoi Books, and the colophon are registered trademarks of Penguin Random House LLC.

Visit us on the Web! GetUnderlined.com

Educators and librarians, for a variety of teaching tools, visit us at RHTeachersLibrarians.com

Library of Congress Cataloging-in-Publication Data
Names: Brown, Scott, author.
Title: XL / Scott Brown.
Description: First edition. | New York : Alfred A. Knopf, 2019. | Summary: "Will has always been troubled by his short stature, but on his sixteenth birthday, he starts to grow—and grow, and grow."—Provided by publisher
Identifiers: LCCN 2018017597 (print) | LCCN 2018023478 (ebook) | ISBN 978-1-5247-6624-5 (trade) | ISBN 978-1-5247-6625-2 (lib. bdg.) | ISBN 978-1-5247-6626-9 (ebook)
Subjects: | CYAC: Size—Fiction. | Growth—Fiction. | Stepbrothers—Fiction. | Dating (Social customs)—Fiction. | Self-esteem—Fiction.
Classification: LCC PZ7.1.B (ebook) | LCC PZ7.1.B (print) | DDC [Fic]—dc23

The text of this book is set in 11-point Janson MT Pro.

Printed in the United States of America
March 2019
10 9 8 7 6 5 4 3 2 1

First Edition

Random House Children's Books supports the First Amendment and celebrates the right to read.

For Katie, Zoe, and Harry,

the troop I'd follow anywhere

And for Pat McDonagh,

who loved little things

and made the world tremendous

"THE PROBLEM WITH monsters," Monica (5′10″) liked to say, "is that monsters *win*."

"And we fight 'em anyway," I'd finish. "Unless you've got a better plan?"

"Nope," she'd come back, with a smile and a shoulder punch. "We few?"

"We happy few."

Our motto. Written in flame. Engraved in gold, or bone, or something even deeper. Stolen from all the books Monica'd ever read, which was a lot of books. We'd recite our motto, and toast *us* with any beverage in toasting distance. Us against the darkness.

Then a gorilla would throw its own shit at another gorilla, and I'd make a note of that in the Aggression Log. Those were our afternoons in the Lowlands, the zoo's gorilla habitat, where I interned three days a week, shoveling, slopping, mopping floors, and updating the Aggression Log (which always needed updating). I kept the gorillas company, and Monica kept me company, and we talked about monsters because Monica had a library of monsters in her head and a smile as rare and bright as that sword-of-legend-drawn-only-at-the-crucial-moment. A smile that made the monsters worth fighting. That made you want to be a lover *and* a fighter. Two things I was pretty sure I'd never be.

See, in the thousand or so fantasy books Monica had read by the time she was seventeen, there were, I dunno, a thousand or so monsters. All defeated. By perseverance. By imagination. By faith. And by the big gun: love.

But there's another kind of book. The book where none of that shit works, and the monster isn't beaten. We just live with it. It hurts us, a little or a lot. We hurt it back. Things go on like that. And finally the monster wins. Or at least lasts.

"That's where *we* live," Monica would say, "in *that* book." By seventeen, she was done with fantasy. She loved those stories. But she didn't believe in them.

Monica believed in monsters. Because she'd met some. She believed you fight them, not because you're a hero, not because it's awesome—but because you *have* to. And odds are, the monster beats you anyway. To a pulp or to a draw. Those are your options. Somehow Monica made that sound epic instead of terrifying. Gorillas got us philosophical, I guess.

They don't "talk" the way we do, but gorillas are just as sophisticated, and way more straightforward. Now, I say *gorillas,* and it conjures up all the brochure photos: gorillas grooming, gorillas playing, the stuff zoo-goers pay good money to see. But from Keeper Access? Where I worked? I didn't see gorillas. I saw *personalities.* There was Blue, our resident manic pixie dream gorilla, doing spur-of-the-moment headstands and offering a bite of mango to anybody, ape or human, who looked hungry. There was Magic Mike, the scrawny beta male, the clown, the comedian—strutting, then tripping, maybe on purpose, maybe not. I loved those gorillas. I *knew* them.

And then there was Asshole.

Not his real name. I mean, jeez, who knew his *real* name? Something in Gorillese, something blunt and grunty you shouldn't argue with. He was the alpha male, the biggest, the strongest. The silverback. The zoo called him Jollof. Why, I don't know. In West Africa, jollof is a popular savory rice dish. In the Lowlands, it was the vastest asshole known to ape- or humankind.

Jollof was definitely a monster by Monica's definition—by any definition—and Jollof, with precious few exceptions, did indeed *win*. He'd hoard all the treats distributed to the troop, and when he'd finished stuffing himself, he'd crush or stomp or spoil most of what was left so no one else could have any. Classy. He'd randomly attack the other males, totally unprovoked—a bite out of nowhere, a casual swat (that probably felt like a full-tilt pile drive from the Chargers' defensive line) just to remind them who was boss. Jollof would also mount any and every female at the drop of a banana. And he wasn't much of a romantic, let's leave it at that. But all that chest-beating alpha shit? (Literal shit—'cause throwing shit is a varsity sport among primates, and Jollof was a star quarterback.) It wasn't a character flaw. It's who he was. His job, his place. What evolution built. Nature made a monster, and it was my job to feed it.

And I was great at it. Better than anybody on staff. Because when *I* walked into the habitat, instead of fluffing up his fur, snarling, mock-charging—his usual routine—Jollof would bound up to me, all goofy-sweet, turn his back, and sit at my feet. Like a faithful dog, asking to be scratched behind the ears. Nice. Right?

Wrong. It was a dominance display. Like an emperor permitting a back rub from a concubine. (A word Monica taught me, of course.) It was a ritual to remind me of my place. Not that I needed reminding. My place was obvious.

I was almost sixteen years old. A nice guy, with a nice life, in every way but one.

I was four feet, eleven inches tall.

I was the 1 percent. The *bottom* 1 percent. Peel up the lowest height percentile: I was *under* it. I was the tile nobody bothered removing when they installed the lowest percentile.

And Jollof, from the bottom of his hairy scrotum, knew this. Knew my status. Which made it okay to accept the food I brought. I wasn't *giving* it, after all. It wasn't mine to give. It was Jollof's to take. I was just *serving* it, like a good underape.

Still, I loved the Lowlands, Jollof and all. It was way better than the other ape house I inhabited: my high school. Jollof, at least, was honest. No loincloth of charm or irony or *Lighten up, bro!* draped over the basic, brutal biology of it all. "The loincloth we call Civilization," Monica was fond of saying, "isn't fooling anybody."

It wasn't fooling her, at least. Nothing fooled Monica, or so I thought. She was seventeen, so close and so out of reach, and I couldn't begin to say how I felt about her, couldn't put words to that music even after six sad years of trying. What if the words were wrong? Would she just disappear? Or *ascend*, like the heroes in those fantasy stories she'd outgrown? I was terrified of finding out. Terrified of losing all at once the girl I was already losing a little at a time. I desperately needed everything to change, and I desperately needed nothing to change. I'd almost run out the clock. Monica was approximately seventy weeks from freedom, from putting all the little tyrannies of high school behind her, and she didn't believe in any civilization bigger than "we happy few."

She believed in monsters.

Anyway.

This is the story of how I became a monster.

PART ONE

HOBBIT

ONE

4'11"

I WOKE UP to the smell of fear.

You know what fear smells like? When you're not quite five feet tall? And turning sixteen?

Cake.

Maybe that's just me.

For normal people, birthdays—the cake, the singing, another candle every year—signify impending adulthood, which is so exciting, you actually appreciate the lame-assery that comes attached. But for us Smalls, birthdays never lose that paper-hat vibe ... because that's all there is to them. Seeing your name in baby-blue frosting, year after year, from the same exact altitude—well, it has a way of shaming your testicles right back to where they descended from. In my crazier moments, I used to think the parties themselves were keeping me small. Which is why I'd come to dread the sound of two little words:

"Will! Breakfast!"

My dad is such an awful actor, it's almost charming. He's just too straightforward by nature. His inability to fake anything—it makes him a great dad. Makes him a natural with zoo animals, too—zoo animals like a straight talker—so that works out well for him professionally, as a zookeeper. But it makes him just *awful* at surprise parties. "Will! Breakfast!" was something my father said precisely once a year. On my birthday. My big day. My big, smoking crater of a day. I woke up, smelled cake, and thought, *Oh, God, no.*

Which is kind of a shitty thing to think when a cake's been baked for you.

But consider this: a birthday's a promise. *Something changes today!* By birthday the sixteenth, I'd discovered otherwise. Every promise had been broken, five promises running, because biology, God bless, can be a real dick sometimes.

So I stalled in bed. Faked a sleep-in for a precious half hour. Any longer, and masturbation would be suspected. This birthday, like all the rest, just needed to happen as quickly as possible, then vanish again. So *I* could vanish again.

That was my top-ranked fantasy on the morning of my sixteenth birthday. Invisibility. To be a shadow. *He who slips past, unseen.* With one (very notable) exception, that was as wild as my dreams got. Slipping Past Unseen was how I planned to get through high school, in the hopes that college would be better. And if it wasn't? I'd slip past that, too.

There was just one thing I wanted to take with me. Just one person I wanted to be seen by. That Notable Exception.

She's why I wanted to slip through this day with as little trouble as possible and get to what would happen next, the thing I didn't even dare name, even though I'd spent the last fortyish nights imagining it.

But first: cake. Should I just rip off the Band-Aid? Or attempt evasive action?

I considered the sycamore outside my window. I could shinny down the trunk in twenty-five seconds, if I had to. Which might've been impressive in a dude of normal proportions. When I did it, I looked like a performing lemur. Something you'd reward for the effort with a slice of mango and a pat on the head.

Have I mentioned how deeply, how *furiously* I hate pats on the head?

Anyway, I got dressed, like a good lemur. A grateful lemur, desirous of cake.

I took a deep breath and padded downstairs, right into the teeth of it: my birthday ambush.

"Birthday ambush!" my dad barked, in a voice usually reserved for lemurs that hopped the fence. He came toastering up from behind the love seat—an impressive, slightly scary, always embarrassing maneuver for a middle-aged man, especially one of above-average height.

My father, Brian Daughtry (6'1"), the zoo's chief primate keeper, was the right size for a keeper. He had *presence*, like a force field that didn't feel forced. It was just this funny assumption of control—nothing bullying or desperate about it—that calmed nervous animals and also nervous people who were afraid nervous animals might eat them. He oversaw the primate staff, gave presentations to all the bigwigs and VIPs who toured the zoo, and spoke gently and evenly to reporters when the rare animal died on the zoo's watch. He also had great hair. My stepmother called it That Irish Mane. I called it Humble Hero Hair.

Brian Daughtry presided over things: bad things, good things, anything.

You preside *over* things, y'know. Not under them. Is my point.

Anyway, as Brian presided, Laura (5′8″) glided into the living room with a blazing cake and a half-sung "Happy birthday, Will!" and her perfect yogurt-commercial brunette ponytail swinging. Laura advised food shippers on safety and best practices. She believed passionately in safety and best practices, and she had the greatest handle on stepmomming I've ever seen in a stepmom. She didn't try to mom me, for starters, and she didn't try to friend me, either, or freeze me out. Laura was simply and plausibly Cool, without attempting to be Cool. She was what they call "at home in her skin."

I appreciate that quality in people. Always been a little low on it myself.

"Happy birthday!" Brian sang horribly. "Happy birthday, baby, oh, I love you so! *Six. Teen. Candles!*" No oldies, no matter how golden, were safe from Brian Daughtry.

A little behavioral biology for you: when Large Things advance on a Small Thing, singing screamy falsetto and brandishing flaming baked goods, the Small Thing's natural, paleomammalian reaction is to back up. Which I did—

—and collided with something as solid as a basketball goal.

Something that *was,* in a sense, a basketball goal.

"Whudup, Willennium. Ready to become a man?"

And there was Drew (5′11¾″). Number 38. "The Special." Lewis Keseberg High School junior varsity basketball's pride and joy. Keseberg *varsity* basketball's future. And my almost brother. My near brother, my blood brother.

"What happened to practice?" I asked. Drew, as a rule, did not miss practice. He was grateful for every nanosecond of practice he got, because every nanosecond brought him closer to fulfilling the Plan.

It hadn't started without a hitch, the Plan. But Drew kept at it.

At five foot nine last fall, as a sophomore, Drew hadn't made the varsity squad, got kicked to JV with the peewees. That didn't sit right with him. By February, Drew was scraping six feet and schooling the league, averaging twenty-six points a game. People (randos, not just parents) actually showed up to JV playoffs that season, just to watch "Spesh" dunk on what Monica called "lumpen Lilliputians." Drew was, that very night, widely expected to put away St. Augustine, the Keseberg Junior Harpoons' nearest competitor, closing out an undefeated season. For him, it would be just another game. He'd already enrolled in a postseason league to keep himself sharp for next fall. He wasn't just aiming for varsity, he wasn't just aiming to start. He'd *started*. The Plan was under way.

The Plan was multipronged, and we were all part of it: Drew, Monica, and I.

Drew had his eye on the University of California, San Diego, which had been teetering on the brink of Division I status for years. The Special's plan was to be there when it tipped in, to shine on a Cinderella team, to burn through March Madness and maybe, I dunno, humiliate Duke or something. A boy can dream.

Some can even reach what they dream without a step stool.

UCSD was just one aspect of the Plan. The Plan was bigger

than all of us, even Drew. But Drew was definitely the keeper of the Plan, and Drew's basketball career was a key part of it (his test scores sure weren't), and that meant Spesh had practice all the time. Afternoons, mornings, weekends. Nothing got in the way.

Nothing, apparently, but this one little thing. My birthday.

"Will Daughtry's turning sixteen," he said. "Screw practice."

"'Screw' practice?" Laura said to Drew, arching an eyebrow. She could mom Drew, just like Brian could dad me. Either parent could parent, of course—we weren't anarchists!—but momming and dadding? Those were dedicated lanes. And the first rule of any blended family is *Stay in your lane.*

Now, the fact that Drew was skipping practice to be part of my birthday? My feelings can only be described as *deprazing,* which is Monican for "simultaneously amazing and depressing." Amazing because this was game day, the Finals, a very big deal for Drew, for the whole damned *school,* and he was 100 percent giving up something precious to celebrate little old me.

Depressing because I was so grateful to him for it.

And it was costing him, I could see. Spesh looked solid, serene as an off-duty aircraft carrier resting in harbor. But his eyes were dancing like the world was on fire. I could see it: he was fidgeting to be gone, to be back under the boards.

Like I said: deprazing.

There'd been a time when I didn't have to read Drew's body language. That time was back when there'd been less body language to read, and less Drew overall. Back when we'd been flying at the same altitude. When we'd been happy just to be the brothers we weren't. When nobody had to feel grateful for anything. That was age ten.

When he'd *started*. And I'd stopped.

"William Daughtry," Drew said, backslapping me, "you look like five Benjamins."

"Why, thank you, young man," I said, recovering from the impact and playing my one card. (I'm two months older.) "I'll let you know what fully licensed driving's like. And congrats to you, too: you're pushing three and one-half Benjamins yourself, adjusting for inflation." (Drew and I misspent our youth building this massive rotation of beyond-dumb riffs on the phrase *You look like a million bucks.*)

"I'll be honest, dude: I slipped you an extra Benj 'cause it's your birthday. But if you're going to be a pube about it, I'll have that back."

Laura clucked at Drew for *pube* and put down the cake. I blew out the candles. Everybody clapped.

Nobody asked what I'd wished for. Nobody needed to.

Laura brought a knife over; Brian pulled up a chair. I cut the cake and saw Drew glance at his phone. Yeesh. Time to mercy-kill this sad-ass ritual.

"Thank you all," I said. "Thank you so much. To my family, to my agent, to my pediatrician, who inspired the whole idea. She said, 'What if you got older every year and eventually turned sixteen?' And I said, 'That's brilliant, I'm in.'"

"This guy, this guy!" Brian guffawed daddishly. "What a comedian!"

Hooboy. I wanted out of this lovefest, pronto.

"In short"—*Jesus, did I just say that?*—"I'm very proud. And I love you guys. And now I gotta get to school." I didn't, actually. I'd wangled a first-period study hall.

"Now hang on, hang on." Brian held up a presiding hand. "Aren't we skipping a key stage of hominid development?"

Huh? Brian wasn't above a random lecture, especially where hominids and behavioral biology were concerned. But this seemed *really* random.

"Mobility," said Brian. "Mobility's big with diasporic hominids. And you're sixteen . . . and a birthday . . . implies a *present*. . . ."

And then, out of this word salad, he pulled out . . . the Keys.

I blinked. With my whole Brain and Being. *Wait. Is this . . .*

Drew, grinning, gestured toward the door like a game-show host. "Shall we?"

I walked outside in a kind of daze. The door swung open in slo-mo, sunlight filled the foyer at the speed of honey, and . . . I saw it. I saw it *before I saw it*. Past my climbing sycamore, sitting in the driveway radiating an electric-blue sheen that made the air around it vibrate—

A car. *My* car.

There was just one problem. One . . . *small* . . . problem—

Where was the rest of the car?

"It's a . . . Fiat!" I said, in a way that I hoped sounded *thrilled*, rather than *complicated*. Because this felt *complicated*. I didn't want it to. But it did.

My first car . . . was a clown car.

Of course it was. Why wouldn't it be? Little man, little car. I mean, how absolutely and totally bobblehead ridiculous, how *Don't Let the Pigeon Drive the Bus!* would I look in anything bigger than a Fiat?

"Fiat Ovum, in Orbital Blue!" Brian practically sang. "Color didn't even *exist* when I bought my first Tracer! They didn't have *blue*, much less Orbital Blue!"

But they probably had another five feet of car, I thought.

What I said was, "Oh . . . wow . . . you guys . . . so awesome . . . *thank you!*" because saying anything else would've been the dickest Dick Move of all Dick Moves.

The truth is, any more car, and I'd probably have had trouble with blind spots. Brian had thought of this. Brian designed *habitats*, after all. For creatures great and small.

I approached the Fiat as if it were rigged to blow, while my mind chattered, *I love these people. These are all the people I love most (with two notable absences), and they have done something wonderful for me, and I love what's happening here* in theory, *and yet I'm also totally, irrationally furious at these wonderful people for buying me a* jacked-up Rascal—

I opened the driver's door slowly. *No special pedals please no special pedals—*

No special pedals. I relaxed. Not noticeably, I hoped.

"They've made big improvements to the roll cage," said Laura. "This model year's Ovum is safest in its class." Laura, obviously, had conducted the helicopter-parent portion of the car research. She snapped away with her phone, posted some shots to "Poca Resaca Mom Mafia." I hoped I was smiling convincingly in them. *Safest in its class. Which class was this car in? Pre-K?*

Brian gave my shoulder a meaty shake. "Orbital Blue!"

Hey. Could've been worse. Could've been a Rollerblade. Could've been a Beatrix Potter mouse wagon, freakin' acorns for wheels. Or nothing. Could've been nothing. Probably should've been. Instead: hugs all around, and the wonderful, terrible moment passed.

"Remember," said Brian, "with great power comes great responsibility," and my brain wisecracked, *What comes with a Fiat? A magnifying glass?* because my brain is an asshole, apparently.

Drew, sensing my inner weirdness, threw me an assist: "Hey, drive me to practice? I like riding with the elderly. You guys get all the good parking."

TWO

"AAAAND . . . FOR THE sixteenth year running . . . the award for Most Awkwardly Brian Person Imaginable goes to . . . Brian!" Drew made a vuvuzela sound.

I let a smile squeak through, but it was a tight one, a rubber band ready to snap. I was driving—seat ratcheted up nearly to the steering column so my foot could work the pedal—and I could feel Drew reading my bad simulation of a grin. Smoking me out. Waiting for it. *What's wrong?*

So I gave the ol' shake-it-off shrug. "Just too old for parties and candles and cakes, shit like that, is all."

"But this new ride's okay, huh?"

"Oh, the ride is *amazing*." *Half car! Half car!* screamed Ass Brain. *Freakishly abbreviated! Just like YOU!*

"Whatcha gonna name it?"

"Huh?" *Half caaaaaaar!*

"Gotta name your ride," said Drew, fake serious. "It's a rule. How about . . . the Yacht?"

"Like . . . short for *Fiat*?" Oh, wow. *Super* dumb. I snorted approvingly.

"This car's short even *for* a Fiat," Drew came back, grinning. "HEY-O!"

Aha. *That's* what Drew was up to: kicking off a dumb-joke race to the bottom. I was game.

"Okay, how 'bout: if this car were any shorter, it'd be a dolly."

"Dude, if this car were any shorter, it'd be a *ca*."

And so on. Dumber and dumber, for miles. The morning was getting better.

The whole thing could've been worse. Brian and Laura could've performed the *full* birthday ritual. The ritual we'd skipped since Drew and I were thirteen. Out of mercy.

You see, birthday ceremonies used to conclude with . . . the Doorframe.

The parade would move from the kitchen table to the pantry doorframe, the holy mystic Tape Measure and Sharpie would be brought forth on velvet cushions, and, lo, we would *measure*. As families have measured for millennia, since there have been families, since there have been doorframes.

My marks start getting closer and closer together until they start running into each other, rear-ending until they form a kind of mutant caterpillar, this fat pupa of Sharpie. It looks like some little kid's trying to draw the same line over and over, never getting it right. The dates fan out on the side; there's no room for them between lines.

Then they stop. Just stop.

Drew's marks, in the upper door-o-sphere, stop at the same time, out of respect for the minuscule.

Growth spurt is not a good term. It sounds, I'm sorry, like jizz. That's probably not a mistake. The teenage years are a very jizzy time for the human male, and whoever came up with *growth spurt* was, most likely, a human male. Personally, I prefer *chondrocyte proliferation, hypertrophy, and extracellular matrix secretion, organized by complex networks of nutritional, cellular, paracrine, and endocrine factors,* but that's just me. I may have done a *little* too much reading on the subject. Everyone else seems totally fine with *growth spurt.*

Sadly, this jizz-sounding term was my last hope for a normal life.

The whole family held out hope. After a while, it was like a religion: the Church of the Spurt. Built around something so improbable, it required serious faith.

"I think the Church of the Spurt may be shutting its doors for good."

Drew set his mouth funny. Didn't like the sound of this. "Meaning?"

I let out a big exhale, went for it: "Nobody even made a move for the tape measure this time."

Now Drew got it. "Will . . ."

"Because *obviously* we don't measure anymore, because *depressing,* right?"

"Will . . ."

"But usually somebody goes for the tape, y'know, like, out of habit, then tries to play it off. Usually Brian. *Oh, I was looking for the dry-roasted peanuts!* This time? He never made a move."

"Will . . ."

"Never even looked at the pantry. It was almost like he was trying *not* to. Look, Drew, it's fine: they've given up. *Good*. I'm glad. They *should* give up. I mean, *I* gave up—"

"Will . . ."

"—like, last year. Time to start working with what we have, right?"

Drew squirmed in his tiny bucket seat. Drew was not meant for this car, and he did not like this conversation. He was stuck in both for me and me alone.

"You all done?" he asked.

"Uh. Yes."

"Okay, so nobody's 'giving up' on anything. Nobody's *expecting* anything, either, and nobody's *not* expecting anything. Everyone's expecting you to be you, and that's it. No conspiracy, no church— just us, man."

It was a really, really nice thing to say. I'd go further than *nice*, actually. I'd go *noble*. That was Drew. Noble. Always worried about me, about Monica, about the people in his orbit, which was a powerful orbit. There was something else, too, something . . . a little sad, maybe? I'm not sure what the sadness was, or how there could even be room for it, with all the winning and the worrying about others Drew had on his plate. Maybe it was just the shadow somebody as great and good and noble as Drew naturally casts. Maybe it's just the way flags look nobler when they're lowered out of respect.

Or maybe I was projecting. Maybe I was the sad one. The one who needed a flag lowered.

"Know what you need?"

Drew wasn't asking. He knew. So did I.

"BoB, my blood brother, BoB," he said, and he was smiling again. "I know, I know. We're a few hours early. Change of plan."

I grinned at that. "A change of plan? From Spesh? The shot caller? My *God*! It is truly the End Times."

"*Slight* change of plan, wiseass. Just drive."

BoB.

It was a secret, too good to share. So we kept it. We happy few.

BoB happened one wild, wonderful afternoon. But really, like a lot of things, it started happening before it happened. There'd been stages. The first was a nightmare.

When I was eight, my mother died of a rare, aggressive bone cancer that the doctors at UCSD had never seen. That had never shown up outside of mining towns, apparently.

The day she died, I was at basketball camp. Brian came to get me. He was crying. It had been "sudden." Unexpected. I mean, obviously. If it had been "expected," I wouldn't have been at goddamned basketball camp.

I remember holding a basketball and watching my father cry. I remember thinking, *I have to get rid of this ball,* but there was no one to pass it to, and dropping it seemed wrong for some reason. So my father cried while I just stood there with my feet planted, ready to pass.

I cried, too. Of course I did. But later. It seems like nothing back then happened when or how it should. Mothers shouldn't die young. If they do, their sons should cry, and cry right away. Right?

My clearest memory of Mom, after it got bad but before the very end: She's in her hospital bed, propped up, but crooked because she can't get comfortable. Her hair hasn't fallen out from the chemo yet, but it looks stringy, wilted. Her skin's the same bad-milk color as the hospital wall, like she's fading into it.

At that point, the doctors were still saying things like *cautiously optimistic.* They were also saying things like *TACE inhibition* and *GHBP production* and *epiphyseal lesions,* and I suddenly needed to know what all those things meant. I started reading biology textbooks that were way over my head, trying to catch up with the thing that was eating my mom, eating her life, eating mine. That, I guess, was my way of being cautiously optimistic.

Still is.

And then she was gone.

Two months after the funeral, this kid I'd met at basketball camp, Andrew Tannenger, shows up with his bike and says, "You want to ride?" And strangely enough, I *did,* for the first time in weeks.

Drew and I were camp friends, and good camp friends, but *only* camp friends. He was small, like I was, and aggressive, like I wasn't, but also generous with assists. He practiced harder than anyone. That's how we became friends: I'd go to the gym to avoid some kumbaya social event—back then, shyness was my biggest problem—and I'd find Drew in there, practicing. We'd shoot around for hours, and shoot the shit for hours. It wasn't the deepest friendship, maybe, but it was steady. And somewhere in there, we discovered we lived in the same basic region of the Poca Resaca burbs, and we said what kids always say at the end of camp: *We'll keep in touch.*

Drew actually kept in touch. And he did it—reached out—at the most important moment, for both of us.

While we were riding, Drew told me his dad had left to fill a prescription for antidepressants . . . and then left. As in, *left*-left.

Called from Belize. Yeah. The *country*. He'd "met someone." He wasn't coming back. It'd been a year.

Drew told me that story, and nothing else. He didn't ask me what I thought of it. He didn't ask me if I "identified." Drew didn't generally have a speech prepared. When he did say something? He meant it.

I remember just one specific thing about what happened next: the hill where Shalina Boulevard meets Magic Avenue. Steep old bastard. Kids'd ride a half mile out of their way to avoid it.

But Drew said, "Shall we?"

I looked at the hill. It hadn't gotten any flatter since the last time I'd avoided it. "Let's go around."

Drew leaned on his handlebars, picked at a faded sticker on the frame with his thumbnail, some cartoon hero whose face had worn off in the rain. He said, "Here's the plan."

The plan? We needed a *plan*? No. We needed to go *around*.

"We do it in zigzags," said Drew.

"Like . . . switchbacks?"

"Yeah, that," he said. "Less steep."

I just looked at him.

Then Drew said, "And we don't think about *them*. Until we're at the top."

Them.

And then I got it. Then I knew we *had* to do it, climb it, just the way he'd said.

So we did. According to plan. In zigzags. All the way. And at the top, we just kept going, didn't look back at what we'd just conquered, didn't even slow down. We *rode*. I don't remember where. I don't remember coming back.

I remember Laura was there when we did. Laura and Brian, in the driveway. They were worried, but not *worried*-worried. Laura looked at me and Drew, saw something—if you want to call it a "bond," go right ahead—something *we* hadn't even seen yet, and said to Brian, "Guess we should have each other's numbers?"

That's how, two years later, our surviving/remaining parents—Brian and Laura, who'd gradually become feed-each-other's-cats friends, and then more—married each other. And Drew and I became brothers. No, better: blood brothers, which was *epic*. We cut our palms with pocketknives, cut them right along the lifelines, and swapped hemoglobin out behind the swing set in Drew's old yard. Did it the same day we watched our parents swap vows at the San Diego county clerk's office.

Then we all went to Chili's.

And somehow, even though everything was ruined, even though everything was wrecked, even though everything had *ended*... everything went on. And was sort of okay. More than okay, in some ways: without knowing it, we were on our way to BoB.

Not too long after our families blended, when Drew and I were ten, we started expanding our bike range over Los Peñasquitos Lagoon, then bushwhacking into Torrey Pines State Natural Reserve, which is one of those rare places in Southern California where you can still pretend you're the first to see the Pacific. So suddenly we were explorers, and the world was bigger, and the days were longer, and so was our leash.

You can see whales from Torrey Pines—gray whales, for the most part, but in the last couple of decades, more and more blue whales, too. They come for the krill, which for some reason (thanks, climate change?) show up here in greater numbers than they used to. Blue whales—the largest animals ever to take lunch on this planet—are something you really, really want to see in this life, just instinctively. Which is why millions of people come to San Diego to do just that.

And to see gray whales, too. I'm not shitting on gray whales. They're great.

Just . . . *smaller*, you know?

You know.

Anyway, we'd seen the whales before, so we barely looked at the ocean as we picked our way across the marsh, up the bluff trail, through the rip in the busted-ass hurricane fence, and up to the End. We called it the End, but it wasn't a name, really, it was just a fact: where we ended up. It was where the trail stopped, so we stopped, too.

We didn't know there was more. We had to be shown.

The End was a jawbone of rock hooked out over the surf, and the park service had bolted on this rusty iron afterthought of a safety railing. There was always dog shit at the End, always in precisely the same spot. Somebody came here to gaze wistfully off the edge of the earth while his/her teacup Doberman did its filthy business.

From there, the world just dropped away, and you felt pretty alone and pretty excited, and maybe even a little scared, and you suddenly understood why the old mapmakers drew monsters in the water past the parts they knew.

That's where we were at ten till five one afternoon, probably staring at dog shit, making dumb jokes, when we heard it for the first time: the call to adventure.

"What's past the dog shit?"

(So it wasn't exactly "Call me Ishmael.")

Drew and I turned at exactly the same time, like a comedy team.

And there she was. A girl. She looked older. And also ageless. She went on: "Just more dog shit? Or is there a way down?"

Drew and I hadn't done a lot of talking to girls. Definitely not in the wild.

Drew spoke first. He said, "Hey."

The girl was looking at me, though, when she said, "You gentlemen wanna be accessories to a victimless crime?"

I had no idea what she was talking about. But *yes*, I did. On gut instinct alone. I wanted to be an accessory to anything and everything she had in mind.

She was taller than both of us then, and a year-plus older, we'd find out. Darker, too, with deeper-than-olive skin, slashes of it visible through her ratty Raiders jersey and torn board shorts. She was drenched, and smelled like ocean, which was weird, because there was no beach access here, forty feet above the shore. Yet here she was, dripping brine, hair that deep iridescent blue-black with the Superman sheen. But hers was *wild*, sparkling with salt, over eyes as green as an angry two-day bruise.

I think I was trying to classify her, and failing, when she walked right by me and climbed over the guardrail, like a goddamned crazy person.

"Did you ever look? Like, *look*-look?"

What I finally said, when I found my mouth again, probably qualifies for the Worst Opening Line Hall of Shame:

"But there's a guardrail."

The girl laughed. And leaned out over the chasm.

Drew and I simul-gasped, a pair of stroller moms. The girl took no notice. She was studying the cliffs below. "Uh-huh," she said. "Yep. That'll work."

In that moment, I knew two things:

1. This girl is a lunatic, and
2. I will follow her anywhere.

Drew moved toward her. Grabbed the railing with one hand, extended the other in the crazy girl's direction. "Here," he said, in a voice that sounded two thousand years older than Drew. I remember watching him reach for her and thinking, *Drew's brave Drew's brave Drew's brave.*

"You should come back."

The green-eyed girl looked at him, confused. Not worried. Just confused.

Then she saw Drew's hand. Then she saw me.

I was holding on to Drew. Bracing him. I'd done it on pure reflex . . . but was trying to play it off, like this was something we did all the time: offering human chains to wayward girls with dysfunctional self-preservation instincts.

We must've looked so *serious.*

She didn't laugh. She just kind of noted it, like a primatologist watching chimps—*a touching if peculiar display of concern*—and then she took Drew's hand—

—and shook it. And grinned. Like they'd just struck a deal. Then she *saluted.* And dropped—

—*gasps from the stroller moms*—

—about two and a half feet.

There was a ledge. A nice wide one, curling down to the beach, almost like a perfect switchback. It'd been there all along. We'd never looked.

The green-eyed girl was already feeling her way along the rock face.

"If there's this much," the wonderful crazy person said, "then there's more."

And that was Monica. And nothing was ever the same.

It was ten minutes later, when we were, no kidding, halfway down the cliff face, sneakers squealing and slipping on the rocks, before I even thought to ask where or what this alleged "more" was.

"This rock we're on?" Monica said. "You can't tell from here, but from out there? Looks like a sea monster. Right now, we're about mid-snout."

Drew and I, clinging to the cliffside like terrified baby possums, looked at each other. From *out there?* Out *where?* From the *ocean?* The ocean past the cliff was always on the boil, torn up by two crooked jetties and this batshit skeleton of hidden reefs. Huge waves stumbled in drunk from three different directions and swung nasty haymakers at each other. Where the jetties nearly touched, all that chaos balled itself into a single fist—a vicious-looking wedge wave—and punched the cove right in the mouth, over and over, never hitting it exactly the same way. But always *hitting*. Hard.

"You were . . . out *there?*" Drew's jaw dangled like its catch was broken.

"Well," said Monica, "I got close. Swam out and had a look."

She gestured casually down at the chasm, at the chompy jaws of Satan's Cuisinart.

"I mean, I haven't *ridden* it."

Ridden?

"Yet," she added.

I looked at it again. It wasn't surf, it was puree.

My talent for stupid remarks at ridiculous moments revealed itself again. "Are you a . . . a *trained* surfer?"

She laughed. And free-dropped again.

A better question might've been, *Why are we following you?* But I'm glad we never asked it. We might've missed out on the next six years.

"I was out there"—she gestured vaguely toward the churn—"and I saw a bird fly out." She calculated her next jump. "In, then out. And again." Another drop to the next shelf. We followed her lead. "It's got a nest here. Cormorant, I think. Big seabird. So whatever's there, it's, like, spacious. And sheltered. Pretty cool, probably."

And guess what? It was all those things. And more.

BoB.

Belly of the Beach.

That's what we ended up calling it: our secret, sacred sea cove, with its jewel-bright tide pools and its domed cavern notched in red rock thirty feet down the cliff face, not two feet above the waterline at high tide, the entrance hidden behind a sandstone tusk. There was a nice little beach, too, a carpet of golden sand ground extra soft and fine by the Sawtooth. (That's what the old kahunas called the monster wedge wave we'd seen out beyond the cove.) The Sawtooth had been chewing every stone and shell and fish skeleton to powder for however many jillion eons, and we got here just in time to walk on the perfect beach it made for us, the gentle sweepings of all those little bones. Technically, BoB was made of death, I guess, a hundred million years of finely milled *death*. But it felt so alive.

I was happy just being there, just being one of three who knew this place.

In the cave, there was this long tongue of rock to sit on. Three could sit comfortably, for hours, talking about basically nothing.

Which we did. For six years.

We had rules. The place was secret, for one. It had to be. To find a place like this and *not* keep it secret? Would be just wrong, somehow. We had rules, because why risk chaos? All three of us had lost something, or someone, to chaos. Now we'd found something precious, right next door to chaos. We needed to protect it. So we made a Plan. A Plan, which was really just a promise to each other: that BoB was ours, and we were BoB's, pure and simple. All other plans, all the later drafts, flowed from that one Plan. I built my first bonfire at BoB. Sipped my first beer there, experimentally, disappointedly. (It was Rolling Rock.) I read all of Tolkien there, even the frickin' *Silmarillion,* under Monica's watchful nerdship.

And I fell in love at BoB. With the best and wrongest person. In violation of the Plan, of the promise.

So yes, it was the end of the world, and the greatest place on earth, and it was also in biking distance of our subdivision, had been all our lives. We'd never have known it was there, if Monica hadn't dared us.

It was also where Monica spent most of her nonschool time. She never went home. For reasons she didn't talk about, and didn't need to.

We had whales to watch. Down here, they seemed very, very close.

"There's no place safer," Monica liked to say, "than *inside* a sea monster."

That's how we started Whaling.

"I couldn't love youuuuuu," Drew caterwauled, *"aaany beeeetterrrrr! I love you just the waaaay you aaaaaaaaaaaaaaarrrrrrrrrrre-ruh!"*

Drew held the last note as long as he could, looking for a fluke, a spout, anything. You only win Whaling if a whale breaches during your verse. Combining the Zen of whale-watching with the screech of karaoke, it barely met the definition of game, and P.S., none of us could really sing. The *real* object of Whaling was to irritate the other players until they picked you up and dumped you in the ocean.

Monica was reigning champ. She had serious lungs and always sang "Honesty," which is a real milking machine of a slow ballad, horrifically extendable.

Drew nearly collapsed trying to hold that last note. He finally had to take a knee, gasping, his terrible serenade declined by whale-kind.

"Whaddaya think Coach Guthridge would say if he knew you were skipping practice . . . for *this*? On game day?"

A jolt of very real worry arced across Drew's face. Then the broad smile unfurled again and caught the wind. "Coach Gut? He'd be down. He's, what, fifty? Old people love them some Joel. These whales do, too, you'll see. Whales are old as shit, Will."

I laughed. He laughed. We were ten again.

But . . . I could look in the mirror and be ten again.

Well-meaning middle-aged women still approached me at the

mall and asked, "Where's your mother? Are you lost?" (Sometimes that made me so mad, I answered honestly.)

That's why I had my own plans for tonight. Plans I hadn't shared with my blood brother, who'd skipped practice and changed his plans—plans he didn't take or make lightly—all for me. There's no other way to say it: I was betraying him. Maybe not fatally. Maybe just a little. Just technically. An asterisk, really. No big deal.

Except that, till now, there'd been no asterisks between us.

Thunk, thunk.

Two books hit the sand, and then *THUNK:* the Asterisk herself. Monica Alegria Bailarín.

"Gentlemen," said Monica, picking up her books and heading toward the cave for her board and wet suit, her sword and shield. I couldn't see the book covers, but lately Monica always traveled with two beat-to-hell paperbacks from her two preferred categories of lit: People Are Garbage, and People Are Flaming Garbage, Beautiful to Behold but Only from a Safe Distance.

"Thought you had practice, Spesh?" Monica kicked off her Keds and vanished into the cave.

"Thought you had history first period," Drew called back.

"I did, I did," came Monica's voice, ringing off the cave dome. "And then, suddenly, halfway there, I just *didn't*. Because, guys, *look* at this *day!*"

"It's San Diego," I said. "This is every day."

"Wrong," said Mon, emerging in her battered wet suit, so many patches it looked like a map of Conflictistan, with her second-least-beat-to-shit surfboard under her arm. "This is a special day. Today, William of Daughtry, you become a man. American-style. Sixteen! Car mitzvah!"

"Did you just say *car mitzvah?*"

Monica took a bow. "Speaking of which: what was that beautiful blue blob of white privilege I saw parked on the access road? Looked suspiciously unbikelike."

"We call it the Yacht." Drew grinned like he'd invented sugar.

"*He* calls it the Yacht," I corrected.

"Short for *Fiat?*" Monica rolled it around gravely. "Mmm. That's terrible."

"Oh, but *car mitzvah* is genius."

"It *is* genius."

"I thought 'the Yacht' was very clever," said Drew, "for a meathead athlete."

"I think," said Monica, heading for the water, "that meathead athletes should be held to higher standards. And one day, God willing, America will have its first meathead-athlete poet laureate."

"How about surf-bum history skippers? What kinda standards for them?"

"Sorry, WHAT?" called Monica, paddling out.

"They get to just drop a *car mitzvah* and take a bow?"

"I can't hear you over the MONSTER WAVE I am about to BEND with MY MIND."

She was paddling toward the Sawtooth, all snarling foam today. The Sawtooth was never *nice,* but today it seemed especially irritable—indigestion from some far-off Pacific cyclone, I guess.

We both knew she wouldn't go all the way. That she'd pause, mid-cove, like she always did. Straddle her board and just study the tangle of mindless murder. And then . . . she'd settle for the ankle biters closer to shore, the Sawtooth's scraps and leavings.

Still, Drew said, "She . . . won't." With this wisp of a question mark, this tiny squiggle of worry. He said it every time she paddled out. I'm not sure he even knew he was saying it.

I wasn't worried. I knew she wouldn't. Not today. Not ever.

"There are two waves you don't get to surf," Monica always said. "Yesterday's, the one you missed, the one you weren't in time for. And tomorrow's, the one you keep in front of you, the one that dares you."

The Sawtooth was always tomorrow's wave for Monica. It was berserk, barely a wave at all, no pattern or math, just gnashing violence. Guess wrong, and you'd get held under and raked over the cheese grater of rock reefs that was BoB's red carpet. The Sawtooth was no murder virgin. Monica'd poked around, found some obits. Dead kahunas from the '50s. From before the guardrail. That's why it was actually (shh, don't tell) illegal to surf here.

Monica always had one eye on the Tooth—and one eye on what she once called the Madwoman Theory. She liked to keep people guessing. Liked a little churn. Churn meant an underdog had a chance.

Drew, on the other hand, did not like churn. Drew did not surf. Drew barely swam in the cove, which was a bathtub. Drew, though he didn't talk about it, had a Water Problem. "Most plans aren't water-resistant," went another Monica maxim, "but all water is plan-resistant." And Drew liked plans.

By *plans,* I mean: if you popped the hood on Drew's head, you'd see an octagonal table with eight little Drews around it, debating the pros and cons of eight different scenarios, then throwing a ninth into the mix, just to be safe. He had plans within plans, plans that Legoed neatly into any number of potential futures, plans for college, career, and beyond—and all of these plans featured the three of us, together, hanging out at BoB our entire lives. Now, technically, we *all* made those plans, and we all liked the idea of never losing each other, but Drew? Actually gamed out the scenarios that'd keep us safely enBoB'd forever. He didn't share them in real time or force them down anybody's throat, but if you casually asked him what he thought? You'd receive a detailed presentation, with footnotes.

When Drew looked at water, he saw long odds. Broken rules. Plans dashed, ass up and skewered on reef jags. He and Monica were about as polar opposite as two people can be, and I was somewhere in the middle, refereeing, making the chemistry work. That was my niche, that was my place.

It wasn't enough. Not anymore.

I picked up one of the books Monica'd left on the sand, felt its shifty old spine squidge a little in my hand, read the title— *Leviathan*—and just enough old-timey speak in headache typeface to know it was not my jam. Drew kicked a pink nugget of beach glass into a tide pool, where it disturbed some delicate tiny creature, something that wriggled away from the ripples and would probably be dead by lunch.

"She's gonna fail history," fretted Drew. "Irvine's not gonna love *that*."

"Irvine's not the be-all, end-all, man."

"Irvine's got the BFA she wants."

"Irvine's got *a* BFA," I corrected, "for sure."

Drew got the drift.

"Okay, okay," he said, scratching his scalp three times fast, claws out, *scritchscritchscritch*, the way he did when he admitted an own goal. "I'll relax. Nobody's asking my opinion. I just ... y'know."

"I know."

And I did. I knew Drew's Risk board of alt-futures as well as Drew did, all the scenarios he'd drawn up for us. How he'd get the full ride at UCSD, how Monica'd teach surf camp for work-study at Irvine, how I'd intern at the Scripps Research Institute and become the next E. O. Wilson. And we'd all spend our weekends at BoB. Like always. Perfect.

A little *too* perfect, maybe, a little too romantic, and even Drew knew that, but still: how beautiful was this thing we had, the three of us?

How beautiful was this thing I was about to put just the teensiest, tiniest, most innocent little crack in?

"So, dude," said Drew as we watched Monica shotgun a three-footer, "don't let her know I told you—she likes to surprise you—but we've got something a little better than beer for tonight. And there might be presents. I know, I know, we said no presents, but . . . Anyway, I know you don't like surprises."

I smiled. They were so careful with me. Like I'd break.

"Great," I said. "Let's say . . . nine?"

And just like that, it was half-done. My itty-bitty betrayal. My li'l semi-Judas.

"Perfect," said Drew. "Time to spare. It's just St. Augie. I don't foresee OT."

Course he didn't. "Just St. Augie." Just the Final. Just a whole season undefeated, just another record, no big deal. Drew knew he'd win, and win handily, inside of regulation.

I had no such assurances, in sports or life. Thus: semi-Judas.

* * *

Drew was halfway up the cliff when Monica rode in. I was still putting on my shoes.

"So don't let him know I told you," said Mon, squeezing out her hair and nodding up at Drew, "but our thing tonight? We got you something better than beer."

"Ah."

"Also, there might be presents. Even though we said no presents."

"Okay."

"I know you don't like surprises."

She studied my face. Was there something on it to study? Shit.

"Aaaand . . . Drew told you already, didn't he?"

I relaxed. "You got me. He spilled. Everyone's just so super respectful of my deadly allergy to surprises."

"You literally said, 'I never need another surprise in my life' last year."

"Last year, you kidnapped me and took me to Medieval Times." *And everyone thought I was in the show* was the part I didn't need to add.

(A fellow medievalist at the next table, blotto on mead, had pointed at me and suggested a "dwarf tossing," and later, Monica'd "accidentally" hip-checked the guy into a pile of authentic medieval horseshit. That *almost* made it a fun memory.)

"Fair enough," said Mon. She grabbed her books. "What time?"

Deep breath. Steady, Daughtry.

"Eight-fifteen?"

All done. The Full Judas.

"Eight-fifteen it is," said Monica, heading into the cave. "See you guys then. Don't become a man without us."

I couldn't summon a comeback that didn't sound creepy, so I asked, "Which kind of book is that?" Nodding at *Leviathan*.

"It's a People Are Garbage," said Monica. "The *bible* of People Are Garbage books, actually. I'm reading all People Are Garbage books right now. Don't take it personally. I'd never lump you in with 'people.'" She flashed that conspiratorial smile of hers, the one that'd been clearing my brain buffer for six years. "Anyway. Just a mood I'm in. It'll pass."

I grinned. "Like history."

"Like history. Wiseass. Don't you start. Mother Tannenger up there is bad enough."

"Will!" called Mother Tannenger, from his aerie.

"Coming!" Then, to Mon: "So, what: no more fantasy books? Like, forever?"

"The real world's full-on fantasy nowadays, you noticed? I'm getting the milk for free." She went into the cave. Then came right back out. Eyebrow cocked. Antenna up.

"You okay?"

"I'm fine," I said. "Why, do I seem . . . ?"

"You seem quiet."

"Can't a guy be quiet?"

"Not this guy. This guy is several dumb puns behind his daily quota."

"I'm saving up for tonight."

Monica smiled. I smiled back. I smiled *up*. The neck strain of basic human interaction: I barely noticed it anymore.

"I'll hold you to that," Monica said.

"WILL!" called Drew, far up the bluff by then. "Afterburners, man!"

* * *

I was a very *forgivable* Judas, I'd decided. That was my whole plan.

My whole plan was to tell Monica I was in love with her. To-night. At BoB. Holiest of holies. Just the two of us, no Drew. I would tell her I wanted to be her boyfriend and do boyfriend-girlfriend things, not just friend-y all-three-of-us things.

Yes, I thought that might go well.

Hear me out:

Monica and I already loved each other. Friend love, sure, but love. Solid foundation. On top of that, we were clearly the weird outliers in a friend triangle Drew had become the undisputed fulcrum of. (Do triangles even *have* fulcrums? Ours did.) Monica was a nerdy surfer-sage from Barrio Nacional, poor and weird and aloof from just about everyone at Keseberg High except for me and Drew. And I was, well, what little I was.

But to Monica, I was more. At least I hoped so. Lately, since basketball had started looming ever larger in Drew's Plan and daily schedule, Monica and I had been spending more and more time on our own, at the Lowlands, or here at BoB, surfing. (She was teaching me. I wasn't bad. A low center of gravity has its advantages.)

There was nothing in the Plan that said we couldn't fall in love. There was also nothing that said we could. The Plan (first draft) was written when I was ten, after all.

Well, *new plan:* I'd confess my love, Monica'd see my point or at least think it over, and then Drew'd arrive, forty-five minutes later, and maybe we'd break the happy news over "something better than beer."

Obviously, this strategy of mine (if you can call it a strategy) was risky. Or, if you like, stupid. Obviously, it upset the delicate ecology of our little tide pool. But I told myself Drew was bigger than our tide pool, bigger than the Plan, even. As a budding sports titan, he had new worlds to conquer, worlds more in proportion with his newly embiggened huge-largeness.

And with Monica, my time was running out. She was a rising senior, and just plain rising. From the minute we met, she was leaving me. Same as Drew. Rising away.

There are two basic kinds of quests, according to Monica. There are quests when the hero's after a prize—glory, justice, revenge, love. And then there are quests to lift a curse. To relieve a burden. I wasn't sure which one this was. What I knew was, if I didn't say something? I'd explode. What I knew was, I had to stick to the plan—*my* plan, with all its minor, forgivable, surgical betrayals—and that nothing, least of all my better judgment, was going to stop me.

THREE

AND THEN I was in biology.

But hey, we're *all* in biology, right? Forever. We never pass. Until we, y'know, pass. And then we're *really* in it, I guess. Intimately. Compostably.

I'm not a dwarf, by the way. If the Medieval Times story made you wonder.

Not that there's anything wrong with that, to quote ancient television history. Just as a matter of accuracy, of taxonomy: I'm not a dwarf.

I'm not a midget, either. That's not really a thing anymore, bio-medically and scientifically. So don't say *midget*. It's just offensive.

"Proportionate dwarf" is a thing, but it sounds like a bad indie band, so no.

What I have (and I don't really *have* anything, my problem is what's *missing*) is called idiopathic short stature, which is just a long way of saying, *You're short.* The short way is ISS.

You're short, nobody knows why, here's an acronym, there's the door.

I'm very short. And I'm also not on fire.

These topics are connected, I promise.

One thing I like about biology is how it looks so messy on the surface, but everything's connected pretty elegantly underneath, like a rhizome or a mycelium. (Go on, look 'em up, your time isn't that precious.) The logic's always there, even if you have to dig for it.

It's there, and it's ruthless. Like, just plain *mean*. For instance, go online. Find some creepy personals. Creepier the better. The creepier they are, the more honest they are.

I was addicted to creepy personals. It's not what you think! I read them for the *biology*. And I found it, in abundance:

Looking for a tall guy . . .

Hey, big men . . .

Please be tall.

Hey, at least she/he said *please*.

In the brutal wilds of the untender internet, *tall* correlates so strongly with *handsome,* they might as well be synonyms. (As for *dark,* well, that's a split decision. Were you aware the internet is insanely racist? What's that? You *were?*)

Why are anonymous, self-interested creatures, operating in a realm beyond shame, *still* selecting for above-average height? Maybe they're just products of a heightist culture. Or maybe something more fundamental's at work.

Fact: Small things don't live as long. They've got faster metabolisms. They have to breed fast, or they burn out quick.

Fact: Small people—shit you not—don't make as much money. Don't live as long.

No use getting upset about it. Small things have their appointed life cycles, such as they are. And big things have ... well, everything.

Big things pace themselves. Because they *can*. Big things have every reason to take it easy. The bigger they grow, the more chilled out their metabolisms get. The less they have to worry about. The less they anticipate OT against St. Augustine.

The more they've "got this." And know it.

And it's a good thing they chill out, too, 'cause—not to biologize your head off, but let me drop a little metabolic theory on you—if an elephant maintained the same go-go hump-and-run metabolism as a mouse? It couldn't radiate the excess heat generated by its own cellular processes. The elephant wouldn't have enough surface area to cool itself, even with those flapping air-conditioner ears, because volume, see, is cubic, and surface area's square, and that means—

Okay, I'm biologizing your head off.

(I am—not to brag, but okay, to brag—kind of the Drew of biology.)

(And yes: that's my best brag.)

Let me cut to the chase. That poor unlucky elephant? With the revved-up mouse metabolism? Would—and I'm not exaggerating—*burst into flames.*

Which would probably make zoos *way* more popular with Keseberg students.

But wouldn't be great for elephants, I don't think.

That's kind of how I felt in those days myself. Like I was always on the verge of bursting into flame. Lucky for me, I wasn't any bigger, right? Flameout dodged. Lucky, lucky me, the guy natural selection plus the internet had already weeded out for extinction. The guy elected by biology to fade away, not burn out.

These are the thoughts that brush-fired through my head in biology while I was knuckles-deep in dead amphibian.

"Careful," whispered Sidney, "you're nicking the spleen."

Sidney Lim was my lab partner.

"That's no spleen. . . ." And that was Rafty Royall. My other lab partner. Frogs are frickin' expensive, even in the wretched hive of Audis and yuppiedom we called Keseberg. Three kids to a frog is just a fact of life in public school, even a rich one.

Sidney studied the tiny snot-green nuggets at the probing end of my tweezers. "That *is* a spleen."

"It's a joke," said Rafty. "I'm doing Obi-Wan. When he says, 'That's no moon!' In *A New Hope*. See? That's the joke."

A moment of merciful silence reigned while I tweezed, resisting the temptation to spleensplain.

"I'm no comedy expert," said Sidney, "but that *is* a spleen, and that *wasn't* a joke."

Rafty sniffed. "Will laughed."

"I kind of . . . exhaled."

This was one slippery spleen. I was concentrating hard. Trying to, at least. My lab partners (maybe I oughta put that in air quotes) weren't making this frogtopsy any easier.

"He *exhaled*, Rafty," said Sidney. "And just saying some random-ass thing from *Star Wars* isn't a joke. Is it *Wars* or *Trek*, Will?"

"*Wars*."

"Okay, well, I want you guys to know," said Sid, serious-faced, "that the only reason I mix those up? Is because I don't give a shit about either of them."

46

"Getting that loud and clear, Dr. Lim." I tweezed the spleen, mounted it on the Styrofoam, just the teensiest feathery hem of connective tissue trailing. Best hands in the business. Best, because *tiniest*.

I always did the dissections. Sid and Rafty handled the debate.

We must've looked like quite the album cover, huddled around that autopsy tray at our lab station: me on the bottom, redheaded Rafty (5′4″) a relative colossus to my left, Sid (5′7″) on my right, statuesque in every sense, towering over both of us.

"Hating *Star Wars* doesn't make you cool," noted Rafty. "It makes you sexist."

"Whoa! 'Splain me, bro." Sid was officially amused.

"Well, it's what's called a 'dog whistle,'" Rafty 'splained, "to man-haters everywhere. It rallies a certain element to attack our *culture*."

"Your *culture* . . . okay, Rafty. Plenty of females like both the *Star*s, the *Wars* and the *Trek* one—"

"Not the preferred nomenclature," Rafty tsked.

"—but I do not happen to be one of those females. That makes me sexist?"

"Look, when you've worked as long as I have in the media-slash-promotion-slash-advertising field—"

"You sell yearbook ads."

"—you become a student of human nature. You hear certain slurs over and over."

"You hear 'I don't like *Star Wars*' over and over? Where? In what secluded corner of the internet? I want to go live there."

"Such hatred." Rafty shook his head, Yoda-style, in mock disappointment.

"Hey, guys?" I put down my tweezers, pulled off my safety goggles. "We're done."

And just in time. Mr. Sulak was back from the supply closet to check our work.

"Mr. Sulak?" Sid asked. "Why aren't there cruelty-free tablet games for anatomy lessons? Oh, wait, there are."

"Too expensive," sighed Sulak. He communicated mostly in sighs. "License fees are nuts, freeware's garbage. You wanna save the frogs? Ask your parents. They're the ones who don't like taxes." He scratched his bald spot—it got a little bigger every time he came out of the supply closet, I swear—and peered at our tray. "Nice job, Will."

"It was a team effort," I said.

"No, it wasn't. Ms. Lim, what's this?"

"Spleen."

"This?"

"Gallbladder. There's the pancreas. Up here, conus arteriosus. All this, over here: ancillary fat bodies."

"Well done. Okay. Mr. Royall, what am I pointing at?" Sulak indicated a lung. A real gimme.

Rafty shook his head. "I cannot answer that," he said, "without incriminating myself."

Sulak sighed. "C'mon, Rafty. Try a little harder? Don't make me fail you."

"I feel like we're failing *each other*, Mr. Sulak. I just don't see how any of this benefits my future in the media-slash-promotion-slash-advertising field."

"Let's get you to the end of the semester, then we'll worry about your . . . field." A long sigh. And then Sulak was back in the supply closet.

"What's he *do* back there?" Rafty asked.

"I've got ten dollars on compulsive masturbation," said Sidney. She was already deep in her phone. Sid's parents were in imports, whatever that meant. What it seemed to mean was that they spent a lot of time in Singapore. Which meant Sid spent a lot of time at parties. Parties and volleyball were 90 percent of what she did. She was an A/B student without having to try too hard. Sid was one of the beautiful people, for sure—her dad had been some kind of clothing model in Hong Kong, and she'd gotten a healthy dose of those good-bone-structure genes—but she didn't carry herself in god mode like a lot of Keseberg's upper-caste jerks.

"There's a betting pool?" I asked. "On Sulak's closet mysteries?"

"Pot's up to thirty-five dollars."

"You guys, check it out," said Rafty, slapping down a flyer. On it was a confusing train wreck of shitty clip art—a microphone, a brick wall, and a chess piece, a queen. *LAUGH YOUR BISHOP OFF! CHESS CLUB COMEDY NIGHT! BUN YIP'S!*

Sid raised an eyebrow. "Yip's does comedy? Isn't it just a Chinese restaurant?"

"They've made a lot of changes since the health department thing last spring. I'm repping them now. Crisis management. Repping the chess club, too. Synergistic cross-pollination."

"Wait..." Sidney wrinkled her nose. "The chess club... they're... performing? *Comedy?*"

"Uh-huh," said Rafty. "Full disclosure: I wrote a lot of their material. It's risky shit. Pushes back against their clean-cut image. You want a free sample? Okay, this joke, it's about a mouse and an elephant. I'll warn you: *it is sexual in nature.*"

The joke *was* sexual in nature, and also sexist in nature, and really just kind of confusing, logically and spatially. I don't really know what the punch line would've been. Mercifully, the whole thing was interrupted by the bell.

"Will?" Sid said. "Thanks for the autopsy." She cut her eyes at Rafty on her way out. "Watch your back around Mouse Joke here."

"I have a very edgy energy!" Rafty called after her. "You know this about me!"

Later, in the hall, Rafty said, "Sidney Lim is so beautiful."

"Yep." It was undeniably true, and also completely irrelevant to individuals on our level, in our position. But Rafty was building a PowerPoint presentation.

"And she likes us."

"Within reason, sure."

"So what we'll do is we'll challenge each other: you have to ask her out—"

"Slow down, Rafty."

"—ask her out on a date inside of *two weeks,* or else . . . *I'll* ask her."

Rafty—and maybe this was part of why he aspired to a life in media-slash-promotion-slash-advertising—thought impossible things could be made true and real just by saying them or printing them on very ugly flyers with stock images and bad clip art. Rafty thought he was a marketing wizard in the making, but really he was just an optimist, and his "marketing" was a form of prayer, and I guess that's why I liked him: I'm not really an optimist, and ever since Mom died, I have trouble with the whole prayer thing. (I wasn't particularly good at it before she died.) But there are moments (like, say, when you have a go-for-broke plan to confess your love for a good friend) when even a pessimist needs a little optimism, and some prayers you can't say for yourself. Rafty'd been optimizing hard enough for both of us since sixth grade.

"I think, Rafty, that whatever it is you're imagining—"

"A campaign. I think of it as a campaign. We're not *really* fighting. It's more like the cola wars—it lifts everybody's stock—"

"Okay, the *campaign* you're imagining? Probably ends with Sidney requesting new lab partners."

"I find your lack of faith disturbing." Rafty grinned. "*Star Wars,* dawg! Oh, and hey, happy birthday! I got you something! Some *things*! Plural!"

He pulled out two individually wrapped presents, baby-blue paper, silver bows, each the size of a small trout.

"Rafty! Dude. That's amazing, but . . . we don't do presents! Do we?"

"We do now, *mon frère.* I was reading this whole thread about how it's good for men to give each other presents. So c'mon! Unwrap, unbox, go! Go!"

I unwrapped. I unboxed.

It was a two-inch lift. For my shoes. On the back, in gold letters, were the words *WE HOOKED UP ALREADY.*

"Shit!" said Rafty. "I was supposed to hand you the other one first."

The other one said *IF YOU CAN READ THIS.*

"Riiiight?" Rafty grinned and nodded. "Try 'em on, I wanna see if they work. My theory is: Be the change you want to see in the world. Walk tall, and you *are* tall. Mind over matter. C'mon, try 'em on!"

I looked around at the crowded hallway. "Here?"

"Okay, good point. Wear 'em to the game tonight! Test my theory!"

Rafty and only Rafty could get away with giving me a gift this awful, this clumsy. Once upon a time, I'd had no words to describe Rafty. Then Monica called him "tactless but harmless," and Rafty didn't mind that. "Truth in advertising is good," he said.

We were a funny pair, Rafty and I. United by stature, and a mutual, only somewhat rational hatred of the Duke Blue Devils, and an impossible dream of dunking. (Ever since Drew shot up, I'd played hoops only with Rafty, using the rusty Pro Slam in his driveway.) Roderick Raftsman Rhinehardt Royall, a little kid with a long, stupid name, tried for years to get people to call him Rod, or Rowdy Roddy, or (for a brief, strange time) Ted, but Rafty is what stuck. ("My early branding strategies, I now see, did not bear fruit.")

Rafty and I had both been called many things, all of them worse than "Rafty." We'd been the two littlest guys in middle school, see. We'd been bullied together. That was the other thing we shared. Drew and I, we had a lot in common, but not that. Bullying is a foxhole bond.

Jared Zigler. Spencer Inskip. Eric Forchette. I'd attracted my fair share of assholes, shit-hearted young swains who saw a lot of comic potential in my tiny body. Some of their routines were pretty inventive. The Display Case, for example. A classic of physical comedy.

There was a large display case in the hall outside the wood shop—intended, I guess, for objects made in wood shop. Either it hadn't caught on or people weren't that proud of what they made in wood shop, because it sat derelict, the catch on its glass door broken.

All those big, empty display shelves had given Jared Zigler an idea.

He and some minion from his doom squad of neckless griefers rounded us up one day, Rafty and me, carried us up a rolling ladder, and placed us on the highest shelves. Get it? Two elves on shelves. Too scared to move. Too funny, right?

Then they'd thrown tennis balls at us. Hard.

So that was a very bad middle school day. But it also turned out to be my lucky day.

Lucky, because Monica had school-choiced her way into our district. (She'd decided it was the only school for her, and she'd figured out, on her application, how to make the San Diego school system see things *precisely* the same way she did.)

Lucky, because Monica was a genius.

And also a bit of a maniac.

Monica had been in wood shop that day.

She spent most of seventh grade in there, cutting her first longboard from the blank. That's what she was doing when she heard the *thwock!* of tennis balls and the frightened yelps of captive shelf elves.

She'd moseyed out of shop—I remember this so clearly, in such brilliant HD, that it hurts—and she was wearing a beat-up hoodie the dull red of road rash, Wranglers she'd rescued from a Goodwill bin, a beige shop apron, and a brindled earflapped knit cap of her own creation, with jagged spikes of black hair peeking out. Her eyes were the green of burning copper, the green of illegal fireworks.

And, oh yeah: she had a circular saw swinging at her hip.

Suddenly it was just the five of us in that hall. A tumbleweed blowing through might've been a nice touch. Instead, a distant toilet flushed. Nice.

Monica hadn't said anything. Just stared at Jared and company.

"What?" Jared said finally.

"I can't find the teacher," Monica said, in her deadest, flattest zombie voice. "I don't know where he went."

"That's my problem?"

"It's so dangerous," Monica said, "to leave seventh graders alone with working shop equipment."

VRIMMM!

The saw hopped to life in Monica's hand. And that's when Jared finally noticed: it had been plugged in the whole time. Shit was *live*.

"Unsupervised seventh graders," Monica went on, "are responsible for sixty-two percent of wood shop accidents nationwide. It's very sad. We can do better."

VRIMMM!

She took a step toward Jared.

Jared took a step backward. His wingdouche followed suit.

"We *must* do better," Monica said.

I remember Jared laughing. I remember him saying, "Peace out, psycho chick," and Monica answering, "Peace out, Neandertool."

I also remember how quickly he left.

Then Monica got the rolling ladder from shop, and down we came.

"Welp," she'd said, "back to class. Everybody be good."

And back she'd moseyed, saw and all, into the classroom. Just like that famous painting *Athena Returning to Wood Shop After Battle*.

"That girl," Rafty said, "is a legend," and for once, he wasn't spinning.

She wasn't done, either.

Later, after school that day, Monica found me, and we went surfing at BoB. It was . . . *medicinal.* That was the first time I got a glimpse of what Monica saw in the water, why she trusted it even though it cared nothing for her or for anyone, even though it was too big to care. She trusted it *because* it was too big to care. That's what made it dependable.

I was not quite twelve. She'd just turned thirteen. I'd tried surfing before, hadn't even managed to plant my feet on the board. I was always pretty sure the waves would kill me. Seemed a simple matter of scale. And they weren't ankle biters that day. Something had stirred them, something big and far off.

"This is where the storm waves come to die," Monica said, "and I'm the undertaker." Before I could properly assess the badassery of that remark, she was already teaching: "You're gonna draw a line from here"—straddling her board, she pointed to the tip of a shorter, blunter jetty—"to there"—a jut of beach inside the cove— "and that's the magic line where this wave and this wave agree. That's the pit, the pocket. I call it the *fold.* That's all you've got. Place like this, the waves are never gonna be corduroy, nothing's ever gonna be smooth. We didn't choose that beach. We chose this one. The fold is narrow some days and fatter others, but it's always there. You gotta trust the water." She rose on her board, those Raggedy Ann patches on her Goodwill wet suit gleaming like medals of honor.

I stood up, too stiff.

Wiped out. A cross wave took my legs out from under me like a broadsword, and when my knees met the reef finger, I felt the sting of the cold salt letting me know that there was blood, that the teeth of the break had nicked me through the suit.

Monica wanted me to try again. Monica said:

"Trust the water."

It was the first time I'd managed to stand up on a board.

I felt eleven feet tall.

"See?" said Monica.

After that, we surfed once a week, every week, usually while Drew was at practice. We went to the water, and the water took it all, all the dirt and shit and blood of land life. Next to the ocean, it was nothing.

A baptism. I'd been saved. It wouldn't be the last time.

Jared Zigler, I think, was cursed after that day, the day of the circular saw. His bully career peaked in seventh grade, and he began his slide from popular meathead to pudgy stoner joke. People called him Jazzy now, I think because he'd tried, for about a week, to get his friends to call him Jay-Z, and this had backfired spectacularly. He'd fallen from grace, if you can call Peak Bullydom "grace," but he was still useful to the Keseberg social machine. His parents owned this huge mansion on the beach, and they liked to fly to Vegas every weekend because apparently they had too much money and some of it needed to be vented into the cold vacuum of Nevada, for safety's sake. So every weekend, some party or another—the ones that lost their original venues or never had any in the first place—would find its way up Jazzy's driveway. People called his house the Party Toilet, because every floater ended up there.

Jazzy was a tool, perhaps a Neandertool, but at least he still *existed*. The same couldn't be said for yours truly. I existed only at BoB.

By eighth grade, thanks to Monica's mama-bearing, the bullying had ceased—and I was grateful, so disgustingly grateful. But the world was starting to get "civilized" as high school set in, and I was starting to fade away. In other words: I was safe, but safely *invisible*. I spent about a year enjoying not being bullied. And then? Part of me, a weird part of me, started *missing* it. When you're bullied, at least you know you're *there*. Solid enough to take a punch.

Species usually don't disappear overnight. Evolution is supposed to be gradual, so gradual a creature doesn't actually notice he's being eliminated. Evolution is supposed to be courteous that way.

That courtesy was not extended to me.

I had this stack of old zoology textbooks, castoffs from the zoo library. There was one that was nothing but extinct species. I marked the page for *Malpaisomys insularis*, the lava mouse, which was a pretty unremarkable mouse, except for the fact that it lived in volcanic rifts in the Canary Islands. But volcanoes aren't what killed it off. People did. People kill everything. People are hungry. That's not the mystery.

The mystery is why the lava mouse was so small. There's something called island gigantism, see. When a smallish species gets thrashed off the mainland by a storm or something and washes up on an island, clinging to driftwood, it starts to change, over the generations. On the island, in isolation, without its usual predators, it starts to evolve a larger and larger body, until it's a shit ton bigger than its mainland cousins. Theoretically, given proper time and conditions, a mouse species on the right island could end up the size of an elephant. But the lava mouse stayed small. Like it knew what was coming. Like it figured, *Why bother?*

Under the entry for *Malpaisomys insularis,* there was a diagram of what the mouse might've looked like, reconstructed from fossil remains, along with a little note that said *Figure Not Drawn to Scale.*

Well: that was my whole life. Figure not drawn to scale.

I was a lava mouse on my own lonely island, clinging to a volcano that could erupt any second, and that volcano was my deep and unscientific love for the fierce and fearless and unflappable yet always earflapped Monica Alegria Bailarín. It was a massive love that was, absurdly, headquartered in a ridiculously tiny body.

Monica was many things. And one of them was tall. Almost a foot taller than I was. *Almost a foot taller.*

That's practically a *species* difference.

I'd watched the girl I loved *leave* me—in not-so-slow motion—on an *evolutionary* level. At twelve, Monica was five foot seven. Within a year, she was five eight . . . five nine . . . headed for five ten. I watched her go, and I watched Drew go. I was ground control watching them head spaceward. Pretty soon, she was tall in my dreams, too—but Dream Me stayed the same size. I couldn't even *dream* big. The most basic cliché: failed. When even your *dreams* are drawn to scale? It's a bad sign. That's why I had to risk this one teeny, tiny betrayal. A minorly shitty thing for a majorly noble goal: Lava Mouse, on his way to extinction or explosion or whatever awaited him, just wanted love to conquer all. Just once. Just this one little grease fire of a miracle. That's all.

At age sixteen, I desperately needed my life as I knew it to explode. And I needed the flaming debris from that explosion to fall to earth just so, in the shape of a heart. And then everything would be fine. Cue strings. Roll credits.

It wasn't my most scientific theory.

I got the exploding part right, at least.

FOUR

MAGIC MIKE WAS balding prematurely. Nobody could figure it out.

I had my theories. But I suspect they were tainted by bias. It's why I hesitated to publish. That, and my complete lack of qualifications.

I shoveled gorilla feces and watched Magic Mike pace his studio apartment, a flattish boulder on the far side of the habitat that Jollof hadn't deigned worthy of pissing on. Mike was a comedian whose day job was Victim, with a sideline as Punching Bag. He didn't mix too much. Spent a lot of time in his apartment. Paced a lot. Waved his arms around. Hooted softly, almost to himself. I said, *He's working on his material.* The primate behaviorists said, *This is something to keep an eye on.*

My theory? Magic Mike was in love with Blue. It was obvious. Dude wasn't subtle. He watched her from his rock for hours, turning away only when Jollof was "romancing" her. He brought her things. And Magic Mike had nothing. He barely even had produce. Jollof bogarted the best stuff. But what was left over? Magic Mike brought it to Blue, laid yesterday's vegetables at her feet like a dozen long-stemmed roses.

Blue was older, wiser, and Mike loved Blue—

—yes, nerds, Biology Boy is well aware he's anthropomorphizing, bringing his own speciesist idiom to an animal's Umwelt, so report me to the ethologists, why don't you?—

—and Magic Mike had absolutely nowhere to go with that love. Jollof didn't field a lot of challenges to his rule. A full-on play for dominance, a rush for the throne—that's rare in captive gorilla troops. You're more likely to end up with a solitary male, a guy like Mike, who doesn't have the status, brawn, or coping skills to deal with his conspecifics.

Especially if the biggest, shittiest conspecific has demonstrated an interest in killing anyone who eats his fruit or so much as looks sideways at his harem.

Some of those solitary males? Go nuts.

Seriously. They can self-harm. It can be ugly.

Now, I didn't think Mike had a secret cigar box full of razors. But I did think he was pulling out his hair. And there was nothing we could do about it. There was no higher power that could reorder ape society around a nicer set of rules.

Mike was a nice guy. Good to Blue. Good to me. Good to everybody. Quick to make himself the butt of his own jokes. His pratfalls were legend. They made the keepers laugh. I think they even made Jollof laugh, which was the point. (The point of all comedy, and most sleight-of-hand magic, is to help the weak survive the dictatorship of the strong.) But the Lowlands just isn't all that nice to nice guys.

Was Mike nice because that was his nature? Or because that was his context? Because he was born small, into a silverback's big, badass world? I thought about this sort of thing a lot on afternoons when I put in my ape hours between the end of school and the opening tip of Harps vs. Harpmeat.

"How's our boy?" Brian was beside me, tapping his Ketch-All restraint pole against his boot.

"Not good."

"What's your scientific opinion?"

I shrugged. "Sad. Lonely. In love. Balding."

"Sounds about right." Brian checked his watch. "Give your old man a ride to the game?"

"I'm worried about Number 19," said Brian. "He's a different animal."

It'd been a surprisingly rough night for the JV Harps. They were down nine at the half, and Brian and I sat on the Keseberg side—a little subdued that night—trying to figure out what was going wrong. There'd been few occasions for Harps fans to spring to their feet, which meant I'd actually gotten to see a decent portion of the game. (Even a sitting crowd, though, meant a lot of partial views for yours truly: I'd mastered the art of watching basketball between lolling heads, through wispy scrims of hair.)

Word was getting around about Drew, I guess, and other squads were finally devising anti-Drew measures: double teams, hard fouls, anything to jam him up. And here in the final hour, St. Augustine looked like it might've found a way: Number 19, a quick little combo guard (by *little*, I mean five eight or so) who'd nabbed a steal off Drew in the first quarter and taken it down for a three, and that was just the appetizer. This kid was *hitting*, he was fast, and he was a demon rebounder for a short stack, winning way more than his share of fifty-fifties. His hands were a blur.

Not bad, little man. Not bad.

He'd even caught the attention of the sports photographer for our yearbook, the *Pequod*. The shutterbug was this skinny white kid who showed up at every game (I could never remember his name, or I'd subliminally forgotten it out of spite because he was always click-click-clicking over me) and was now sprawling on the sidelines to get a low angle on the St. Augie guard. Looked like Drew's new nemesis had already made *Pequod*'s "Worthy Adversaries" page.

"But watch," said Brian, "Drew'll come out of the locker room a new player. They came here with a perfectly good game to play against him, but in five minutes, he'll be someone else, playing a new game, just watch. *Adaptation.* Name of the game."

My dad applied a lot of evolutionary biology to high school basketball, maybe a little more than it could bear. Maybe a little more than *I* could bear, sometimes.

"That's why invasive species throw everything out of whack. Often, they're overadapted to their new environments. Everybody in town's got all these automatic assumptions, how big you have to be, how fast, etc. Then in comes the tegu, or the northern snakehead, or Japanese knotweed—and bam! None of it matters anymore...."

Truth is, I loved my father's zoo stories, even when they were what one might call *patronizing* (if one were an unbridled ingrate dick face). Brian's fables tended to have morals, pretty unsubtle ones, which always boiled down to *Don't underestimate yourself!* Needless to say, Drew did not receive lavish inspirational animal fables packed with scientific facts, because he didn't need them. He was doing just fine in the adaptation department, thank you very much.

I loved the animal stories, because they were a language only Brian and I spoke.

But it was already time for the third-quarter tip. Back to reality.

"Consider the tegu, for ex— Uh-oh, here it comes, here it *comes!*" And Brian was suddenly on his feet, because biology in motion is tons more fun than biology in theory, and Drew was making his move. Adapting.

First he hit a big three off the dribble, and the stands exploded. Then, very next play, before our eyes stopped vibrating from the last shot, Drew zeroed in on St. Augie's little guard, who was in the process of reading the bigs inside, deciding how to come off his pick. Drew came off his man unexpectedly and just *stripped* Number 19, candy from an armless baby. Spesh then proceeded to lope downcourt for a casual dunk that took the roof off the joint.

Meltdown. The bleachers combusted. The shutterbug jerked excitedly, practically in seizures, as he snapped away. As the third quarter passed into the fourth, the stands could feel the game's tectonic plates sliding in the Harps' direction, and so could the St. Augie guard, who was obviously off his axis. Rattled. Slinging brick after brick. He was a more than competent player and had put on a good show, but now, all of a sudden, he was a different person, just like Drew was. But not in a good way. He wouldn't pass, couldn't see the lifelines his teammates were throwing him. In a matter of seconds, he'd gone from giant killer to just another victim of Number 38, the Special.

Next play, the defense tried to close over Drew, tried to swallow him, but he wouldn't be swallowed. He Euro-stepped, launched himself, rose from this tangle of minor giants, and found the free air above the paint. Then fed the hoop again with a satisfying *GA-GONG*.

Now Keseberg was only down by two. Thirty seconds to go.

Brian stood up. "Do it, Drew! C'mon!" And I got the strangest feeling. . . .

Sympathy.

For the devil.

I felt really bad for that little guard.

I wanted him to show Drew that he was still the same person, underneath. That he was still the winner he'd seemed to be just fifteen minutes ago. That he couldn't be so easily shaken, so forcibly changed.

It was not to be.

Because Drew suddenly, humiliatingly stole the ball from him *again*.

He was on a breakaway for an easy tie, the little guard scrambling in pursuit. The clock had seven seconds, plenty of time to even the score with a safe, uncontested layup. But Drew stopped—

—*and pulled up for the three*. Released. Just as the little guard—as surprised as the rest of us at this move—plowed into Drew from behind . . . and bounced off harmlessly. The ball was at the top of its parabola . . .

. . . and I realized . . .

. . . suddenly, demonically, and out of nowhere . . .

. . . that I was praying for a *brick*.

Swish.

And the foul.

The stands went insane. The shutterbug's camera had a grand mal.

Drew drained the free throw.

Of course he did. He was 90 percent from the line.

With two seconds on the clock, the little guard launched a half-court Hail Mary. It landed in the pep band with a cartoon clatter of cymbals. A witty Keseberg trumpeter made the *waaaah-waaaah* with her horn mute, and Harp Nation thundered down the risers to the court and dog-piled my blood brother, who stood a head above all comers until he got pulled down into the boil. Before he disappeared into it, his eyes found mine. He looked right at me, raised a fist, and pointed a finger.

You, he was telling me, *that was for you.* Which made me feel so grateful.

But by now you know how I feel about feeling grateful.

He'd just dedicated his JV championship win to me. To the guy who'd just prayed for him to brick, who'd just prayed against his own brother. I watched the St. Augie guard slink out the side door of the gym, out of the light, out of the gene pool.

I was glad my prayer hadn't been answered.

But I still had a kind of faith that night. Faith in my own adaptation.

Adaptation's a funny word for betrayal.

* * *

I was changing.

An hour early, I'd lemured down the rock face to BoB, vanished into the cave, opened my small duffel, laid out my Batsuit:

Jeans from the internet, expensive ones, tailored by a guy in LA whose website said he made costumes for child actors. (They'd cost me most of my Lowlands earnings.)

A beige linen shirt, cut for a short torso. (Most off-the-rack shirts blouse on the little man, making him look square and low and boxy.)

I stared at Rafty's lifts for thirty solid seconds, asking myself, *Really?* before slipping them into my sick-ass brand-new Bred Jordans (boys' size 7, the *Space Jam* logo carefully blotted out with Liquid Paper).

I fussed, I straightened. I flossed and Listerined.

Then I waited.

And waited.

For over an hour.

Eight-fifteen came and went. No Monica.

Nine came and went. No Drew.

There's one inconvenient thing about BoB I forgot to mention: no signal.

I know, I know: *Hold up, halfling. Why didn't you just head back up to civilization and check your messages?*

Two reasons. One was logical. There was more than one way down the cliff, and I didn't want to miss them, a whales-passing-in-the-night sort of thing.

The other reason was less logical, and little unhinged: I didn't want excuses. Short of apocalypse, they should've been there. No excuse was enough.

She'd bagged. So much for love.

He'd bagged. So much for brotherhood.

My greatest friends in the world (whose trust I'd planned to betray, but only a little, only surgically, and for all the right reasons) somehow couldn't find a way to make it to the most important night of my life.

Maybe it was a sign, or just evolution taking its course. This was a half plan by a half man. Nature had eliminated it before it could even climb out of its shell, and that was for the best, probably.

The moonlight shivered on the water off the reef as I sang ancient Billy Joel sea chanteys, and the whales ignored me. Rightfully so. I was a solitary male. Pulling my hair out. Talking to myself. Out of step with my conspecifics. Stranger in a strange biome. I'd asked just one little favor of the universe: for everything to change. And the universe had *blown it*. Big-time.

I stomped back into the domed cathedral of the BoB cave, looking for the ceremonial beverage, that which was allegedly better than beer. I found it, behind a boulder: Cap'n Chad's Apricot Spiced Rum.

Deprazing.

I almost opened the bottle. Maybe that'd be a proper response— get trashed, then try to catch a wave. Die mythically, like a rock star. But no, cliché alert: teen drinking tragedy. With an absurd twist:

TINY DRUNKEN CORPSE WASHES ASHORE AT TORREY

FIRST RESPONDERS BAFFLED, AMUSED

I had happier thoughts, too. Like *Maybe everyone is dead?*

That'd explain it. How both of them could flake on me. Why hadn't I considered it before? Ebola outbreak. Terrorist attack. Nuclear carrier meltdown in the harbor. Zoo jailbreak, mass carnage. I was Omega Man, last of my kind. When the aliens came to pick over what was left, they'd find me and think, *Adorable*. "Zarlok! Fetch our tiniest terrarium."

I was sitting in the cave, calculating how long I could live here on rum—apricot spiced rum had to have some nutritional value, and my dainty metabolism wouldn't need much—when a skittle of pebbles rained off the rock overhead.

I popped up way too fast. Way too eager.

"Monica?"

"Will?"

She was preceded by a smell I did not recognize, not in the context of BoB nor in the context of Monica: *perfume*. I associated three smells with Monica. Ocean. Old wet suit. Hot sauce. This was none of the above.

Then a pair of what can only be described as sexy sandals hit the sand. Monica dropped down after them.

Sexy sandals? Decorative danglies and leather thingies?

It wasn't the last shock of the night. Not by a long shot.

For instance: Monica climbed into BoB wearing the most un-Monica outfit imaginable. Pants that had a silky sheen to them. Pants that had some kind of *shape* to them. Pants that suggested *Monica* had a shape. And what was going on with this shirt? It was bright red, fire-truck red, and sheer, with a lower-flying neckline than I'd ever seen on Monica, and sleeves that flared like little wings and ended halfway down her upper arms. Also: *mascara?!* Was that really mascara? Holy God, it was. She had on enough mascara to fuel an emo revival single-handedly.

What was happening? Had I hit my head on the way down here? Was I dead? Had I already reached the inexplicable finale of my low-rated television series?

Monica's head was cocked a little sideways, like an owl's. She was studying me.

"You look weird. What's wrong?"

"*I* look weird? What's with the sandals and . . . stuff?"

She looked down at her outfit, shrugged. "Not working? Mascara too much? Or just too much mascara? I honestly don't know. Took forever to get this shit on. 'S why I'm late."

"I mean," I said, my mouth suddenly full of cotton candy, "it . . . *works.*" I really had no idea where to go with *that.* What did *works* mean, in that context? For whom? On whom? I just stopped talking for a second, and let the Angel of Awkwardness pass over.

"Well," said Monica finally, "it's my best friend's sixteenth birthday. Is that *not* a special occasion?" And she sat down next to me, in a plume of . . . perfume? I must've winced or something. She noticed. "Look, I never wear this crap. Don't know when to say when."

"What . . . *flavor* is that?"

Monica shrugged. "Some kind of flora." She looked like she was really trying to remember what flower reek she'd bought. That, or gathering her thoughts. Again: a weird look on her. You generally didn't see Monica gathering her thoughts. She came into every situation with thoughts pregathered.

Finally she said: "You didn't get our messages."

"No."

"Why didn't you go back up?"

I gave her the logical answer that didn't matter, instead of the irrational one that did: "I was afraid I'd miss you."

Monica thought about that. "I get it."

"So what happened?"

"Drew got jocknapped."

"Ah. Varsity."

"Varsity. They took him to the Party Toilet. I think he's trying to get an Uber. Could be here any minute."

And it hit me: for all my wailing and gnashing of teeth, and despite four mournful choruses of Billy Joel's "Miami 2017" (to which no whales had responded), this was *exactly* the time alone with Monica I'd imagined. Everything I'd hoped for. Just an hour late.

Nothing was canceled. It was all happening.

So tell her.

Here's what I'd planned to say: *We'll be ridiculously mismatched together! We'll be the weirdest silhouette against a romantic sunset! We'll show 'em asymmetric love in a square world! Robbing banks and surfing!* A lot of this didn't make sense, but the point was: *Hell with everything, let's do this!*

"So . . . this morning, if I was acting a little . . . off . . ." Holy shit. I was doing it. I was starting!

Monica squinted at me in the dark.

Beyond the Sawtooth, something big breached, breathed, dove again.

"Well," I went on, feeling my way into the dangerous fissure I'd opened, "it's 'cause I've . . . I've been thinking a lot . . ."

The moon dove behind a cloud. Like it was taking cover. The night had gone all cinematic, for sure, but . . . maybe the wrong kind of cinematic? Maybe not the romantic dramedy I'd half planned. Wait. Was this a *horror* movie?

Too late. I'd started.

Tell her.

"... thinking about all the times you've ... saved me ..."

"Hey," said Monica, smelling toast burning and coming to my rescue—*again!*—even though she had no idea what she was rescuing. "You know how many times you've helped me through shit with my dad? Actually, you *don't* know. That's what's great about you, Daughtry. You don't keep score."

She was wrong. She was *so* wrong. I *had* kept score. I knew precisely how much I was losing by. It was my worst feature—

Oh, God. Her hand had landed on mine. She left it there long enough for me to feel its weight. Its warmth. I couldn't believe how good it felt. My big love confession, just starting to take shape, began twiddling its lips like a cartoon rabbit.

Blubbityblubbityblub.

Tell her.

The words were live and chambered, and I was opening my mouth with the very real intention of saying them, when Monica asked, "So you want your present now or after the party?"

This was a trick question.

Because Monica gave trick presents.

Once, she gave me, no kidding, *bleached squirrel bones* (culmination of a running joke too complex to go into here), only she'd packed them in a Lego box, organizing them in the little trays, so I was *deep* into unpacking the damn thing (*Legos, that's cool, I'm a little old for Legos but—What the Jesus? Bones!*) before I realized I'd been handed an itemized rodent autopsy.

Before I could answer, she dropped it in my hand: something *warm* from the pocket she'd kept it in (I tried not to think about that).

Small. But heavy. Round.

A ring. Plain. On a leather thong.

On pure nerd instinct, I immediately peeked at the inscription. There it was.

"Not out loud," Monica warned.

Ash nazg durbatulûk . . .

The Black Speech of Mordor. Not to be spoken here.

It was, of course, the One Ring.

And what the inscription said, in the Dark Tongue, was *One Ring to rule them all . . .*

"*Etsy*," whispered Monica, mock mysterioso. "Custom job. Many, many long and confusing conversations with a metalsmith in Venice Beach who, I'm pretty sure, has more pewter gnomes than friends. Anyway. Happy birthday."

I turned the ring over and over in my hand, searching for the right response—in Elvish, in English, whatever. Because this had, for real, cost Monica precious time and money, neither of which she had. And because, for the third time that day, I had no idea how to feel about a birthday present.

There was another reason I was Dark Tongue–tied.

Monica, Drew, and I, see, we'd been dweeby Tolkienoid Middle-earthers together forever . . . but we didn't *assign roles,* y'know?

Maybe the bigger issue was: we all knew what role *I'd* be assigned.

And Monica had just assigned it to me.

Frodo.

I love you and I've always loved you isn't something you say after someone's just made you Frodo. Frodo's great, don't get me wrong. But Frodo doesn't get the girl. Frodo lives in the Shire, which is another name for the friend zone.

I'd come here wondering, *Does love conquer all? Or is it always eleven inches away?* And Monica had just answered my question with *Here is your hobbit ring from Etsy, and also a complimentary ballectomy because no, I do not consider you any kind of man. Now off to Mordor with you! I packed you a little lunch!*

Not what she intended at all, of course. And part of me knew that. The rest of me *still* said the really dumb thing I said:

"You do know I'm *already* invisible. Right?"

Ever watch a building get demolished, like, professionally? One of those detonations done from the inside out? That's how Monica's face looked, the second I said that.

After a pause just long enough for me to regret what I'd said and my whole loathsome existence, she said: "No, dummy. You only *turn* invisible if you give in to the darkness. If you put it on. That's the whole point. You *carry* the burden, you don't . . . Shit. Just forget it."

She looked at the ring. Seeing it from another angle. My angle. My low angle. My low, shitty angle.

Great job, buddy. Drag her down to your level.

"Hey. Hey! I'm kidding," I said. "I love it. I love it so much, I . . . I don't even know what to say."

She squinted. Not buying it, not not-buying it. "You're not a great present receiver, anybody ever tell you that?" she said finally.

My dead mom did once, a long time ago, but that's another story.

"Guilty as charged."

"Okay, Ring-bearer, I guess let's . . . get our asses to Jazzy's Party Toilet, save Drew. His Toxic Masculinity Exposure Badge must be deep red by now."

And before I knew it, we were climbing.

Up the cliffside, away from BoB, away from the amazing moment we'd had, which I'd ruined. Away from my one window, my one chance for everything to change.

I couldn't let it end like this, the moment I'd schemed and lied and microbetrayed into existence.

Near the top, cell service returned, and my phone hiccuped.

Drew. A barrage of old texts (*quick stop at p toilet then to you!*), and a new one:

trying to find a lyft

"Who's that?" asked Monica. She'd already summited, and was getting her strange, sexy sandals back on. She wasn't used to them, and it was a battle, one girl against wave after wave of tiny leather thongs.

The *blurp!* of a fresh text from Drew:

stay put @ bob monica headed your way me too will converge

No. No, no, no. I needed more time.

Project Semi-Judas could still work. On sheer instinct, I typed:

no dont come we will meet u

"Is that Drew?"

Drew wrote back:

would rather go with original will-centric plan

"Yep."

no no no stay where u are all's well

"Says he needs an extract. We should come to him."

The lie came so easily, it was scary.

k brother c u soon chez toilet!

I turned off the phone. Added a white lie to my Ethical Breach Queue.

Now came the hard part.

"Hey! Wanna see something pathetic as hell?"

Monica turned, raised an eyebrow. "Always?"

I kicked off my Jordans. Picked the lifts out of them, like anchovies off a pizza. Showed them to her.

For a second, she just stared.

Then she cracked up. Guffaws. Belly laughs. Snorts. Monica never held back a good laugh.

"Jesus," she said. "Rafty?"

We both laughed.

She handed me *IF YOU CAN READ THIS* and hung on to *WE HOOKED UP ALREADY,* and then together—still laughing our asses off—we ran to the End, the cliff's edge, where the guardrail guarded BoB, and we each pitched a lift into the water below.

"What do I tell Rafty?"

"Tell him," Monica said, "tell him you hooked up with someone. And she stole them."

"What I like about this story," I laughed, almost gasping now, "is the plausibilit—"

At first I thought she'd slipped and bumped into me.

Except Monica didn't slip. Everything Monica did was magic, and everything Monica did was precisely what Monica meant to do in the moment she was living in. So when I felt it, I knew what it was, I knew what it meant.

What she'd done was

Have I mentioned

she'd reached out

how furiously

and patted my head

I hate pats on the head?

like my mom.

We just kind of looked at each other. Like neither of us could believe what had just happened. But it had. It couldn't be taken back. Hobbit hair cannot be unruffled.

That's when the shadow took me.

"*Don't.* Do that." Little fangs and claws sprouting. Ugly. Small.

Monica took a step back. Appalled. At what she'd done? At how I'd reacted?

And the moment—the moment I'd lied and betrayed for, the moment I'd committed so many small sins to engineer—was gone. It heaved, rolled, and took a terminal dive. In its place was just night. Dead night. Water. Rock. Nothing alive down there, nothing worth trying to sing to the surface.

"Hey. Uh. It's been a weird day." I pretended to get a text. "Whoa, Drew must really be drowning in the Party Toilet."

Monica didn't say anything. I saw a real darkness on her. A sticking, tarry darkness. And I'd put it there.

I would've done any lame-ass imp dance to get that shadow off her. Instead, I put on my necklace, my One Ring, my gift and burden. And I said: "Whaddaya say? Off to Mordor?" Then: "It's just . . . the head pat thing . . ."

"No," Monica said quickly, "I get it."

"Promise I won't go Gollum again."

Then she smiled. The darkness lifted a little. "Better not," she said. "Don't make me throw you into Mount Doom."

I was back to being the half-decent half man she knew, instead of the whole and complete asshole I'd just toyed with becoming.

And for nothing. Because I knew now that this person would

never love me the way I loved her. She would love me in another way, one that would make it impossible for the kind of love I needed to exist.

And I would be happy for that. Lucky.

Breaking even: that was going to be my big victory tonight.

And you know what? I was *grateful*.

But the night wasn't half over.

FIVE

THE PARTY TOILET was a porcelain-white trapezoid hung off a beach cliff in Pacific View, the choicest nabe in the school district. It looked like a box of supermarket wine trying to mount a commode. That's kinda what it smelled like inside, too. The whole school was there. And the whole school was *wasted*.

"When the Big Wave comes," Monica screamed over the assembly of raving Harps, "this crock of shit will be the first thing to go." Monica loved the Big Wave. It was her preferred apocalypse. It's probably every surfer's preferred apocalypse.

Nothing makes the short man feel shorter quite like a crowded party. And packed in this tight—cologne and deodorant are pretty stifling at armpit level—it's not a wholesome atmosphere, let me tell you.

Even worse, I watched dudes' heads swivel to Monica as we pushed through that mash of Harps. They were once-overing her, trying to figure out who she was, starting to put it together: it's

Monica Bailarín, Barrio Nacional's own mystic surf bum in training, Cleaned Up Nice for a night. Hooboy. Last thing I needed was to watch shit-faced meatheads and meat-faced shitheads ogle Monica. I wanted to complete our mission—Operation Drew Extraction—and GTFO.

"Where's Drew, you think?" I asked.

"Outside is my guess," Monica yelled, leaning in. He certainly wasn't in plain view—and he'd gotten much easier to find in a crowd over the last year or so.

Monica bulldozed through the throbbing flesh that mobbed Jazzy's massive mead hall of a living room. I followed in her wake, but in the end, there was too much throb and too little me. Elbows. The world's a forest of elbows at four foot eleven. I ducked into the galley pantry for a breather, and when I looked up, Monica had completely disappeared. Two towering, tottering guys—basketball players, I think—passed a keg *over my head* as I took the side door out of the scrum. Felt good to breathe fresh-ish sea air again. But Monica was nowhere to be found.

Outside, there was a lot of suspicious rustling in the bushes. Bedrooms upstairs were full, I guess, so memories that would last a lifetime and/or be obliterated by tomorrow had to be made out here, in nature. I had to step carefully to avoid becoming part of those memories.

I heard the *thwap* of basketball on asphalt, moved in that direction.

It wasn't Drew. It was his future teammate Eric Forchette (6′4″), varsity power forward and unironic rage machine. He was playing a game of horse for a gathering crowd.

His opponent: one Roderick Raftsman Rhinehardt Royall.

And—holy shit—Rafty was *winning.*

As I walked up, he'd just sunk a through-the-legs bounce shot. *Swish.*

Audible gasps. It was H-O-R-S in Rafty's favor. Eric Forchette looked sweaty. (And, it should be noted, drunk. Which explained a lot.)

A growing village of gawkers was gathering now, to watch the runty kid who suddenly couldn't miss a series of crazy trick shots take on the towering jock who couldn't disguise his frustration. Phones blazed.

Everybody loves the exception, so they can go right back to the rule.

"Willy boy!" Rafty yelled, motioning me over.

Forchette barked, "Take your shot, Royall. Let's get this over with."

"One sec, E-Money!" Rafty turned back to me. "My friend, I'm so glad you're here. Top of the Toilet, Ma! We made it!"

"What's going on here, buddy?" I felt an obligation to apply the brakes, knowing Rafty never would.

"I'm in the middle of a *major rebrand* is what's going on. I, uh, I may have been . . . preparing? For this moment? A little?"

"That's great, Rafty," I said. "Just watch out, okay? Forchette's a psycho when he's drunk."

Rafty grinned. " 'Be cautious and bold.' Barnum."

"Okay, but: 'Hulk smash.' Hulk."

"Last chance, asshole!" shouted Eric.

"William?" Rafty snapped his fingers. "Camera, por favor. I would like the following archived for future generations."

And Roderick Raftsman Rhinehardt Royall squared up and—

I'll be damned—drained another no-look, over-the-head bucket, twenty yards out, from behind the azaleas.

Forchette dropped a muddy, slurry series of f-bombs, then released his shot . . .

. . . which toilet-bowled into the neighbor's yard.

The crowd went wild. Forchette sulked off, grabbing a bottle of Cuervo from the first beta male he saw, mumbling, "Goddamn circus act."

That it was, Eric Forchette. That it was.

I saw my friend and fellow halfling, my war buddy and co–shelf elf, hoisted onto the shoulders of near strangers. Rafty pointed down at me. "Are you not entertained?! Post the long version! I'll edit it down to a twelve-second spot tomorrow! *Tomorrooooooow!*"

With that, Rafty was carried off in the direction of the keg. After we found Drew, I figured, we'd do a Rafty sweep, try to pull him out of here before Forchette got drunk enough to seek revenge.

That's when I heard two sounds that, together, bothered me.

Vomiting. And laughter. Male laughter. Low and throaty, from multiple sources. The kind of laughter that comes in packs.

There are various theories about how animals sense danger. Stories of worms boiling out of the ground before an earthquake, elephants fleeing from the coast five minutes before the tsunami crashes through. It's what serious science would call interesting but anecdotal. Hard to run that experiment, y'know?

But I felt it. I felt, in the soles of my feet, what those elephants must've felt. The unmistakable vibration of Trouble. And the undeniable urge to run.

Hehehehehehe . . .

It came from back in the pines, a wooded lot that was Toilet-adjacent. I looked around. As far as I could tell, everyone who'd been watching the Rafty show had gone back to the house. Biology told me I should do the same. Civilization agreed with biology. *Back to the light! Back to the cookfires and piddling rules of society, shitty though they may be! It's better than whatever's out there!*

More laughter now. And more vomiting.

On instinct, I pulled out my phone. Only one bar of battery, and flickering. Power drained by BoB, from reaching for a signal that wasn't there. I flicked it to Airplane Mode to save whatever juice was left.

So there I was: one of those behind-enemy-lines-without-a-radio moments. Go find reinforcements? And risk letting the bad thing that was clearly in progress happen? Or go in, half-cocked? A half-cocked half man?

What would Drew do? What would Monica—

Vomiting. Laughter.

Without a plan, I walked into the pines.

There was a fallen tree and a shaft of streetlight, enough to see a bunch of guy shapes, faceless in the shadows, standing in the ancient ritual semicircle of Guy Evil. I braced for what I'd see in the middle of that semicircle: some poor girl, blotto, in God knows what state of—

But no. It was the shutterbug.

Now his name came swimming back to me: Neville Ethan. No! *Ethan Neville.*

And there was his steampunk Leica, his pathetic hipster accessory, the world's last film camera, on the ground. In pieces. Ethan wasn't in pieces quite yet, but it looked like he was headed that way. They had him draped over a pine like a duffel bag. His shirt was off, and his fish-belly-white torso glowed in the moonlight. He was heaving in weird ways, like he wasn't quite conscious. Even from a ways off, I could smell him. Had science found a way to distill Jolly Ranchers into liquor?

"The Human CamelBak," someone funnied, unfunnily. "Coming to a theater near you."

"Not too near, man. He's gonna—"

Ethan upchucked some noxious, unreal color, the kind of atomic green found only in low-budget science fiction and high-toxicity cleaning products. They'd pumped him full of one of those candy liquors. Probably convinced him he could be one of the pack or something.

"It spilled," another voice observed. "Refill!"

And now I recognized the voices.

It was the football team.

Unhappy, perhaps, with their lack of yearbook coverage?

Of course it was the football team: Spencer Inskip and his lineup of beefy mediocrities, my most fearsome middle school foes. Worse than Jazzy, even. Jazzy enjoyed humiliating people, but Spencer and Co.? Those dudes *hit*.

Aside from Spencer, I'd blocked out their names, but I remembered their *shapes:* rhombus, rectangle, doucheahedron—shapes I often saw coming at me in my nightmares. Jesus, how much Pucker had they funneled down Ethan's gullet to get him to take his shirt off?

Leaves crunched underfoot, announcing me.

Six pairs of drunk-but-not-nearly-drunk-enough eyes swiveled to me: together, the assembled shapes were a giant mutant spider in the dark. Well. Here we were. Half Man vs. Acromantula! Me and Shelob down by the schoolyard! I spoke the following in my testosteroniest voice:

"Hey, uh, what's happenin', guys?"

Triangle shrugged. "All's well, little man. Just having fun." This voice was silkier. It belonged, I knew, to Spencer.

"You okay?" I asked the kid, whose name, in the midst of staving off a full-scale panic attack, *I had forgotten again*. Ah, there it was: "Ethan? *You* having fun?"

"Private party," Rhombus growled, in defiance of the dangerous lack of self-awareness it takes to *actually growl* the words "private party."

I felt the nearly dead phone in my hand and, on pure reflex, lifted it. And hit Flashlight. Bathed the woods in a clean white Gandalfian glow.

"Shit," said one baller, and started edging off, back toward the party. Another followed him. Wow. Instant reaction. I would have felt downright powerful if I hadn't been so busy shitting myself. How long would the light last? Not long.

Rhombus came forward on his knuckles, or seemed to. "Give me the goddamn phone, shit twist."

I stepped back. "Sure," I said, "but I'm live-streaming, and it looks to me like Ethan might need a ride home. So—"

"*Oh my God!* What did you assholes *do?*" The voice came from behind me: familiar, but my adrenalized brain couldn't run the plate until I saw my lab partner, Sidney Lim.

Oh, thank God.

Sidney ran to Ethan's side. By that time, he was out cold.

"The hell's wrong with you?" Sidney muttered to the remaining meat stacks.

Sidney and Ethan Neville are friends was my initial, idiotic thought. *That's weird.* Brains get strange when they think they're about to die.

"Jesus. I'm calling an ambulance."

"Sid," came Spencer's silky, triangular voice again, "don't be dumb."

"Dumb?! Dumb was when you dick warts poisoned him. You know how he is."

"How is he, Sid?" Spencer's voice was a creepy, even hum. "You two close, or is this just another one of your rescue puppies?"

They locked eyes. Spencer. Sidney. Another idiotic thought drifted through my head: *Spencer and Sidney. They used to date. Huh.*

"You're torturing my friends now?"

"This derp's not your friend," said Spencer. "You collect these betas, Sid." And here he gestured vaguely in my direction. "They worship you. It's sad."

"Get medicated, psycho," Sid spat. "Ethan? Can you hear me?"

"I dunno," and his voice was the low hum of a white noise machine. "I seem like the calm one here, Sid. You're the one— What are you doing?"

Sidney held up her phone, showed him the 911 she'd already dialed. "And I hope the EMTs call the cops on every last one of you Pop Warner date rapists."

"Hey, bit—" growled Rhombus, but Spencer held up a restraining hand. With a nod from him, the shapes began to disperse. Best to be gone when the ambulance pulled up.

Sid was already hoisting Ethan, staggering low to get his right arm around her neck. "Can you help?" Rectangle, the most soul-enabled of the ballers, started swooping in, but Sidney shook her head. "Not you. Will? A little help here?"

A little help. I almost made the joke so I could be the punch line. Plain old derision felt much safer than this. But instead, I got under Ethan's left side—

Oof. Never in my life, before or since, have I felt anything heavier than Ethan Neville felt that night. I don't even know how I did it.

"Hey, Will," called Spencer, in his most pointed, most triangular voice. "Let's talk later."

"Sounds great," I gasped. I was too busy struggling to lug a limp Ethan up the embankment to worry about any future beatdowns implied.

Sidney and I hauled Ethan into a miraculously empty guest bedroom, flopped him down, and flipped him on his side, like the health class manuals say right after they say, *Don't drink.*

"Should I wait for the ambulance outside?"

"Didn't call the ambulance," said Sid. "That was a bluff. But who knows, someone's probably called one by now, after your live stream."

"Um," I said, holding up my dead phone. "This was a bluff, too."

Sid smiled. "Not bad. You learn that in AP bio?"

"Sure," I said. "Bluffing and camouflage. That's half of biology."

"What's the other half?"

Decent question. "Showing up?"

Sid laughed as she wiped Ethan's face with a Stridex from her purse. "He's really not a drinker." She flicked it into the Pottery Barn trash can under the Pottery Barn nightstand. "And I *am* his friend. I don't 'collect betas.' For the record."

Sid and Ethan the shutterbug: now it hit me. Her volleyball pics in last year's *Pequod*. *That's* how they'd crossed paths.

Sidney was looking at me now, really *looking*. Odd sensation. "How'd you break up their little circle jerk?"

"Laughter and vomit," I said. Then, realizing this made no sense, I added, "I mean: I heard vomiting, and then laughing, and . . . well, it seemed like a bad vibe."

"Yep, that's Spencer," said Sid. "He's a walking bad vibe. Can't believe I dated that sociopath for *four months. . . .*"

She sighed, as if the whole relationship were playing out in her imagination at that moment. It was playing out in mine, too: how'd that even work? Sure, Sidney was pretty, Sidney was popular, and Spencer was captain of the football team . . . albeit a football team so fourth-rate, they were kind of a school-wide joke.

The basic social math added up, but . . . Spencer was *evil*. Always had been. And Sidney just *wasn't*. Sidney was loyal. Open. Cruelty-free, from what I'd seen. She even tolerated Rafty, who tested the limits of tolerance on a semiregular basis.

And Sidney had a unique mutant power, pretty exotic among high school students: Sidney remembered who her real friends were. Ethan Neville, beached safely on Jazzy's fourth-best guest bedroom bed, was (barely) living proof of that.

"Well," said Sidney, eyes on her phone now, "thanks for walking toward a bad vibe." She sighed again. "World's a real pile of shit, huh?"

"I . . . uh, I dunno." I really didn't. I still don't.

All I knew, at that moment, was: I wanted to be with *my* real friends, my home triad. All I wanted, after tonight's many adven-

Her hip slid to one side, giving her body a curve I'd never even seen before, and here was Drew's long arm curving parabolically to compensate. I fixated, for some reason, on that arm, his shooting arm, and I had a strange, strong, not entirely geometric thought: *His arm is bigger than my whole body.* And Monica was bending into that arm like a tree in the wind, bending in ways Monica did not bend.

I remember thinking two equally true things:

No, no, wrong, WRONG

and also

Of course.

Because, well, look at them, I thought. *Of course. Of course.*

Figure Drawn to Scale.

I don't remember how long I stood there.

I do remember leaving before they could notice me.

I definitely remember picking up a nearly finished bottle of tequila from the bushes, nothing left but two shots and a Listerine swig, and thinking, *With my body weight? Should be plenty.*

I remember the pavement under my feet as I walked past my Fiat, my clown car, and kept walking, walked all the way home.

As I walked, I did what all good scientists do when a theory fails spectacularly.

I made a new theory.

The new theory went like this:

Biology had taken its shitty course.

Shitty for me. Beautiful for the world.

Beautiful things had found other beautiful things, as is only

tures, was to return to my oceanside Shire with the people I knew I'd always have in my life, no matter how short or long life was, no matter how short or long I was.

Sid's phone chimed. "Heya," she said, patting Ethan's cheek. "Lyft's here."

Ethan's eyes had fluttered open. And boy, did they look . . . scared. Like Ethan wasn't seeing *me* at all, he was still seeing Spencer and his Killer Polygons.

"Hey! Alkie. Up here," Sid said to Ethan, snapping her fingers. "Will Daughtry saved your ass. Remember that."

"Uhhhnnn," mumbled Ethan, uber-confused. "Oh . . . kay?"

"Sid saved you," I corrected. "I maybe threw an assist."

"Let's get you in that car." Sid touched my arm. "Thank you."

And suddenly—the second she touched me and I got that warm tingle spreading through my capillaries that any heteroproximate teenage boy gets when a girl touches him—I knew just where I wanted to be, just where I needed to go. It was hitting me: *why* I'd done what I'd done, why it'd felt possible to walk toward a bad, bad vibe, solo and small.

Because, in that moment, I hadn't been solo. I hadn't been small. Drew and Monica had been with me. I'd walked in there imagining what *they'd* do. I'd walked in there solid in the knowledge I was part of something bigger than myself.

Low bar, Half Man!

Shut up, Asshole Brain. If it weren't for your bullshit, I'd have seen it all along.

We were three. And we were *one.* And we were brave.

I knew, all at once, how I fit into the world. I belonged with

Drew and Monica. My fellowship. *We* were the rest of me, the lost two-thirds of me. Drew and Monica, who made me want to be more. And with them, I already was.

I'd come so close to wrecking that tonight. And for what? For a change?

I wanted to find them. Right that instant. I wanted to tell them what had happened in the woods. How everything felt possible.

There was a narrow path to the ocean behind Jazzy's, and on instinct, I headed down, the coyote mint that fringed the path tugging at my silly Rodeo Drive mini-jeans. I heard the Pacific down there, breathing low, sleeping with one eye open, and for the first time, I felt like I could run into it, right that second, could wade the hell in, on legs that'd hold against the current. Even in the dark, I felt like I could wade in and not just live, not just float, but *swim*. Swim clear of everything, even fear.

Trust the water. I finally got it.

Thanks, Monica.

Be brave. But have a plan.

Gotcha, Drew.

I was sorry I'd lied.

I was sorry I'd been, for a second there, a shifty little semi-Judas. It had been a phase. Just a phase. I was back. We were back. And we were never going to—

That's when I smelled it: some kind of *flora*. Some rando flower flavor.

Monica's new perfume.

And a voice. Male.

Drew's.

How 'bout that, now. It was like the universe'd heard me.

I came bounding down the beach path, rounding the dwarf firs Jazzy's parents had planted to keep their absurd Party Toilet from eroding into the Pacific, and there they were, the rest of my fellowship. Squabbling, the way gods do.

Drew said something I couldn't hear. But I could tell, from the tone, that it was intentionally crass or intentionally dumb or both. Monica thumped him in the chest.

Drew grabbed at her other arm before she could catch him in the gut. Classic Monica! Classic Drew! I'd seen this slap fight.

Then Monica leaned in. And Drew leaned in. And I couldn't make out what was happening.

Then:

I *could* make out what was happening.

Making out was happening.

The moon exploded.

The Big Wave came.

The Party Toilet was swept away, along with the rest of San Diego. But we were still there. The three of us.

Well.

"Three."

They had no idea I was there, and all of a sudden, neither did I, just by accident, put the One Ring on my finger? No. It was just hanging there.

Heavier than it had been a minute ago.

It hung there, I hung there, everything just hung there. Maybe, I thought thickly, maybe Monica would pull away. And say, *Drew! What the hell was that? Are you insane?*

What happened instead was . . . something *gave way* in Monica's body. Like a whole hillside in one of those Japanese tsunami vi

natural. There's a lovely, vicious logic to it you can't deny, because screw you.

Perfection isn't really a thing, scientifically; it's a bias, like beauty. But efficiency—yeah, evolution's got that. Eventually. Makes a lot of local stops along the way. Makes some mistakes.

Like me.

Like my mom.

You've gotta be patient with evolution, is the thing. All those mistakes, all those extinctions, all those trial-and-error bodies in the discard pile—evolution's *learning*. Sure, it's gonna mow down a few hundred billion insufficiently evolved creatures along the way. Sure, it's gonna send a few losers home with tequila bottles full of backwash. But give it time, and you'll get something pure and wonderful out of all that pain.

As for the rest? The waste? The false starts and the first drafts and the sloppy marginalia? You can find it all in the fossil record, that big ledger of also-rans. Written in rock: *YOU LOSE*.

Oh yeah, I was full-on drunk by the time I got home.

Being a lightweight has some advantages, I guess.

I felt like I'd earned this buzz. For being such a good sport. For playing Biology, the game I always knew I'd lose.

My birthday cake was waiting on the counter. Mostly intact. Laura was on a macro diet. Brian had high cholesterol.

I ravaged that cake. Went at it claws out, ate every goddamned crumb. Then I had what suddenly qualified as a happy thought: *If I'm doomed to be a hobbit . . . that means I get to have a hobbit belly!*

The cake was gone. I wanted more. Of anything. So I ate half a jar of pickles. Very undistinguished sandwich pickles. Was this "drunk hungry"? Was this "eating my feelings"?

Is this what giving in to the darkness feels like? I wondered. *Is Sauron just type 2 diabetes?*

I took off my shoes, curled my toes in the carpet, and took off the One Ring. I threw it into our gas log fireplace. I tried to turn that stupid thing on for the better part of ten minutes before I remembered the gas line feeding it had been shut off a long time ago.

So I fished the ring out of the fireplace. I read the inscription, out loud. *Let the Nazgûl come,* I thought. *What does it matter?* I said this out loud, too:

"I will always be four feet, eleven inches tall."

The Black Speech. It was all getting uttered now. *Sorry, Monica.*

So I'd been deselected. So what? Felt natural enough. Practiced for it all my life.

Monica and Drew. Fitting together. I couldn't stop seeing it. Couldn't stop hearing the *click* of compatible DNA.

Monica and Drew. I'd have to get used to that. Monica & Drew.

Could I be the ampersand? Was that position available?

No. "We" were not a triumvirate or a troika or a trinity or a fellowship. "We" were not godsiblings or co-adventurers. "We" were a supercouple—Dronica? MoniDrew"?

Plus a *pet.*

"Will?" Brian. In his bathrobe. "Are you okay?"

I'd been crying. I thought not audibly. One more thing I was wrong about, I guess.

"Fine."

"Have you been drinking?"

I couldn't even muster a good lie. "Yeah, but I walked home."

He sighed. "It's okay."

"It . . . isn't." I sat on the floor. Crisscross applesauce. Story time. "I'm sorry."

Dad sat on the sofa. And he was "Dad" again. I needed a dad right then, I think, not a "Brian" so much. I didn't *want* to need one, but I did.

"You want to talk?"

No? Yes? It was the last question I wanted to answer.

"Where's Drew?" Dad-Brian asked.

No, sorry, *that* was the last question I wanted to answer. I shrugged.

Dad-Brian ran his hands through his Humble Hero Hair. "Is he with Monica?"

I knew he was asking that only because he'd be less concerned about Drew if Monica were with him. But he could not have picked a hotter poker to slide into my dangling entrails. I just wanted this conversation to end. So I managed to form, with my drunkish mouth, words that caused me actual, physical pain:

"He's . . . with Monica."

My father studied me. Knowing something was wrong. Knowing, too, that I wasn't interested in sharing. But honor-bound by the code of parenting, he tried: "You're sure you don't want to—"

"Not really."

We sat in the dark. Then he said, "Okay," and "When you're ready, let me know," and started to head back to bed. "I'll see you at the zoo tomorrow."

"Dad."

"Yeah?"

"You didn't even reach for the tape measure this morning."

It was quiet. I couldn't see Dad-Brian's face. I didn't need to. Finally he said, "I love you, Will. Let's talk when you feel better."

I didn't know when that would be.

Dad-Brian went back to his room, and I ate yet another limp pickle, like a champ. Then I stumped down the hall, kicked off my liftless shoes, and fell into bed. Screamed into a pillow for a solid minute. Cried into it for five, the One Ring stabbing at my chest. Then I started to go away. Finally. Sweet invisibility, even to myself.

And as I faded, I prayed, to some generic and unverified god, for two small things.

SIX

"WILL? WILL?!"

I don't sleep in much. I'm a morning person. Getting literally *shaken* awake—this was a new one.

"Will!"

Light. Stucco. A dirty, glow-in-the-dark stegosaur decal. My bedroom ceiling.

"Will? Are you okay?"

Laura. Standing over me. Worried. I rose up, a reanimated corpse.

"Wha?"

"You wouldn't wake up."

"Oh."

"It's ten a.m. I thought you were gone already."

"Gone?"

"It's Saturday?"

Saturday. *Shit.* The Lowlands. Internship. *Brian.* I launched out of bed, still in yesterday's clothes, tripped over my shoes.

"Should I call your father? Whoa. You smell like . . . pickles."

"Yeah," I mumbled, sludge-mouthed. "I, uh . . . I ate some pickles."

My shoes were tight. They fought me. AP bio came back to me: Water retention. Bloat. From the booze? There hadn't been much tequila left in that bottle. How much damage could I have done? Plus: I didn't *feel* hungover. And something else was coming back to me:

The Big Wave.

Monica. And Drew.

Like waking up with a leg amputated and thinking, *Oh, right, that was REAL.* And then the pain. That phantom limb.

Day One of the New Normal.

"Uh, Laura?"

"Yes?"

"Can you . . . uh . . . drive me to my car?"

On the way to the zoo, I clocked three texts from Monica (*where r u? u get a ride?*), one from Drew (*u ghosted?*), and one from Rafty (*where u @? u post vid of me skooling forchette? narrow window of virality!*). I mass-texted everyone my official status: alive, late for work. I kept my unofficial status to myself: caught in flashback loop, watching Monica's body melt into Drew's. . . .

"Feeling better?"

Brian leaned on his Ketch-All pole. He'd had a rough morning. Bunch of gibbons off their chow.

I nodded.

"You sure?"

"Yeah."

"Then you won't mind feeding the Family." Meaning the gorillas. Our Mansons. I really didn't want to feed the Family. Being in the habitat required some presence of mind, even for a nonthreatening halfling like myself. Jollof was a wild thing, after all.

But I didn't want to have that conversation with Brian, either.

So into the habitat I went, baskets of fruit under each arm. I tottered a little going up the ramp; my feet were stiff and sore from walking home, and my shoes still felt strangely tight. Under the circumstances, it was easy for me to look submissive—head down, sideways shuffle—which is how you're supposed to look upon entering Jollof's domain. Not that Jollof needed any proof that I was beta to his alpha.

But today was different.

Jollof didn't come greet me. He didn't bound up and turn his back to request his usual back massage. He stayed on his rock, his throne. There was an overhang, giving him some privacy from the concourse if he wanted it. The overhang cast a shadow. Today, unlike every other day, Jollof stayed in that shadow. Watching me. I could see his eyes angle on me, glittering like cold dimes. (I remembered, suddenly, strangely, the wishing well on the concourse, the coins at the bottom. All those little faces staring up at the wishers, as if to say, *Wish away, but this is where we* all *end up. . . .*)

The air felt tight. The breeding females and beta males started to gather near me, near the baskets. I got the sense we were all thinking the same thing: *What now?* Nobody, neither man nor gorilla, knew what was going on. We betas waited for our cues.

But nothing happened. We all just stood there. For a very long time.

Finally Magic Mike got tired of waiting. He shrugged, actually *shrugged*. Looked at me like, *Whatcha gonna do?*

I had no answer for him.

So Mike made a move for the mangoes—

Jollof was on him in a hot second.

Biting, cuffing, and—*whoomp!* Magic Mike went tumbling, then ran screeching for the safety of the bamboo brakes.

I started toward the door, but Jollof cut me off.

I froze. He froze. His silver ruff was fluffed up, spiked, like a live current was running through it. He had, I noticed queasily, an enormous erection. *Welp,* I thought, *this is when I get raped to death by an angry gorilla. What a week.*

But right within arm's reach, Jollof just . . . sniffed. Gave me what primatologists call "the stink eye." (Am I getting that right, primatologists?) He twitched his lips and huffed. Like he was trying to decide who I was, *what* I was. Sizing me up. Satisfying some scientific curiosity. Then he *snorted.* Hard enough to blow my hair back a bit. I don't speak Gorillese, but I'm as simian as the next guy, and this snort said, pretty clearly, *GTFO.*

So I GTFO'd. Fast.

Back in the staging area, my heart still racing, I watched things return to normal.

Jollof snapped at a couple of betas, ate his fill, kicked a few melons into the dirt to make his point, beat his chest thunderously, then mounted Blue. Just another Saturday.

What the hell was that all about?

Theories: Maybe Jollof could tell—or smell—that I'd had a few the night before. Maybe he was Southern Baptist, and judgmental. (This would actually explain *a lot* about Jollof.)

Maybe he just didn't like my new shoes.

No one had seen what happened—Brian had been in the office, and I was so reliable that nobody watched me on the monitor anymore. I didn't share. I picked up the Aggression Log, wrote *attacked Magic Mike* under Jollof's name. I looked at the previous fourteen entries. They were all *attacked Magic Mike*.

I sighed. *That's the story,* I thought, *of the rest of their lives, both of them.* Biology is destiny. And in real life, destiny doesn't have much of a plot. It's just a pattern. Reruns. Then death.

My hand hovered over "Additional Notes," but I left it blank. Left out how he'd gotten between me and the door. Feeders who ran afoul of Jollof were immediately reassigned. This? This was a fluke, I convinced myself.

I couldn't lose the one job I was good at, not today.

"Hey! Belated birthday boy!"

I turned. Drew showed no trace of a hangover except a little squint and a careless choice of T-shirt—*SeaWorld Seal-ebration!* Something from the dirty laundry, I guessed.

"So what'd I miss?"

The laundry. That meant he'd been home. Where'd he slept? *Had* he slept?

I didn't want answers to these questions. Why was Asshole Brain asking them?

"Uh, nothing, you missed nothing," I told him. "Just . . . some . . . great apes. Some really great apes."

Asshole Brain was spitting out frantic junk code: *Where'd he sleep didn't see him at home but the shirt wait the shirt was in his gym bag had they did they did they?*

Pock pock pock. Drew drummed his fingers on the habitat's glass. "How's our little guy?"

"Jollof? Model citizen. Even spell-checks his tweets now."

"You got some downtime?" Drew asked. In his voice, I heard it: the Conversation. He wanted to have the Conversation. Little did he know, I'd rehearsed the very same conversation: my version. With me playing the role of rebel lover. *Drew . . . I know the three of us have been friends forever, but . . . Monica and I . . . we're . . . something more. . . .* It was a Fire Speech, a Break Glass in Case of Emergency Address. There'd been a crisis, all right. Just not in my favor.

I shook my head. "Y'know, I got in late, and I'm slammed. I was just gonna grab a turkey sub. . . ."

Drew wasn't shakable. "Cool. I could eat. I'll come with."

In my defense, I really did want a turkey sub. I'd wanted one all morning.

Maybe more than one.

Something about the combination of being threatened by an erect gorilla and anticipating the most awkward conversation of your life with the best friend who's robbed you of your one true love just makes a guy want a foot-long Gibbity Gobbler from the Kibble Kiosk outside the Chinchilla Experience.

"I could eat." Always hated that phrase. It made me want to snap back: *How nice for you! It's so good to have options!* But that was just Asshole Brain talking, and Asshole Brain was not happy with Andrew Tannenger.

Will Daughtry just wanted a sandwich. *So hungry.*

In line, I waited for Drew to tell me about Monica. I could tell he wasn't eager to, for the same reasons I wouldn't have been. He was noodling through some postparty gossip: how drunk Ethan Neville got, how Rafty Royall beat Eric Forchette at horse. How

Eric gargled trash can–punch and got into a huge screamer with his girlfriend in the driveway. On and on. And the family of five in front of us was taking *forever* to order. . . .

I couldn't take it anymore.

"Hey, lemme just . . . before you go on . . . I think it's only fair to say: I . . . I saw you guys."

Drew looked confused and mildly panicked. I put him out of his misery:

"You and Monica. On the beach path at Jazzy's."

Drew was quiet for a long, long time. He seemed to have trouble meeting my eyes. More than usual, I mean: This wasn't a height-disparity issue. This was a shame issue. I didn't blame him.

No, wait. I *did* blame him.

"Yeah," he said finally. "I was gonna . . . I mean, shit." The fact that they'd been seen, by me—that hadn't been factored into Drew's confession plan, or whatever it was he'd cooked up on the way over here. This new information threw him off. Made him a little mad, even.

Which made me a little *happy*, maybe?

Stop, I told Asshole Brain. *Just. Stop.*

"You could've *said* something," Drew said.

Hooboy. Really, buddy?

I stopped arguing with A. Brain and let it take the wheel. "Uh. Said something? Like what? *Hey, could you two stop making out for a second, I wanna tell you something: I'm watching you two make out!*"

Drew ran his hand through his hair. Stung and humbled. Which A. Brain rewrote as *hung and stumbled*. Now my brain was just trolling me.

But Drew was genuinely brushed back. "Dude . . . I'm sorry. I . . . this is . . . it's kinda like telling someone you made out with your own sister, isn't it?"

"Is it? If it is, that is weird. For you."

I sucked on my teeth a minute. Waited to see if Drew had a reply. He didn't. He just stood there.

"No," I said, "it's worse than telling someone you made out with your sister. Because you're not just telling *someone*. You're telling your brother."

Drew looked appalled. I let it hang a second.

Then I laughed. Punched him gently in the gut, the customary shoulder being out of my reach.

"Kidding. *Kidding!* I've been thinking about it, and . . . I think . . ."

And here it was. The fattest, fiercest lie I'd told in a week of lies.

". . . I think . . . that this . . . the two of you . . . that this is a *good* thing."

Drew . . . laughed.

Explosively. A huge trapped bubble of pure relief escaping his thorax. You could almost see the cloud of relief spell out the word *relief* over his head. Which made me—

Grrrrrrrrooowl.

My stomach. Pacing its cage. Audibly. The littlest kid from the family of five ahead of us actually turned and looked: *What* was *that? Did something escape?*

Drew either didn't hear the growl or chose to ignore it. He was still laughing, still relieved. Couldn't process anything else. "I'm so . . . so . . . glad to hear that, dude. You don't know how much . . . last night . . . Well, we basically stayed up all night, talking about you."

"Me?"

"You, and the Plan."

Of course. The Plan. Can't endanger the Plan!

"I don't wanna pretend nothing's different," Drew was saying. "This is ... Well, it kind of snuck up on us, and I want to make sure we, y'know, limit the, y'know ..."

Damage. I *did* know.

"... effects. I mean. It's so strange. Last night, man, I don't know ... it was just ... different. She was different. She made *me* feel different. I mean, I dunno, coulda been the game, coulda been the beer." He suddenly realized what he was saying. "I mean, it wasn't. At all. It was ... real. It *is* real." He grinned.

The phrase *slap that grin off* started to write itself on the bathroom wall of my bad, bad brain. I quickly erased it. But Drew was still grinning. "Probably a really, really bad idea, right?"

Grrrrrrrrooowl.

Drew heard me that time. "Was that you?"

"Uh, yeah. I'm ... uh ... hangover hungry, I guess?"

Drew clapped me on the shoulder, too hard. "What'd you get into last night?"

I only hated Drew a little at that moment. I was much too pre-occupied with hating myself. How was any of this his fault? I'd never given the slightest signal I felt anything toward Monica but brotherly love. I hadn't confided any of my innermost feelings to my closest friend in the world. Instead, I'd tried to hide those feelings, smuggle them past my blood brother, like a guilty little thing fleeing the light. Which, in retrospect: bad move! Oh, and I'd never suspected Drew of feeling anything other than brotherly love for Monica, either. Which, also in retrospect: stupid, *galactically* stupid!

Why should I have expected him to see what I couldn't?

After we'd yammered awhile about alcohol, as if we were old drinking buddies, Drew said, "You never answered my question."

I was lost.

"Is this . . . is this a really, really bad idea?"

"It's a little late to worry about that, isn't it?"

Drew's eyes darkened a shade. "So you *do* think it's a bad idea."

"I think . . ." What I think I thought was: *I'm being an asshole.* Think, schmink: I *was* being an asshole. I'd somehow stumbled thigh-deep into asshole swamps I'd hoped to avoid. But now that I was there . . . "I think it's risky, sure."

"That's it?" he said. " 'Risky'? You think it's risky?"

"Risky's not the same as bad. . . ."

"I know! But you're supposed to *disagree.*" He shook his head. "Because I think . . . Will . . ."

Oh, Jesus, I thought. *Here it comes.*

"I think I . . . I think she . . . maybe the two of us . . . maybe we've always . . ."

I needed to stop whatever was being said here. I knew I didn't want to hear it. So I slapped a big ol' Band-Aid on this gusher of a burst aneurysm:

"I don't think you'd have done it if you thought it was wrong, deep down. You two are my closest friends in the world. This is . . . new. I just gotta, y'know, stress-test it. Kick the tires. That's my job."

Drew smiled. Appeased. Grateful. We were at the front of the line. "Sub?" he offered. "I'm buying."

Because eventually the silverback lets the betas eat, right?

"Sub me," I said.

Grrrrrrowl.

"Whoa! Right in the nick of time. You better *feed* that thing!"

Drew stared at me as I took the last two bites of my sub. His wasn't even half-finished.

He whistled. "Would *not* want to meet your hangover in a dark alley."

Two pounds of food in three minutes can't be healthy, but Drew offered me his other half anyway, saying he was late for practice. Which left me alone with his sub. Two minutes later, I was just alone.

I finished my shift at the zoo, carefully avoiding Brian. I stared in at Jollof for a while, trying to make sense of his episode. Maybe he'd sensed my mood? Animals can do that. Almost felt bad for ol' Asshole, having to sense a mood like mine.

I clocked the hell out.

Back in the safe zone of my bedroom, I pried my sneaks off my bloated river-corpse feet and fell deeply, deeply asleep. It was two-thirty.

And then I was at BoB.

Except one of the two red cliffs was crushed to pebbles and Monica was there, talking about how the Big Wave had come and gone and had taken a few things with it, a few *people* with it, and not the ones you'd expect. All in all, though, she said, the Big Wave hadn't been as big as she'd hoped. She'd surfed it anyway.

I couldn't tell where she was bleeding, only that she left red footprints.

Behind her, on the water, something was . . . *breaching*. Bigger than a gray. Bigger than a *blue*. Like the ocean itself was splitting its skin, tearing itself apart from the inside, like a birth gone horror-movie bad. And this Thing, whatever it was, rose and rose out of the water, kept rising, volcano-high. Monica took zero notice, even as it threw a long shadow over her, over us. She just kept looking at me. Like she was waiting for an answer, but I hadn't understood the question.

I opened my mouth to warn her, and seawater came out.

"Will?!"

I opened my eyes. Darkness. Then light. Way too much light. Laura'd flipped on my bedroom dome. It was like dropping a safe on my face.

Laura was in her plaid cotton pajamas. What time was it?

"We couldn't wake you up," Laura said. Then she called down the hall: "He's up, he's fine, don't call an ambulance."

"Ambulance?"

"We were really worried."

There was a ridge between her eyebrows I'd only seen at Drew's games, when the Harps were losing. Brian came in. Bit of a ridge between his brows, too. What was going on?

"Will, do you know what time it is?"

I shook my head.

"Seven."

I clocked fresh sunlight peeking through the blinds. "A.M.?"

"Sunday morning. You fell asleep ... when?"

I looked around my room, as if my Visible Human Body mockup or my scale-model gibbon skeleton would provide some sort of answer. "Yesterday?"

"Afternoon. That's not normal," Laura said to Brian, like I wasn't even there.

"Will, how do you feel?"

Grrrrrowl.

"Hungry," I said, getting up. "And fine. I feel fine. Seriously."

I did, too. I felt . . . *great.* Actually. Hungry. And great.

In the fridge, I found an unopened pack of hickory-smoked turkey, ripped the pull tab, crammed a cold handful of wet deli slices in my mouth. They slid down my throat too easily. Drew was in the kitchen, eating almonds and reading *A Coach's Life.* He was looking me over again, the way he'd looked me over at the Lowlands. *Are you okay? Is there anything I can do? Is this my fault?*

It just made me angry.

Grrrrowl.

Which just made me hungry. Hungrier.

"I think we should take him to the doctor," Laura was telling my dad. Laura was always up for going to the doctor. Laura, by herself, was probably one of the top five reasons health-care costs are out of control.

"Now hang on," Brian said. "I think overeating and sleeping in are pretty normal for any gr—"

Brian choked on the word. Then corrected:

"For a teenage boy."

I stopped eating.

He'd started to say *growing.* And stopped himself.

I swallowed the meat in my mouth.

"You can say *growing,* Dad. It's just an expression." Here's the great thing about Getting Angry: it takes on its own momentum. That's why I added: "It's just a *fucking* expression."

"Will!"

"Believe me, nobody in this house," I yelled, plummeting into the abyss, "takes the expression *growing boy* literally! Or seriously!"

"Will, I never meant to—"

"Stop being so careful with me, okay?! Stop pretending!"

I was heading for the pantry. I barely knew why. Instinct, man. Sometimes you don't wanna get between instinct and a basket of mangoes, am I right? Rage has its own rules. I jerked out the second drawer down, the junk drawer, plunged a hand under a layer of greasy, forgotten soy sauce packets. My fingers closed on it:

The tape measure.

When I turned back, they were all watching me. Embarrassed. For me? For themselves? My answer was the same either way: *Good.* Let them feel as embarrassed as I did every minute of every day.

I grabbed a Sharpie off the counter, stood at the doorframe, my back to it, flat against it. Slashed a nice fat black line right at my crown, right at Peak Me. Then I took the tape measure, stomped on the tab, yanked it up for all to see: the awful truth. Data. Brutal. Irrefutable.

"There," I said. "*That's* what's real. Let's just face it."

I faced it.

"Dude," I heard Drew say before I actually read the measurement. Drew was staring at the doorframe with an expression of utter surprise, which was not an expression I associated with the Special.

I stared, too. And what I saw—it didn't make sense.

The slash I'd made was *above* my last line. *Three inches* above my last line, from years back. Which could mean only one thing.

I was five feet, two inches tall.

We all stared at it for a while. This *new* New Normal. What was the proper response here? Part of me wanted to pull a Rafty: pump a fist, take a doorframe selfie, post the evidence to everything postable. Part of me wanted to cry. Because it was so little. And so much.

I settled for "Huh."

"Well," said Brian, with a grin he clearly couldn't control. "Look. At. That!"

I remeasured. Laura remeasured. Brian and Drew remeasured. I made sure we scientific-methoded the crap out of this, scrubbed all bias. In moments like these—fluky, outlier-y, percentile-jumping—it pays to be skeptical.

But the results were pretty hard to argue with. There are only so many ways a tape measure can malfunction.

I thought about playing it cool. Then I thought, *Screw that.* I jumped up, half expecting to stick in midair as credits started to roll underneath me.

Drew grabbed me, lifting me higher. Kinda brotherly, kinda toddlery. But I didn't mind, because: *Five feet. Two inches.* It'd snuck up on me somehow, during those dark unmeasurable eons. Had I been slouching? Consistently? For years?

That made no sense. And made no difference. All that mattered to me was that it was here. It was happening. It was measurable. *I* was measurable.

"Could be a spurt in the last year—heck, even the last six months," babbled Brian, trying to strike a balance between thrilled and insultingly thrilled. "It's not unheard of!"

"I guess it explains why you've been so tired," said Laura, sounding relieved.

I didn't need explanations. I knew what I needed to know:

Today I was a new form of life. A *growing* one.

As the kitchen calmed down, Drew smiled. "So . . . what do you want to do now?"

I thought about that. So many possibilities, all of a sudden. But only one that made instant sense.

"Let's eat."

PART TWO

MAN

SEVEN

5'2"

IF YOU'RE AVERAGE size, the difference between four foot eleven and five foot two probably doesn't sound like much. *So what? You went from being one kind of short dude to another kind of short dude. BFD!*

Let me tell you just how FB a D it was: the difference between four eleven and five two is the difference between being below human radar and being a blip on the screen.

I'll take the blip.

At four eleven, you don't register as anything, unless you're surrounded by clowns and jugglers.

At five two, you're a short man making his way in the world, a short man in a long tradition. Prince. Carnegie. Manson. Men of just over five feet have redefined pop, built steel empires, and started highly successful murder cults.

Me, I was happy just clicking my Fiat's seat back a notch. Tiny little thing, but suddenly? My ride felt like a *ride*. Not a verdict.

The morning of the doorframe, after we'd returned from a

celebratory brunch (at which none of us, not even yours truly, bothered disguising our glee), I went to my room and clinked through the various tubes and bottles of herbal growth supplements I'd been squirreling away for years in a small gray footlocker I'd pushed to the back of my closet. I opened it up, smelled the plume of strange herbs that blossomed out of it. I sorted through the bottles, the many foreign words and characters, reviewing what I'd taken and when, in what order, in what combinations.

Turns out I hadn't been very scientific about it.

My growth supplement habit/obsession/addiction lasted almost two years, and it wasn't pretty. You could even see it, I guess, as a kind of mild self-mutilation. I'd find some new tincture or essence on the internet, gulp it down faithfully for a month or so, see no change, quit, swear, *Never again.* Then, three months later, I'd order more snake oil. But had one of them actually worked? If so, why now? What was the secret sauce?

Was it just . . . *wanting* it bad enough?

That was my least scientific theory. And, I've got to admit, my favorite.

"It was the lifts, obviously," Rafty said.

We were hanging out on his elaborate front porch, which his mom and dad modeled after one they saw on a show called *Epic Porches.* (The apple, in Rafty's case, did not fall far from the epic porch.)

"Rafty, I told you, I wasn't wearing them when I measured—"

"No, man, they, like, *spurred* it. They challenged your body."

"I think my body was plenty challenged before you gave me those lifts, Rafty."

"Whatever, man. Perception is reality."

"Yeah, but not . . . really."

"What's 'really'?" He made a psychic flutter with his hand, which made me snort-laugh. "Speaking of those lifts, where are they? Dude! They'd take you up to, like, five three and a half now! I mean, I'd miss you down here, but . . ."

Obviously, I couldn't tell him that Monica and I threw them into the ocean. So I went with something almost true: "I'm actually good where I am."

Rafty smiled. "I see that. You've got that glow, man. The way, like, pregnant women get."

"Mmm. Thanks?"

"Hang on, got an idea." Rafty ran off.

A few seconds later, I heard the *eeek eeek eeek* of something heavy rolling down the driveway on rusty casters.

Rafty's Pro Slam basketball hoop, set at eight feet, for pee-wee dunking. Rafty'd had it since we were at basketball camp together.

"Okay . . ."

"Hang on," said Rafty. "The pièce de résistance!" He ran off again, came back rolling a trampoline on its side. He let it fall onto its rubber hooves about four feet from the hoop, then just stood there, grinning like an idiot.

"Do we dare, Treetops?"

I grinned back. "We dare."

And we dunked off the trampoline, like a couple of trained monkeys, happy and stupid, for hours.

* * *

"Let's game this out," Drew said. "New plan! Huddle up!"

It was a blindingly beautiful day at BoB, and Drew was already ruining it.

"I like the old plan," said Monica. "The one where we just swim?"

"Did you just say *huddle up*?" I asked. "Right here? In real life?"

"Yes. I did. Sorry to go all team captain on you guys, but we've been avoiding this."

I had been, for sure. For just over ten days, since the Night of the Toilet, the night I'd heard that *click* of MoniDrew DNA coupling, I'd avoided facing the New Normal, because the New Normal *hurt*. Horribly. But I was still glorying in my newfound five-foot-two-ness, enjoying how the world felt different, even if some of it was probably imagined. (I hadn't grown three inches overnight, obviously. Obviously.)

(Right?)

My bed felt like it fit me better, though—less vast, more snug—and my clothes did, too. Even the climb down the cliff face felt different; my feet landed in different spots, in different ways. Half the time, I felt like I was falling; half the time, it was more like flying. I was higher off the water, farther above the sand. I had—very literally—a new angle on life, and I had a lot of catching up to do. So I didn't feel like dwelling on anything that got me down. But Spesh was in planner mode, shot-caller mode, and would not be denied.

"We need *something*," Drew said. "We need, like, rules. Or a referee."

"A parliamentarian," Monica offered, but she was barely paying attention. Her eyes were where her eyes usually were, on the horizon—which, today, was a squiggle of churn. The Sawtooth was restless.

"Yes!" said Drew. "A parliamentarian! Whatever that is!"

"Can I play devil's advocate for a sec?" I asked. "Why do we need new rules? Why do we need referees all of a sudden?"

Drew paced. "Think," he said, "about what happens if we, I dunno, disagree about something. Something more important than *Burritos or burgers?* Like, college, maybe. And then all of a sudden, it's two on one."

I couldn't resist:

"Am I 'one'?"

Drew flushed. Caught. "Well, no. Course not. Not . . . necessarily, no. It could be any two of us against any one of us."

"But that was true before," Monica put in, still turned away, still Tooth-watching.

"Riiiight," Drew improvised, with effort, "but, y'know . . . maybe we need some ground rules about what's, y'know, in bounds. . . ."

" 'In bounds'?"

Drew was looking for any way to talk about our new need for boundaries without mentioning who redrew those boundaries in the first place. And without mentioning that two of the three of us spent a nonzero amount of time groping each other's bodies, while the third ate turkey subs and cleaned ape habitats, and that was why we needed new boundaries. I knew this. Drew knew this. Monica knew it, too, which is why she stood fifteen feet apart and watched waves eat each other.

"Okay!" Drew said, palms up in surrender. "You got me, you two! I am no! Good! With the 'words'! I just wanna think strategically about this. I liked the old Plan. I liked where it was going. Where *we* were going. I don't want that to change."

"I don't want it to change, either," I said, and I was mostly telling the truth. Though part of me thought: *Where we're going? We're not going anywhere.*

That was the whole plan. To stay near each other, to stay put. Thus: UCSD, Irvine, etc.

"I'm all for not overthinking this," said Monica, but her voice was half swallowed by the crushing surf past the jetty.

"Right," said Drew. "So we all agree: no change."

"How about this," said Monica, coming over. And just like that, she drew new lines in the sand, new rules for a New Plan, which was really just the old Plan in disguise, with thicker bumpers bolted on. The rules were:

1. Don't make it weird.
2. If things are made weird, ask yourself: Would things be *weirder* if the third person were here? Or would things be *less* weird if that person were here?
3. If the answer to *either* of those is yes, don't make it weird.

"But," I noted, "we are weird. We've always been weird."

"True," mulled Monica, "so . . . remember your Ben Franklin."

Drew was lost. "'I put a key on a kite, so now there's electricity somehow'?"

"No, dude," I corrected. "She means the famous Ben Franklin saying: 'I love freedom and hate syphilis, but I also love French prostitutes, so sue me.'"

"He didn't really have syphilis," said Monica.

"WHAT?! I was lied to! There goes my childhood!"

"Actually," Monica rolled on, "I was thinking of 'Three may keep a secret, if two of them are dead.'"

"Yikes," said Drew.

"Except for us, I'd paraphrase it: Three can be weird, if two are weird and the third is willing."

We stared at her like broken slot machines, matching sets of lemons.

Monica tried again: "We can *be* weird. As long as things don't . . . *get* weird. Huh? Whatcha think?"

I rolled that one around. "Well . . . it's definitely . . . weird."

"Yeah," said Drew. "I'm pretty sure none of that made any sense."

"Well then, how about we just do what we already do," said Monica. "Stay out of each other's way. While simultaneously always being there for each other. Right?"

Was that what we always did? Yeah. It kind of was. I'd never thought of it in terms so clear. But then, clarity was a Monica specialty. You just had to let her get there.

I concurred. "That sounds good to me. Drew? You turn your key on that?"

Drew's phone started screaming an alarm. Practice beckoned.

"I turn my key," said Drew, heading for the cliff. "Grabbin' a Lyft. You two okay?"

"We're fine," Monica said. She gave him a quick peck. I made a small opera of not noticing, of catching sight of something off the coast. *Oh, look! Gray whale!*

Drew climbed the cliff trail. Monica stayed.

"Come surfing with me," she said. "Got both boards, and your extra suit's in BoB."

I hesitated.

She saw me hesitate.

Five minutes into the New Old Plan, and shit was already getting weird.

"Can't," I lied, thinking, *Maybe I need to make some rules of my own, just for me.* "Got a thing with Rafty. Promised."

"Okay." She hugged me. Solid and platonic, friend hug of death. Not hard enough to feel the One Ring under my T-shirt, luckily. I didn't want her to know I was still wearing it. *I* didn't even know why I was still wearing it. "I swear to God," she said, "you're . . ."

She didn't say *taller.* She just let it hang.

It's funny: Monica never mentioned my height. Ever. Until that moment.

We hadn't really talked about it, the Heightening. I wasn't telling people. Telling people you're now five two is like telling people you're no longer obese, just overweight.

But I knew Drew had told Mon about the tape measure. Was that weird? Pre-MoniDrew, it wouldn't have been. It just would've been How Information Travels Between Friends.

Monica smiled, shrugged. "Anyway: whales and waves wait for no woman."

"Pick you up later?"

"Nah. I'll take the bus."

"You sure?"

"I like reading on the bus."

"Hipster affectation."

"For *you,* maybe, Daughtry. I'm actually *poor.*"

And with that, Monica Bailarín dove into the surf.

Athena Departing an Awkward Conversation.

* * *

Later, I was gathering behavioral data from questionable sources—building a histogram from creepy old-school internet personals, the really gross kind—on female interest in men who were five foot two (a small but noticeable uptick!) when I noticed my fingernails clicking against the keyboard. They needed trimming.

Again. But I'd trimmed them just the day before. That seemed notable.

I went to the bathroom and trimmed. That's when I noticed my scruff—my sparse and slow-growing scruff, which needed attention only every three weeks or so, and then only on my upper lip and a few patches hither and yon—was scruffier than usual.

That seemed notable, too.

It'd been eleven days since the Doorframe Revelation.

I wondered.

I went downstairs, marched into the kitchen on a mission, became briefly distracted by a large Tupperware full of spaghetti Bolognese, quietly, guiltily washed the empty tub when I was finished, and *then* approached the doorframe. Carefully. Respectfully. As if it might bite. I put my back to the pine, slashed a new mark. Measured: five foot two . . . and three-quarters.

Eleven days. *Almost an inch.*

An obvious operator error, any reasonable biologist would conclude.

So I checked it five times. I almost went to find Laura, to get her to check.

But I didn't. I knew it would worry her.

By then, even *I* was a little worried.

EIGHT

5'8"

IT'S WEIRD, AND not particularly fun, spending summer vacation getting examined (and examined, and examined) in the same hospital where your mom died.

I don't recommend it.

It was also weird hearing my physician, Dr. Danielle Helman (5'9"), inform Brian and Laura (in the quiet, controlled tones I knew from experience to be the Voice of Very Bad News) that it was "probably pathological."

Since my birthday, I'd grown six inches. In about three months.

I knew what that meant.

That meant cancer.

Pituitary, more than likely. Maybe adrenal. Gigantism.

Maybe late-breaking Marfan syndrome, if I was lucky.

I wasn't feeling so lucky, all of a sudden.

Before my smallness became statistically bizarro (she didn't live to see my nonstarter of an adolescence), my mom liked to tell me about her father and grandfather, both under five six and decorated war heroes. They learned (in Mom's telling, at least) that being not-the-biggest man teaches you how to be the bigger man. That "modest stature" wasn't the worst thing in the world.

Then, later—also via Mom—I learned what the worst thing in the world actually was.

Now the same genes I'd complained about making me a midget were sending me skyward at a growth rate far beyond the norm. Now my weird genes were probably going to kill me, same as they'd killed Mom.

UCSD had a topflight Human Growth and Endocrinology Unit (or HGEU, which my brain always respelled as HUGE). That was the good news. The bad news was that UCSD was where Mom spent her last nine weeks. So I was very, very familiar with UCSD, in the worst way.

I noticed immediately that they hadn't updated the vending machines. The Grandma's cookie that clung to its ring by one desperate, mangled corner of wrapper, ready to fall any second—had it been hanging like that for the better part of a decade? I remembered trying to shake it loose one long, bad night when Mom was starting her terminal dive. Was it the same cookie? It couldn't be, right? What was the life span of a Grandma's cookie anyway, preservatives notwithstanding?

So many memories in this wing. HUGE was adjacent to Oncology. Which seemed ghoulish. Yet correct.

I was fed into the same MRI tunnel she was. Got my blood drawn on the same chair, arm tied off by the same nurse (well, I think it was the same nurse—similar scowl, similar vampiric pallor), all while wrapped in the same kind of soothing-floral-print hospital gown my mom was wearing when she slipped softly out of this world like laundry down a chute.

I talked to my mom a lot in that MRI tunnel. There wasn't much else to do. What did we talk about? Topics ranged. *Mom, don't let me be sick. Mom, don't let me die.* Natural enough thoughts. But the big one, strangely, was:

Mom . . . on the off chance I'm not dying . . .

. . . please don't let them stop me.

Because this had already been discussed: responding to the Heightening with a Stoppening. Braking my growth, gently, with hormones. Hormones fighting hormones. I was not in favor of this option. It seemed . . . contrary. Not to mention dangerous. Cock-blocking a miracle—isn't that a special kind of crime? Unless it wasn't a miracle. Just a disease. You'd think somebody could tell the difference.

But no. The doctors asked a thousand questions, exploring the possibility of an environmental trigger. Endocrine disrupters, that sort of thing. What was a typical meal in our house? (Answer: organic *everything*, light on meat, free of pesticides, herbicides, hormones, antibiotics.) Was I on any medications? Had I shown evidence of any strange new allergies? Had anything new, anything *nonstandard* been introduced into the household in the last year? Was I huffing Roundup? Did I meditate?

No, no, no, no, no. Very, very, very slowly, everything was ruled out.

By the time all those tests were done, I'd grown another inch.

Brian and I waited for the (partial) results of the (initial) tests in Dr. Helman's office, where several generations of healthy, hardy

Helmans were running around on her bookshelf in tasteful Pottery Barn frames, playing soccer or tennis, celebrating birthdays, graduating from things. There's something really strange about doctors (especially ones who deliver a lot of bad news, and Dr. Helman delivered a *lot* of bad news) showing off their evolutionary fitness to sick people.

"It's okay." Brian patted my leg. "This is all just—they just need to be sure, that's all."

Brian was more worried than I was. I had my worries, sure. I wasn't an idiot. Any kid who's watched a parent die knows that life can't be trusted to deliver a happy ending. But I wasn't worried on a gut level. On a gut level, I felt damned good. Empty, as always; hungry as hell. But basically, fundamentally good.

In came Dr. Helman, and Brian sat up like a German shepherd. I felt bad for him, being back here—all those feelings stirred up, all over again.

Dr. Helman pushed her glasses up her short, upturned nose as she read my chart. She looked like a pig—and I mean a nice pig, a cute pig, a Muppet pig. But a pig. Her face was hard to read. Could be: *Kid's a goner.* Could be: *Do these glasses make me look like I want truffles?*

Your mind goes to dumb places when you're waiting to hear if you're dying.

"Well, gentlemen," she said finally, "I'll be honest: I'm stumped."

Brian leaned in. "So his hormone levels—?"

"Normal. Which, frankly, makes no sense. And the MRI's clean. There's no evidence of a pituitary tumor." I watched my dad relax. "Now, respirometer's off the charts. His body's eating oxygen like a grease fire. Why? I've only got theories, and they're not great." Dr. Helman shook her wise porcine head again. "Thirty years here, I've never seen anything like this."

That was saying something, because HUGE, from what I'd witnessed just today, had seen a lot. A cruel person might even deploy the term *freaks*, perhaps in conjunction with the word *circus*. In the waiting room before the respirometer test, I'd met a twenty-six-year-old just three feet tall, with normal-size arms. A nine-year-old girl who was creeping up on 6'3"—gigantism. Hands the size of baseball mitts and heart problems that could kill her in her late twenties, if not before. It was a real Tolkienopedia in here, everything from hobbits to orcs. I was at the time the most "average" guy in the room.

And I was thrilled. Not just because I didn't have a pituitary tumor (although, not for nothin', *bonus*), but because the normal hormone levels and otherwise healthy readings meant maybe, just maybe, they'd leave me alone.

"Now, none of this is conclusive or dispositive," said Dr. Helman. "We'll need weeks to analyze the data. We're still looking at the adrenals. All we can tell you today is that it isn't a pituitary tumor. But there's a lot of lab work we're—"

"That's something, that's wonderful," Brian said, shaking Dr. Helman's hand too hard. All he'd heard was *not a tumor*, and for right now, that was enough. I shook Dr. Helman's hand, too. She held it a little longer than necessary, looking at me like I was a prizewinning steer.

"Really, now: No joint pain? No restless legs? Sleepless nights?" No, no, and no. She scrunched her eyes, gave me the medical once-over. "How do you feel?"

"I feel . . . well, actually, I feel *amazing*."

That seemed to worry her. She made a note.

I swung into Rafty's driveway, late for our hang; the hospital visit had taken most of the morning. We were supposed to go to the Portola Embarcadero, where Rafty promised me a "full reupholstering." I was leery of that. But I desperately needed new clothes. Lately, I needed new clothes every couple of weeks. As I set the parking brake and hauled out legs I was rapidly running out of legroom for—time to move the seat back another notch—I heard a digital *click* right next to my face. Rafty had appeared at the driver's-side door. Phone at the ready, he was documenting.

"Let's get a shot right here by the Yacht."

"Sorry I'm late. . . ."

"Will. You. Are. A *celebrity*. You're *supposed* to be late."

I yanked my backpack out of the passenger seat, tossed it into the back, marveling, for the fortieth time, at how easy that had become, how weightless the bag seemed now.

Rafty rattled on. "So I checked *Guinness*, and this is on track to be the *huge-largest* growth spurt ever."

"Is *huge-largest* English or metric? I forget."

"Dude. People are gonna notice. People are already noticing." He pulled up some randomly sourced fact sheet on his phone. "Dwight Howard: thirteen inches in a year. Impressive! But slower than you. Adam Rainer: guy from old-timey times, went from four feet tall at eighteen to over seven feet in his thirties. Bonkers. But! It took him almost fifteen years. Adam Rainer can't touch Will Daughtry! And so, for the sake of our children's children's grandchildren, you gotta let me document your excellence. Now stand next to the Yacht. We're doing this every day from now on."

I rolled my eyes. "No, man, I don't wanna be one of those—"

"You have to. For posterior generations."

"For *posterity.*"

"Them too!"

I sighed. "How long do I have to do this?"

"Until you stop being amazing or the internet dies! Until forever!"

So I stood by the Yacht, and Rafty clicked away.

"Um. How many of these are you gonna—"

"Perfection is not an accident, Highlander," said Rafty, changing angles. "This is Photo Mark I, gotta set a precedent here. Chill with your huge self."

Click. Click. Click click click.

Rafty was a clown, but he was right about one thing. People *were* noticing.

More to the point: girl people were noticing.

Or maybe girl people were just the ones I *noticed* noticing.

I wasn't getting ogled or eye-groped or anything. It was just . . . acknowledgment. Maybe a little curiosity thrown in.

On a more practical, less sexy level: Rafty and I walked through the Portola Galleria now without zigzagging or fighting the current. Humanity parted for me, like I was actually *there*. Was this what walking was like for the average-size human?

Passing Mister Vape, we saw Jazzy, huddled with two of his frowsier co-bongoliers. Jazzy wouldn't meet my eyes. Funny, because it was easier now than it'd ever been, altitudinally. But when I nodded at him, I saw something new on his face, something I'd seen on many an ape face: *uncertainty*. About where he stood.

That made me so happy, it was almost embarrassing.

"So . . . ," Rafty said, "I have to ask again. In fact, I'll never stop asking. What'd you *do*? To make this happen? It's 'roids, right? If it's 'roids, you can tell me. I'm a vault. Feds'll never crack me. This is just between us Smalls."

"I didn't 'do' anything."

"C'mon. You can tell ol' Rafts."

"Ol' Rafts, if I knew? I'd be tall *and* rich."

There was no scientific answer to Rafty's unscientific question.

But after failing to declare it to a series of UCSD doctors, I knew I had to show Brian my *contraband*. The box.

Even in the face of cancer, I couldn't bring myself to tell the white coats about it. I could barely admit it to myself. It was so shameful. Desperate. And potentially important to the path report, so it was time to tell *someone*. So Brian and I sat on my bed with the open box. He examined each bottle and vial, sniffing, rubbing some of the dried herbs between thumb and forefinger. Trying to figure out what to say. He settled on:

"This stuff—it's completely unregulated, Will."

"I know, I—"

"Incredibly dangerous, messing around with this kind of—"

"Dad. I know."

He sighed. Put the bottles back in the box, gently closed the top, and left his palm on the lid, heavy and flat, like he was swearing on a Bible or trapping a small, snarling animal. "I wasn't there for you. Was I?"

"Dad . . ."

"I had . . . *no idea.* And I should have. I feel . . . *terrible.*"

"Don't. Look. I wasn't . . . telling anyone." It was weird having a conversation like this with my dad—a real soul barer, about my *body*—under any circumstances. It was especially weird having a conversation like this because I was rapidly acquiring a different body, becoming a different person—and yeah, I mean proportionally, relative to Brian. A few months before, Brian had to tilt his head down to look me in the eye, even if we were sitting. Now I was gaining on him, fast. Fathers and sons usually have years to adjust to that kind of leveling.

Brian and I had weeks.

"Look," I told him, "I don't think any of this is, y'know, significant."

"You can't *know* that—"

"Because I'd stopped. Taking any of it."

"When?"

"I dunno. A year ago?"

"And you stopped because . . ."

"I gave up."

Brian was giving me the sad eyes, the sea turtle eyes that make you think, *Damn, my parents are old* and also *Did* I *do that to them?*

"Anyway," I said. "I don't think powdered monkey testicles are . . . *timed-release* or anything."

"Oh, please," laughed Brian. "You think that's *really* powdered monkey testicles?" He picked up the box. "We'll have the lab run it all anyway. There's enough here to keep UCSD busy for quite a while."

I watched the box leave the room for the last time.

And, not for the last time, I prayed they wouldn't find anything. I didn't want the box to have anything to do with what was happening to me, good or bad.

I wanted the only reason for what was happening to me to be Me.

Looking back, I'm pretty sure I got my wish.

NINE

5'10"

SUMMER WENT ON while I waited on the toxicology analysis—
the pituitary tumor had been ruled out, but more "exotic" possibilities hadn't. I was still, potentially, a cancer grenade, pin pulled,
waiting to blow. I wasn't really *celebrating*.

But I was still growing.

I knew this because it had started to hurt a little. Not much,
not excruciating, but it was there: this kind of pleasant ache, like I'd
just run a mile. At night, though? My shin splints were exclamation
points.

And I kept tripping over things. Things that weren't the right
distance away anymore. Stairs. Rock outcroppings at BoB. Kitchen
chairs. I was a figure drawn to a slightly different scale every day,
it seemed. The world was doing a terrible job of adjusting to me.

Dr. Helman had suggested, of all things, a weight lifting routine.

"Gentle," she said. "Easy. Nothing NFL. The important thing
isn't the weight you're lifting; it's the routine. Living in your body

every day. Building out what they call your proprioception, your body awareness. Like an invisible scaffold."

I took Dr. Helman's proprioception prescription and handed it to my physical therapist, Dr. Andrew Tannenger, B.o.B. And he gave me a weight lifting regimen.

We lifted together, actually. Well: not *together*. Drew was lifting a lot more, and for different reasons. He was getting ready for varsity, staying in shape, playing in the La Jolla Summerhoop League. I was getting ready for . . . well, I didn't really know what. I just wanted to stop tripping over my own feet. To stop being quite so surprised every time I passed a mirror.

So I lifted. And I watched. I watched Drew burn through the Summerhoop League, where his team was a thinly veiled test run of the Harpoons' varsity lineup. They were even called the Poca Resaca Mobys. (Not super subtle.) The Mobys had been unstoppable out of the gate, but in the last three games, Drew'd averaged fewer than eighteen points, which was considered shocking. Fans were chattering about "hype," the way fans do. I didn't think it had gotten to Drew.

I was wrong.

One night, against the Portola Warthogs, Drew was off from the jump, turning over the ball five times in the first half and shooting three for fifteen, crazy low for him.

"What's going on?" I asked Monica. Laura was covering her eyes. (Laura didn't like suspense.)

"No clue," said Monica. Her typical game face, which I'd call Focused Detachment, had been replaced by Obvious Worry. Monica, in the previous incarnation of our trio, liked to affect not caring about the game of basketball overmuch. Basketball had been *our* thing, Drew's and mine. I surfed with Monica, played hoops with Drew. Now Monica had to be a basketball superfan? Was that the New Plan? Or was that just . . . weird?

"He's psyching himself out," muttered Brian. "Trying to solve problems he doesn't have."

Grotesque and inelegant ball sprawled before us for the better part of forty minutes. Finally, mercifully, it was halftime.

"Will?"

And there was Sidney. Holding two giant sodas.

"Hey, Sid!" Yikes. It came out a little *Disney World!*

"I got two," she explained, regarding the twin sodas, "but Ethan's off sugar, something about his Adderall. You want this?"

"Sure!" This wasn't bullshit. I craved sugar water all the time. "Please, hand me some sweet, sweet diabetes."

Sid grinned, passed me a missile silo's worth of high-fructose corn syrup, and sat down. Her hip touched mine, and to my surprise, the place it touched heated up to about nine thousand degrees Celsius.

"C'mon, Mobys, c'mon!" Brian said, standing, clapping. He was the only one standing and clapping, because it was halftime. Brian was melting down a little.

"Your dad's had a long day," Laura explained. "The chimpanzees started making spears."

"What?" Monica raised an eyebrow.

"Yeah, apparently it's a big deal."

"It *is* a big deal," Brian editorialized. "It's never happened in captivity before. Not just tool use, *weapon* use, in a zoo environment. C'MON, MOBYS!"

"Brian? It's halftime."

"I think I need popcorn," said Brian. "Popcorn? I'm going for popcorn."

He sidled out of the bleachers. Laura sighed. "I'm off to talk your father down from his tree."

"Don't give him a spear," said Monica.

Laura turned to Sidney. "I'm Laura Tannenger, Will's step-mom."

They shook hands, as if something had just been transacted, and a small eruption of butterflies, for some reason, blew through my stomach. Laura scootched down the bleachers, caught up with my dad. Whispered something to him. I saw him turn, take in Sidney. Eek. My face, I imagined, cycled through six shades of red. I hoped nobody'd noticed.

Monica was looking at Sidney, too. Just . . . looking.

Sidney said, "Monica? Right?"

"Monica," said Monica. "Right." She said it in her flat assassin voice. Monica regarded all rich, popular kids with suspicion, but I was a little surprised at this. Open hostility (except in special cases of self- or friend defense) was not Monica's jam.

"You tutored me in algebra? Seventh grade?" Sid attempted.

"Mmm," said Monica. "Yes. Algebra. The killing fields. One sec, gotta drain the dragon." Monica stood, began sidling out of our row.

Sid flipped back to me. "Crazy, huh?"

"What?"

"The game."

"Oh. Yeah. Ugly ball."

"Refs are kinda obviously anti-Drew."

"Well," I said, "to be fair, Drew is a little anti-Drew tonight."

Monica, in the aisle now, shot me a look as she headed for the bathroom: *Uh. Traitor?* She had a point. Why had I said something even vaguely Drew-critical? To an "outsider"?

Maybe because Sid wasn't *quite* an outsider these days. We'd been hanging out that summer, even without frogs to dissect.

I wasn't really sure what it meant, this new attention from Sid. Was it height-related? Better question: was it *only* height-related?

"So if you're serious about that anti-cruelty petition to ban dissections," I said, flapping my lips on instinct, "we'd better file it now. Or else another generation'll be subjected to Sulak's mindless butchery. I mean . . . think of the fetal pigs. . . ."

I rattled on about pigs and petitions, and Sid just looked at me like she was looking *at* me, but just looking, not really listening. Because, Jesus? Who would? I was talking about pig parts! Why was I talking about pig parts?

Sid stopped my hogalogue with: "What are you doing this weekend?"

Honest answer: Riding the bench of life. Waiting for test results. Dunking on Rafty's low goal. Maybe some BoB time with two people who'd probably rather be having se—

"Uh, I dunno," I yammered, "still in the planning stages . . ."

"'Cause there's this thing at Jazzy's. The volleyball squad's going to scrimmage at sunset. On the beach."

On the beach. This meant beach volleyball. This meant a lightly clothed event.

"Will loves volleyball!"

My father's voice. My blood ran cold. Brian was back, with popcorn. Leaning over us. Some kernels spilled from the paper sleeve

and fell on Sid's blouse. I wanted to die. What the *hell* had Laura said to him?

"Will's a big volleyball fan," Brian told Sidney helpfully. "We used to play on the beach a lot. You play volleyball?"

"Yeah. Varsity. And intramural, just for fun."

"In-tra-mu-ral!" said Brian, with the kind of overenunciated wonder normally reserved for alien first contact. In my mind, I was strangling him to death with a volleyball net. And he wasn't finished! "Y'know, a while ago, we took a road trip to New England, and we visited the Volleyball Hall of Fame in Holyoke, Mass. It's very near the Basketball Hall of Fame in Springfield. Remember that, Will? Our 'Hall Crawl'?"

"Yeah, we didn't call it that—"

"Two Halls of Fame! In one day! Have you ever been? To the Volleyball Hall of Fame?"

"No," Sidney said, "but it sounds cool." She got up. "See you this weekend, Will?"

"Um. Sure! Enjoy the rest of the, y'know . . ."

"Yeah," said Sid. "Drew'll bounce back, I'm sure."

And then Sidney Lim took her soda and left, just as Monica was coming back from the dragon drain. She watched Sid go, sucking her teeth thoughtfully. "So. You and Sidney."

"Huh? What? We were in AP bio together."

"Indeed." Monica grinned. But it wasn't—how to explain this?—the nicest grin. It was just lips over teeth.

The team was filing back onto the court.

Monica spotted Drew and screamed: "C'mon, Harps! WOOOOO!"

Wooooo?

It felt less like a sincere fan hoot and more like a javelin thrown

at my face. *What the hell happened on the algebra killing fields?* I wanted to ask Monica. But that might make things weird. So I just watched the game, sipped my free soda, and thought warm, happy thoughts, and some of them were about Sidney Lim, for a change.

The second half was even worse. Drew came out strong in the worst possible way: aggressive, but dumb about it. He got in foul trouble early and rode the bench for half the half. For the first time that Summerhoop season, the Mobys closed a lead *without* him. I watched him on the sidelines, tapping his foot, head down, eyes floorward.

With twelve seconds left and a chance to tie, they brought him back in.

He went for the three. From way out. For no good reason. *CAROM!* The ball hit the front of the hoop with stunning force, delivered itself into the hands of a Portola shooting guard, who ran out the last five seconds. The Portola bleachers went absolutely bug nuts.

And Drew *cursed*. Audibly. F-bomb-inably. It sounded like a gunshot.

That was . . . strange. Uncool. Un-Drew.

"Ah, jeez." Brian shook his head. "Not good. So hard on himself."

We watched the coach call Drew over, watched him lean in and give Spesh what I can only assume was a talking-to.

Monica and I went into triage mode.

"Let's kidnap him. Take him Whaling."

"That," said Monica, "is precisely what I was thinking."

On reflex, we still knew how to circle the herd.

So we waited for him in the parking lot, Monica and I, with Brian and Laura bringing up the rear.

"Refs, man," said Monica when Drew finally appeared, rumpled, showered but uncombed, and slumping toward us.

Drew didn't say anything. He was digging in his gym bag for something, or pretending to. He hadn't met anyone's eyes.

"Lotta ticky-tack fouls," Monica went on. "I mean, what's the accreditation for these high school refs anyway—"

"They did their job," muttered Drew. "I didn't do mine."

Brian pursed his lips. "Sometimes you eat the bar..."

"Thanks, Brian."

Laura was nodding. She'd seen this before in Drew. I saw her touch Brian's elbow, a small warning. "We'll see you at home," she said to Drew. "Shake it off."

"Okay, Mom." Drew was back in his bag, still looking for the fake thing he pretended not to have found.

When they were gone, Monica said, "All right, Tannenger. Get your ass in the car. This is a *Hot August Night* night, methinks. We've got cetaceans to serenade."

Drew just blinked at her.

I stepped up: "You heard the lady. Time for some Whailing."

"It's actually time for some *practice*," Drew snapped. "So you two go sing to the whales. I've got to fix this."

He walked off through the parking lot and onto the soccer field, and a small but dangerous crater opened in the parking lot. All our words fell into it.

"Oh. Kay?" I was running plays in my head, trying to figure out how to salvage this. How to unweird that which Drew had made weird. "Not a Neil Diamond fan, I see."

Then I saw Monica. Her eyes. *Wet.* I saw them before she had a chance to turn away.

Not possible. I'd never seen her cry. Maybe once. Watching *Fellowship*, when Gandalf bites it on the bridge with the Balrog. That was the last time I'd seen the mist roll in. But never because of something *real*. Not even when she got rolled and ate shit at BoB and left a long scroll of skin on the cheese-grater cove bottom.

Not even when her dad had one of his weekends.

"He's not mad at you," I told her, and started to reach an arm around her shoulder, pure instinct, before thinking better of it (*CAUTION: WEIRD!*) and veering off.

"I know." Neutral voice. Scary neutral. She was still turned away from me and was drifting toward the bike rack.

"Throw the bike on the Yacht. I got a bungee—"

"No, I'm good." She stopped. "Tell Drew: I get it."

She was already on the bike, swinging toward the mouth of the parking lot, the reflector on her busted-ass helmet catching the streetlight. Her face, in the half glow, was restored to its resting state: detached, room-temperature amusement.

"Just another crazy week, Daughtry," Monica called as she wheeled by. "The chimps are making spears! Extraordinary times!"

"Mon says to tell you she 'gets it.'"

The ride had been silent. I was just doing my best to fill a void.

Drew didn't appreciate my best.

"Do me a favor," he said, "and don't talk to Monica about me behind my back?"

Ker-chunk. Sound of a spear sinking into a blood brother's sternum.

"Um. Okaaaay. That's a . . . rule? Bylaw? Part of the New Plan?"

"Maybe," Drew said pissily, chewing a finger and staring out the window. "Maybe it should be. I know how new this is, it's new to me, too, but . . . what happened to *Don't make it weird?* Seriously, man: boundaries."

Wow. WOW. Boundaries.

That was . . . that was . . . *choice.*

Yeah, Drew was a real font of dickery that night.

And part of me—out of nowhere—wanted to snap that font right off and feed it to him.

So Dr. Helman calling?

At that precise moment?

Was fortunate, I think, for all involved. The call Bluetoothed automatically onto the Fiat speaker and interrupted my Vesuvius-in-progress—

"I wanted to call right away, Will," said Dr. Helman. "I just spoke with your dad, he said you were out. . . ."

Oh, God. Here it was. The verdict that I supposedly wasn't waiting for, that (I suddenly realized) I'd completely, totally, and panic-strickenly been waiting for.

"Count is normal. Scans are normal. Everything's normal."

THANK YOU. Thank you, all generic and nonspecific deities! Thank you, Science, thank you, Chance. Something bubbled up inside me, something I hadn't even realized I'd been tamping down, something warm and grateful, and it didn't matter to whom or for what exactly.

"What's abnormal is how damned normal you are." She made a sound that was half relief, half exasperation. I, on the other hand, just grinned like an idiot. "But we're going to monitor you for the next six to nine months. At least. Okay?"

"Okay."

Dr. Helman, having sentenced me to life, hung up, and I started involuntarily bouncing in my seat as I drove.

Drew was grinning, too. The icky, icy shitscape of six minutes ago? Gone. Forgotten. I realized that this little question of *Will Will die?* had been hanging over both of us. And now? The clouds were parting.

"Pull over," Drew said.

We were passing a playground. I pulled in, next to the monkey bars, and Drew came over to my side, hauled me out of the car. Hugged the living hell out of me.

I remembered then: we were two people who'd lost people. We both knew what losing was like. Nothing else—not tonight's stupid fail against Portola, not the *New* Plan or the new awkwardness, not even Monica—was as important as not losing someone.

"God*damn*, you're heavy," said Drew as he let me go. "So okay: can you officially start enjoying yourself now?"

"I . . . I think so? I think maybe I already started. Enjoying myself. Even before I stopped dying."

Drew smiled, smacked my shoulder. "Brother of blood, you are the opposite of dying. You're a goddamn tragedy in reverse." His eye caught on something over my shoulder. "C'mon," he said, and popped the hatch. *Thump, thump.* Ball on asphalt.

"C'mon where? What's happening?"

"What's happening," said Drew, "is my jumper was a goddamn garbage fire tonight. And I can't sleep until I work it out. You mind . . . helping? With a little defense?"

I cannot overstate how crazy this was.

Drew wanted me on D. He needed a sparring partner. A *partner*. If not an equal, then at least equal enough.

As you may have noticed: *I like basketball.*

I like the pick-and-roll, I like the give-and-go. As the poet says.

And I watched basketball. I *studied* basketball. But did I *play* basketball?

Sure. All the time. But only with Rafty, in his driveway, far from prying eyes.

I hadn't played with anyone *bigger* than Rafty since . . . well, since basketball camp. With Drew. Eons ago. Back when we were players of roughly similar size and skill.

That night? The night I was sentenced to life? We were eight again.

Play was still pretty lopsided. I lost by six. But at one point . . . I *led*. By as many as five. For ninety whole seconds.

Against Drew, this was a *phenomenon*.

I mean, he was holding back. Obviously.

For sure. A thousand percent.

I think?

"Not bad, right?" I said, panting, after draining a lucky fadeaway over Drew's block. "Pretty fly . . . for a five-ten guy! . . ."

"You're not . . . five ten. . . ." He was panting, too. Not quite as hard as I was, but still. "Guard who was all over me tonight, *he* was five ten. When was the last time you measured?"

"Uh. Weekend before last."

Drew shook his head, flicked off some sweat. "You're my height, I'd put money on it."

We sat down on the blacktop, passed a Powerade.

"Can I, uh, admit something?" I panted.

"Anytime."

I gulped at the bottle. "I . . . don't think I'm in the right body."

Drew squinted. "Explain."

"It's like . . . I'm six and wearing my dad's shoes. And it's hilarious."

"Well," said Drew, "if you play like *this* as a six-year-old in your dad's shoes, then by fall, we're starting you at center."

We laughed. Because that was funny.

And the truth is, that night? Going one on one with Drew? Was the first night I started feeling at home in that new, possibly wrong body. Like my proprioception had finally started . . . *propriocepting* again.

Drew clapped a hand on my shoulder, and I noticed: my whole torso didn't jerk forward when he did it. Sea change, right there. All of a sudden, I could absorb the normal impact of brotherhood. I could survive a backslapping.

"You're gonna clear *me*, Will. You realize that, right?"

I just nodded, noncommittally. I'd been trying not to think of where this was heading.

"You know why I lost tonight?"

That snapped me out of my reverie. Drew was reflecting.

"I lost . . . for the same reason I was a dick to you and Monica in the parking lot. I wasn't playing Portola. I was playing the next game, see. In my head, I'd already beaten Portola, I'd already moved on to the next game. Problem is . . . I didn't beat them. And by the time I realized that . . . I was already back at practice, at least in my head. Instead of standing in a parking lot with my two best friends." He smiled. "I am clearly in need of serious Whailage. And maybe a smack in the face."

I loved Drew in those moments when he felt the need to explain himself. Because Drew was very bad at explaining himself, and he knew it. He only did it when he felt something important was at stake. So once again, not for the first time: I was flattered. I was grateful.

I was probably looking for my reflection, in his reflection.

Drew wanted to be known. So did I.

People worry so much about being *known*, don't they? We think: *Will anyone ever find out who I really am?* As if *we* know.

You think you're already someone: this fully formed, all-done organism, completely evolved and adapted.

Like you already *are* who you'll end up being.

So sorry to break it to you, but you aren't. You never will be. You're a phase. Forever and always a phase.

Take it from a phase.

TEN

6'1"

⟨jack⟩: hey

WillD: Hi!

⟨jack⟩: saw ur page

WillD: Cool. Thanks for following!

⟨jack⟩: dont thank me save ur strength

. . .

WillD: sorry?

. . .

⟨jack⟩: ur going to die big man

WillD: ⟨YOU HAVE BEEN BLOCKED⟩

. . .

⟨jacksback⟩: me again nice try c u soon

BY SEPTEMBER, I was a changed man. The *man* part being the biggest change.

Being seen as one. Being seen, period.

I'd left for summer vacation almost five foot six—strange enough, considering I'd started the year four eleven and under the impression I was likely to stay that way forever. Other than the fact that my two best friends, one of whom was my secret crush, were quite possibly having sex with each other (and no, I never asked, and not just because I didn't want to know—I was *determined* not to be the Weird Maker or Plan Breaker), I had a very normal summer for a growing boy of sixteen: I lifted some weights, played some hoop, hung out with friends, and monitored my endocrine system.

The next fall, I came back to school six foot one. Not just taller, either. Not just the bone scaffold of a Big Person Coming Soon—*Watch This Space!* No, I was a fully filled-out, height/weight-proportionate male human of above-average size. Dr. Helman's weight lifting routine had paid off, and not just for my proprioception (which was getting better all the time: I was still growing fast, but my brain had started anticipating it, I guess, and I stumbled less, missed fewer stairs). I was barely recognizable. And people recognized that. People *looked*. Not just the kids at school.

"Is this you?"

People in the waiting room of HUGE noticed. People with a dog in the fight.

"Is it?"

A small hand on a short arm held a phone in front of my face. On the phone I saw myself. Doing my thing. *Growing.*

It was the time-lapse video Rafty had shot for "my" fan page, wittily titled "Will Daughtry Gets High." (*Not* my idea. Neither was the fan page. But . . . c'est la Rafty!) In the video (since shared under tags like "Grow-liath," "DamnSamwise!," etc., etc.), I stand next to my Fiat every day for ninety days, getting taller. In the process: my jaw squares off, my arms and chest thicken. I watched them become more like Arms and a Chest, less like American Girl doll parts. The view counter said I'd done this about 235,000 times since the video'd been posted.

(Only 5,000 of those views are mine, I swear.)

The video starts on March 4, my birthday. I'm five foot two (even though I don't know it yet) in my birthday photo, taken by Laura: a boy and his Yacht. Tiny car, tinier boy.

By July 4, I'm five seven, and Sidney's there (Rafty: "You gotta put a girl in the video, dude, if you want views, that's just basic") and she's five seven, and the Fiat's a Fiat.

By September, Sidney's still five seven, the Fiat's still a Fiat, *and I'm sailing past six one.* Averaging two inches a month. A handful of NBA players have kept up that pace, but only for two or three months, tops. There are some similar cases in China, Mongolia, Russia, but as far as I could tell from my hunt-and-peck research, I was among the fastest-growing humans on record.

Got questions? Some totally legitimate but still slightly creepy questions? Here are all my standard answers off the FAQ, from those giddy early days of the Heightening:

No, I don't "feel" it.

No, it doesn't hurt. Not really. Not that much. A little.

Yes, I'm hungry all the time.

No, I won't answer questions re "foot" size. Or "hand" size. Or "proportions."

(Fella's gotta preserve some mystique.)

I'll say this: Mostly? It was *great.*

But the FAQ didn't cut it for some folks. Like, for instance, the kids in the waiting room of HUGE.

"So?"

The voice asking the question didn't quite match the hand holding the phone, and the hand holding the phone didn't quite match the arm attached to the hand, and the arm didn't match the torso. She was about fourteen, I guessed. Pituitary dwarfism.

"Yep." I nodded at the screen. "That's me."

I waited for it.

"Tell me how."

Yay. My favorite conversation.

"I don't know," I said. "I wish I did."

She gave me the hard look I knew too well, the look of the Overdiagnosed and Undercured. Then she said the same thing *I* would've said (or at least *thought*) six months ago:

"Liar."

And for some reason, I really *felt* like one.

"Will Daughtry," the nurse called, too late.

"Thank God," whispered Monica, closing the *Entertainment Weekly* she'd been pretending to read, and in we went to find out what I wasn't dying of that week.

Lotta check-ins at ol' HUGE for young Will Daughtry. Weekly monitoring: it comes with every medical mystery. It's the part they leave out of those X-Men movies. Probably because it's deadly dull. And not fully covered, insurance-wise. And a giant buzzkill.

The upside was that Monica drove me there. Technically, it

should've been a guardian, Brian or Laura, and they were all too eager to oblige, believe me. That's why I begged them not to.

"You two," I told them, "no offense, but you freak me out."

"I'm not trying to freak anybody out!" Brian came back. "I just want some answers."

"They don't have those there," I said. "They have tests. And questions. And then more tests. When they have answers, you'll know. We'll all know."

"We don't mean to hover, Will," Laura said, in her smoothest and most soothing yogurt-commercial voice. "We really don't."

"I know," I said. "Believe me, I appreciate it. Everything you're both doing. But . . . there are going to be a lot of these tests, a lot of these appointments. And . . . every time I look at you two in that waiting room, the looks on your faces, I see the crash cart and defib paddles right around the corner."

"That's not what we—"

"I know! I know! It's not you, it's me. But . . . can it be Monica? For a while? Just for a while?"

So it was Monica for a while, driving me to my weekly bleedings. And after, we'd go to the Lowlands, or surfing, where the water would take it all, make it all go away.

Dr. Helman closed the door to the exam room. "Roll up a sleeve and stay awhile."

The nurse—always the same nurse, always the same vampiric complexion—laid out his medieval phlebotomy tackle and swabbed my good bleeding arm (I'm a lefty for bleeding, a righty for everything else) while Dr. Helman went down her checklist: Any joint pain? Shortness of breath, chest pain? Migraines, bad headaches?

ling," said Monica, throwing her salt-rotten
 sand and dropping after them. "It's a cliché,

llof and I are over for good."
 possibility," said Monica. She'd disappeared
 board. "Jollof doesn't like deviations from the

 male gorilla of a certain age. So I'll bet he watches
u are, after all, What's Weird in the 858. . . ."
iseass. Enough."
news had come a-calling when *Guinness* started
h spurt for a potential record. Rafty tipped them
or several weeks. And that's how I became "What's
" (which is the real, actual, not-shitting-you name
or our local news station. They shot a short inter-
htry driveway, me next to the Yacht, intercut with
e GIF.
y days after my spot aired, [jack] showed up.
k Jollof is [jack]?" We were waxing our boards.
ok her head. "Jollof's too evolved to be a troll. And
ive."
jack] explained to me—was a giant killer. He was a
s troll. That much was verifiable. He systematically
ious platforms, registering under dozens of names—
s of [jack]—and spouting off various mumbly, am-
case threats, which everyone encouraged me not to
while simultaneously insisting I alert the police.
 was always the same:

Visual "shimmers"? Strange sensations that may or may not be mild seizures? Loss of appetite?

Nope, nope, nope, nope, nope. And to that last one: quite the opposite. Given the chance, any time of day or night, I could and would eat my weight in Ranch Corn Nuts. At the end of that day's session, we had what we always had: another few pages of data for Dr. Helman, another five vials of blood for Vampire Nurse.

"You're fine," said Dr. Helman. "That's the headline. Again."

"I feel fine," I said. "Unless I'm here. Here, I feel like a time bomb."

"Well, there's no evidence you are. We're just keeping an eye on you. For, y'know, 'science'!"

There are very few doctors who can get away with putting *science* in ironic air quotes, and Dr. Helman wasn't one of them. But I didn't blame her for trying to lighten things up before saying what she *really* wanted to say:

"In all seriousness: would you like to talk to a therapist?"

I always gave that question four seconds of serious thought and concluded: *Less than anything.*

"I mean . . . I already *have* a therapist?"

"Oh!" said Dr. Helman. "Well, that's great."

Dr. Monica Bailarín, B.o.B. (also my driver, as luck would have it), was skilled at what she called the Talking Cure: a treatment that involved no drugs stronger than Pibb Xtra and Tabasco, but did require a great deal of surfing.

After a long Saturday at the bleedorium or phlebodome or

whatever, we'd drive to the zoo, I'd put in an hour at the Lowlands, then we'd head north to spend the last light at BoB, waxing our boards and just waxing. Drew was there sometimes. But mostly not. Practice, practice. The Plan demanded Wins. And thus: practice.

One day, on the way to postbleeding therapy, I left Monica in Keeper Access and opened the air lock (what we called the security door leading into the habitat) to take the chow to the Family. The usual routine, same time, same everything.

Except right away, I knew something was different.

Jollof was nowhere to be seen. Not on his throne. Not in the yard. Not on the concourse ledges. None of his usual haunts.

I sat the food down where I always did. Blue watched me from over by the observation window. Gave a shy wave. I waved back.

Maybe that's what did it.

As I turned back toward the air lock, the bushes twenty yards to my right *exploded,* and Jollof, propelled by forces of nature we upright bipeds can only guess at, came galloping at me fast, only one of his four sets of knuckles touching the ground at a time. I had zero chance of making it to the air lock, so I just froze.

He'd gotten between me and the door again. But this time, he seemed less unsure about what he planned to do. This time, his canines were bared, fangs as long as switchblades.

A trickle of perspiration made its way all the way to my tailbone—where my tail, if I'd had one, would've been firmly between my legs.

This wasn't a dominance display. This was just *dominance.* The Full Jollof.

Lucky for me, that's when Mike started pilfering the mangoes.

Lucky for me, that was th   s counse
Even if he was in the middle   wn to th
While Jollof wrote a sca   ."
with fists and fangs, I slipped   think Jo
In Keeper Access, Brian   's anothe
the cavalry—and two other ke   ve for he
guards, hands on their pistol p   t?"
Brian grabbed me, hugged   ."
Then Brian said, "Okay, inte   Jollof *is* a
I was fine with that.   s. And yo
I watched Jollof lose intere   y, okay, w
he always did. Mike was good a   the local
taking the blows, rolling with   my grow
parting cuff to the ear, took a bi   e a day. F
to his throne room.   n the 858!
Mike stumped unevenly bac   egment) f
and bowed, his goofy gait subd   the Daug
ezoid. I swear he looked back at r   time-laps
nod, so tiny I might've imagined   t too ma
pomorphize apes, I might've inte   o you thi
You and me, bro.   onica sho
Or *You owe me, bro.*   xually ac
Or maybe both.   ack]—as
                                  industriou
                                  ked my va
It was a gorgeous day at BoB, a gre   lly versio
"I don't know what got into hin   ous lowe
picked our way down the red rock   seriously
weird with me that one time, but I t   The them

u r not 2 big 2 fail

juice-box-size juicer = still a juicer

will daughtry—now with 30% more derp

Super lame shit. None of it bothered me, honestly. Internet gonna internet.

Then [jack] got less entertaining.

bigger they r . . . hardr they die

6-letter word for rapid growth? C-A-N-C-E-R—ask ur mom

That last one rattled me. It meant there'd been some deep, deep googling.

It meant commitment.

It also made me suddenly, explosively furious. I mean, anyone would be upset, reading that. But this kind of anger—it was a *temperature* I'd never felt before. I felt it in my *hands*. I'd never felt anger in my hands before.

Was it because they were bigger now?

And then I'd come down. Come back to myself. *Mood swings.* One of the things Dr. Helman had said to watch out for. But was it really so strange, was it really so pathological to get angry when a stranger talks shit about your dead mom?

Drew didn't think it was strange. Drew got angry enough for both of us the first time he saw one of [jack]'s fan letters.

"Tell him to meet us behind the gym, and I'll pound his little lowercase letters into the dirt."

Drew was brave. Drew was protective. And Drew was, of course, joking.

He didn't really believe in violence. He believed in the Plan. But he wanted me to know how angry he was, and I appreciated that. I was grateful. As always. And a little irrationally annoyed, at the same time.

Because I was Drew's size now. I actually edged him by a few pounds that September. I could do my own troll rolling, thanks, if things broke that way. Part of me wondered if they would. Part of me was curious. Not a super admirable part: the part that wouldn't mind settling scores.

I didn't want that part of me diagnosed, maybe. I was already the subject of too many attempted diagnoses. Half the time, I felt terrified of dying, even after my clean bill of health, maybe 'cause *You're fine! But we'll be monitoring you forever!* doesn't really feel like the cleanest bill of health.

Half the time, I felt like a god. A minor god. Demi, for sure. But a god.

And all the time, I worried about bursting into flame.

I worried the anger I felt in my hands came from someplace so deep and metabolic, I wouldn't be able to beat it, or outrun it, or outgrow it.

Sometimes I just wanted to be weightless.

Dr. Monica had a prescription for that.

We floated in the BoB cove, on our backs, on the beat-to-shit Goodwill boards she kept in the cave.

"All this talk about cancer, about stalkers—we're leaving it at the cliff top," Monica was saying. "It doesn't belong down here. I won't have it, William. I will *not* have it." And then, in her best grizzled-cop voice, she rasped: "Not on *my* BoB!"

I laughed, because it was the dumbest nonjoke in the world, delivered perfectly, and I felt the board jiggle and pitch, felt the cold tickle of Pacific seawater. There was more of me on the board than there had been before. Every time, there was always more. I felt unwieldy.

"Okay," I said. "I'm cured. I'm not afraid anymore. Of anything. *Except hypothermia.* Can we please paddle in?"

"'Nother ten minutes," said Monica. "Trust me, this is thera-peutic." She stretched on her board, actually managed this kinda yoga-ish backbend, then went flat again. "I have . . . *utter* faith in you, Will Daughtry," she said. "I always have. So you're changing, so what? We all are, right? *Trust the water.* There's a good plan. One of my faves. Oh, and also: *bend your knees.* Very good plan. *Always bring a book.* Decent plan. Hey. Were you telling Dr. Helman the truth?"

"About what?"

"That you feel good?"

"I feel . . . *really* good. I feel . . ."

"Strong?" The green eyes were scanning me hard now. Couldn't quite tell what for. It made me warmer, though. Hearing her say that word, *strong.* While looking at me.

"Yeah. I feel . . . strong."

"Then: *be strong.*"

"Also . . . hungry."

Monica laughed. "Now *that's* a plan. That the hormones talking? Is it Grow-liath's time of the month?"

(Grow-liath, I'm sorry to say, was Rafty's "brand name" for me.

Monica couldn't get enough of repeating it, because it was heart-stoppingly abominable.)

"It's apparently always Grow-liath's time of the month."

"Y'know," said Monica, zagging. "I was looking at my freshman yearbook the other day."

"Okay. Non sequitur. So, apropos of nothing—"

"Of something. Wait for it."

"Apropos of something, you were gazing at an actual, physical print yearbook. Very romantic, very steampunk."

"Indeed," said Monica, to the sky. "Anyway . . . I flipped to the back page, and somebody'd written, *Don't ever change!* Which should've been funny to me. But . . . wasn't. Because . . . why do people say that? And write it in yearbooks? Why is that on birthday cards? And not *Eat shit and die? Don't ever change* is, like, the king of all curses! That's like saying, *Don't breathe, please. For me?* I mean, it's the procrustean bed of yearbook clichés!"

I wasn't about to slow her down to ask about the crusty bed thing.

"Shit, Daughtry," she rolled on, "everyone *changes*. Everyone who *can*." Monica made a surf angel with her arms, finning the water, and then floated off vaguely in the direction of the Sawtooth. "Except me. I am eternal. Me and BoB. We are magic. We are legend."

I didn't argue with her there.

We floated. Then I said, "What do *you* worry about?"

"Lots of stuff."

"College?"

"*Don't.*" She splashed me. "Drew's bad enough. Don't *you* start."

"What? I mean . . . you're a *senior*—"

"That I am."

"So you're down with the Plan."

"I'm down," Monica said, looking out at the Sawtooth, at the froth and churn, "with *my* plan."

Monica was already halfway up the cliff. I was about to follow when the sun hit the inside of the cave just right and I saw it:

Her sleeping bag. Her kerosene camp stove.

What do you *worry about?*

Lots of stuff.

She was sleeping here. Again. She'd done it before. When her dad had one of his "off" weekends.

I usually made a point of asking about it, even though Monica hated that, even though she got annoyed. And I almost asked about it that day, but then I saw, next to the sleeping bag, a duffel. A simple, unassuming, just-minding-its-own-business duffel.

Drew's duffel.

Maybe she was just borrowing it? Doubtful. It was Drew's favorite duffel, his lucky duffel, the one he took to playoff games.

This particular camping trip wasn't dad-driven. It was Drew-driven.

Sex at BoB. I felt a fresh wave of betrayal.

Then I got over it.

But I still wanted to know: dad or Drew?

Also, I wanted *not* to know.

Also, it was moot, I realized, because I couldn't ask either of them. It would Get Weird. Fast.

Drew would be embarrassed because he didn't know Monica

was bunking at BoB, or because *I* did, and Monica'd be furious at me for checking up on her, either behind her back or to her face. Well-intentioned paternalism was her least favorite kind of paternalism.

But there were worse paternalisms.

Here was Monica's official line on her dad, as long as I'd known her: "He's just a goddamned mess, but he's *my* mess, and I don't want him in the system, *comprende?*"

In other words: *Back off. I've got this.*

In innocent ancient times—before the Heightening, before MoniDrew—Drew and I had made it clear to Monica: *Our door's always open. Crash away, if shit gets bad. Surf our couch, for a change.* Monica listened, nodded, appreciated the gesture, I think—but was also mildly appalled. She'd blown it off. "You guys don't have enough bookshelves," she'd said finally, "to handle me and mine."

Me and mine, meaning Monica and all her books.

What she really meant was: her dad was all the family she had left. Sometimes, though, she had to get away from him. Thus, her BoB overnights. "It's an oversad kind of thing," she'd reassure us. "Not an undersafe kind of thing."

I looked up at her, hanging off the cliff, halfway back to civilization, that wobbly empire of fear, and—*SMASH!* went the Sawtooth—away from nature, that boiling cauldron of fear.

I probably should have said something, should have asked, but ... what was I asking? Was I asking: *Are you okay?*

Or *Are you and Drew hooking up? As in,* hooking up–*hooking up?*

Nature frothed over the barrier jetty, kicked up sand, mixed the land with the sea. I didn't know where I stood anymore, only that I stood more than a foot higher than I used to. I looked up and watched Monica disappearing over the cliff top, watched the moment slip away, like all those other moments. *Tomorrow,* I thought. *I'll find a way to ask tomorrow.*

Looking at that worse-for-wear sleeping bag, curled like a grub in the sacred cathedral of the BoB cave, I couldn't put what I felt into words. But the fewer words I had to work with, the more I felt it in my hands: heat.

I needed to put it somewhere, that heat, that wordless heat.

I think that's how I found my way into the middle of the Oklahoma.

ELEVEN

6'4"

"FROM SHALINA BOULEVARD in Poca Resaca, Will Daughtry! Come on down!"

I was in the ring. The ring was about eight feet across.

And there was this guy in the ring with me. He was about eight feet across, too.

This, apparently, was football.

"And from Sutter Ave. in U City, Jaylen Teixiera!"

We were all suited up, pads and helmets (mine borrowed from the department, a loose fit), and we were on wet grass, in this big black Hula-Hoop together, Jaylen Teixiera and I. The idea was: in forty seconds or so, one of us wouldn't be.

It's like sumo wrestling, only with turf instead of sand, and more concussive helmet butting. And no tea after.

Coach Whately called it the Oklahoma.

This is what happens when Monica Bailarín tells you to be

strong. One Ring hanging around my neck, inside a borrowed jersey, bouncing against my chest like a second heart, answering the one inside knock for knock—*thump, thump, BANG, BANG*— I'd decided to test-drive this new body.

Turns out the football squad had suffered some injuries that season. Even mediocre football, it seems, leads to injuries. So the fall brought walk-on tryouts.

I'd decided to try football first because I didn't actually *like* football. I thought I'd be less disappointed if I washed out. I thought that would lower the stakes. What's it matter if you fail at something you don't even like?

The other side of it was: I'd always been a little scared of football, and I wanted to do something about that. The universe had called my bluff, and presented me with Jaylen Teixiera, all two hundred pounds of him. I knew him a little, I guess. Well: I knew his shape. This was Rhombus, from the Ethan Neville affair, the night in Jazzy's woods. And from countless roughings-up in remote hallways during middle school.

I took comfort in the fact that the Keseberg High football team was (how to put this gently?) *not very good.* The Harps had a semi-storied basketball team, but we weren't a football power. I assumed the bar would be lower.

Maybe it *was* low. I had no comparison.

Great plan, Daughtry. If Brian knew, he'd tranq-dart you and drag you home with his Ketch-All. Hell, if DREW knew . . .

I tried a little levity. "Hi, Jaylen. Come here often?"

Jaylen gave a mad-bull kind of snort that said, quite clearly, *You will soon be not-alive, beta snowflake.*

"What do you think this is, Daughtry?" barked Coach Whately.

This was obviously a trick question, but I was a guest here, so I tried to answer politely: "I was guessing . . . football?"

"This is the Oklahoma!" Coach Whately crowed to his meat sticks, and they went all hooty. *Hoot hoot hoot!* Whatever was about to happen to me? Was apparently hilarious.

Coach roared: "Bull in the ring, sudden death. Set!"

I didn't much like the sound of any of those words.

If this'd been a movie, a distant eagle scream would've pierced the air, but all I heard was the shriek of the whistle—

—and the *CHOCK!* of my helmet (and head) connecting with the helmet (and head) of Jaylen Teixiera.

URF.

Okay. Lesson. Learned.

Bar. Not. Low. Enough.

A blast wave passed through my new body, energy rippling through meat, bone, and better judgment as Jaylen Teixiera's eyeless, mouthless face slot bulldozed into the curve of my left shoulder. My feet were briefly off the ground, both of them, and then came down, but they were slipping, trying to find traction in the wet grass. I dug in with my unfamiliar cleats, panicky little divots of turf flying like confetti.

Then.

He let me go.

Huh. That's weir—

ORF.

Fresh impact. Harder this time. Didn't seem possible. But. Yes. *Harder.*

And now I was off balance.

My knees folded like lawn chairs. Muscles in my back and arms, muscles I didn't even know I had, started screaming bloody murder at me—*Why are you doing this?!*—and for a second, I was knocked right *out* of this shiny new body and back into my old one—

I'm four feet, eleven inches, ninety-six pounds, and a monster's crushing me to death—

And then a voice:

William. Be strong.

And then I was *back.*

Back in the moment. Back in the flesh. My flesh.

We were just two guys, Will and Jaylen, head to head on a football field, and this was just a drill. A test. Nothing serious. That's all I came out here to do, right?

So I tested.

An inch from the edge of the ring, I got low. It was pure instinct, the getting low. I dug in. And I pushed back, with everything I wasn't sure I had.

When I did . . . I felt that unstoppable Rhombus . . . *stop.* And reverse. Just a tiny little bit, just enough. I felt Jaylen Teixiera *give.*

I'd never felt anything like that before. Feeling someone else give . . . under *my* strength?

Feeling that changed, well, everything. Muscles that'd been flashing *ALL DONE!* three seconds before now felt irrigated with jet fuel. Strength from God knows where surged through them, and Jaylen Teixiera—who'd maybe gotten a little cocky when I was three inches from oblivion—now found himself with the higher center of gravity and a surprisingly strong force at work underneath it, tipping him toward the opposite side of the circle. He jujitsued out of my clutches just in time but couldn't quite reclaim his momentum, and we were stalemated for so long, Coach finally called it.

For a second there, I was that guy in the movie who says, *I could do this all day.*

"Not bad, Daughtry," said Coach, not meeting my eyes, but smiling as he flipped the sheet on his clipboard. "Beginner's luck. Awright, *next*! From North Laurenzi Ave. . . ."

For reasons I can't explain—something having to do with adrenaline and maybe something deeper than adrenaline, something I've felt only one other time in my life and never want to feel again—I said to Coach Whately:

"Lemme go again."

Coach raised an eyebrow. But before he could say no, another face slot stepped out of the scrum. Not quite as wide as Jaylen, but taller. Like Jaylen, he wore the full-face-eraser sun visor. Unlike Jaylen, he had a cocky posture that asked, *Who's your silverback?* And there was . . . something else. Something . . . familiar.

"I'll go." Player Y cocked his head. "Hi, Will."

Before I had time to place that voice, Coach said, "Awright, ladies' choice. Set!"

The whistle screamed and Player Y came in fast, a human scimitar, looking for a quick decapitation. I absorbed the hit into my padded shoulder, and for a second, I thought I'd capsize like some torpedoed ocean liner—he hit so hard and fast, one of my legs lifted off the ground, and a dam broke inside me, cold panic flooded—

But then I came down.

And as soon as I got traction—

—my muscles seemed to figure out what was really going on: *it was a bluff.*

This guy didn't have the bulk of Jaylen, or the power of Jaylen, or the stability of Jaylen. He'd come in hard and high, trying to take off my head. I realized I'd seen this before: this matchup, these stances, this exact species of push-and-pull. And I knew just what to do.

I hooked.

I scooped.

I got under him, *lifted.*

And suddenly Player Y was on his back. On the ground. Outside the ring, wriggling like a stag beetle.

Which is where I got the idea.

(Don't mess with Biology Boy.)

Player Y spent what seemed like a slo-mo eternity on the ground. Then he ripped off his helmet, came at me, skunk-stripe highlights flashing in the sun. The other players restrained him.

Of course it was Spencer. Sidney's old Spencer. Spencer from the woods at Jazzy's party.

"Fuck was that?" he screamed, and Coach blew the whistle.

"Inskip! Language! You wanna sit out a game or three?"

Spencer shook off his restrainers, turned, mumbled under his breath, "Like you'd bench your star quarterback."

Coach was suddenly in close orbit of Spencer's face. "If I had one," he said, "no, I wouldn't bench him."

More hoots, and a few *daaayums.* Spencer reddened. "Coach," he said, in a voice dangerously close to a whine. "What that little freak pulled—*that wasn't football!*"

"Nope," I said—and unless you're Monica Bailarín, there are very few moments when life hands you the perfect line at the perfect time, and this happened to be one of those moments. "That was the Oklahoma."

It wasn't the kind of thing a nice guy would say. But then, nice guys don't usually get the chance to settle old middle school scores wearing new grown-up bodies.

The hoots bloomed again. Coach shut everybody up with a whistle, and I walked off the field for the first and last time, gloriously backlit by victory, quitting while I was ahead.

Yep, that was my football career, from beginning to end.

I *really* don't like football.

(I'll always have a soft spot for the Oklahoma, though.)

I was toweling off when a familiar shadow fell over me.

"What the hell?" asked Drew. "What the *hell*?"

He was in practice sweats. Trying to look casual, like he'd just happened to run across me here, in a locker room I never, ever visited.

"Football?"

"Tryout for walk-ons, big deal."

"Yeah, big deal. I heard you almost got the shit kicked out of you."

Now that got me a little riled, I'll admit. Because there's no version of what happened on that football field in which the shit was almost kicked out of me. "Who told you that?"

Drew had on his most annoying face: Dad Face. I braced for it: the Sonning.

(I'll fill in his *son*s for you. They're silent—even Drew couldn't hear them, I don't think—but they're most definitely there.)

"Spencer Inskip is an effin' sociopath, son. And, son, football is not your game. Okay? The team is bad news, son. The harder those guys lose, son, the shittier they treat people, and those guys lose *hard*. You've got nothing to prove to them, my sonny son son."

Ah, but he was wrong, son. I *did* have something to prove.

Not to *them*, maybe.

"Okay," I said, not bothering to disguise my irritation. "So what you're saying is, *Don't get too big for your britches?*"

When we used to argue, I'd always been a foot away from Drew's face, no matter how close I'd been standing.

Now, even sitting down, I was a lot closer to his airspace.

We weren't *fighting*, though.

Were we?

Drew was quiet for an almost-too-long time. Then he said:

"I would . . . *never* . . . say *britches*."

And we both laughed. Fighting? Who, us? Nah!

"What I'm saying," said Drew after we'd laughed, "is maybe slow down."

And because he'd just been so funny, I tried really hard not to hold that buzzer-beater Sonning against him.

I had a deep think on the way home. Drew. Monica. All the *helpful advice* my new body was attracting. Seemed to be this thing's single function lately: advice stimulator.

Slow down, Drew said.

Be strong, Monica said.

Don't make it weird, the Plan said.

But! But Monica's sleeping bag was in BoB! *With Drew's lucky duffel!* That was already weird, right? That needed addressing! My central processor was melting down, barfing out feedback: *Slowdownbestrongdon'tmakeitweird . . . slowdownbestrongdon'tmakeitweird . . .*

Rafty had a different perspective. He shared it with me one afternoon as we dunked in his driveway. The Pro Slam had been set back to regulation, for my benefit. The trampoline had been pushed to the side. Rafty sat on it and philosophized.

"My friend," he said. "With great power comes great responsibility."

"Feel like I've heard that before," I said. "What does it mean? In this case?"

"It means you have a responsibility to your body."

"Okay."

"You have a responsibility to use your body . . . for sex."

"Hmm."

"You need to have sex with that body, Will. If I had that body? I would have sex with it."

"Hmm."

"I mean . . . I don't mean . . . you know what I mean! And I mean: Soon. Imminently. Tonight, maybe. There are takers, dude. So many. The girls in the hall, you walk in, and it's like . . . it's like they're at Red Lobster, and the waiter says, 'Ladies, pick your lobster.' And there's this one really big lobster, and you know they all want it. That's a bad metaphor—I lost my grip."

"You did. And now I'll never eat lobster again."

"My point is, you're all in your head about this. When you should be . . . all in your bed . . . about this. . . ."

"Now, *that* rhymes."

"In bed *with* someone. Less thinking. More sexing."

"Says the virgin."

"As a virgin, I have clarity on this."

"Well, as a fellow virgin, I'm vomiting. On the inside. Because of words like *sexing*."

"Sure, go on, be a nozzle about this, but you know I'm right." Rafty stood up on his trampoline, looking very *friends, Romans, countrymen*. He bounced a little as he speechified. "You're off surfing and doing whatever it is you do at the zoo," he pointed out, "when you should be turning the back of your car into a frickin' *sex museum*."

"There is very little back of my car," I said. "So that . . . would be one tiny sex museum. . . ."

"Will. Be serious. Focus."

"The exhibits would have to be, like, *modest*—"

"Now you listen to me, you giant ass prolapse!" Rafty was hopping up and down on his trampoline. Every third or fourth word he delivered to me eye to eye. "You are living a life most of us can only imagine. Sitting on a freakin' jackpot, doing jack shit about it. That is . . . a *betrayal*. You are a *celebrity*. You have *responsibilities*. And as your manager—"

"Raf, this 'manager' thing, we gotta talk about it—"

"—as your *manager*, my managerial advice is: strike while the lobster is hot. You're gonna be a *Guinness* entry in, like, a matter of weeks. You need to do something with this. You need a goal. Preferably a sex goal."

Rafty didn't know my secret: I had a goal in mind. It wasn't a sex goal.

It was: six feet, seven inches. That was my goal.

Not very scientific, I know, banking on a conclusion before the experiment's over.

For some reason, though, six foot seven had become my Goldilocks height: tall enough to be taller than just about everyone (99.7th percentile, if you're interested—the *ceiling* tile of percentiles), yet not so tall that people would think *freak* or *How sad!* or grasp for the names of glands they only dimly remembered from AP biology. I had no evidence to support six seven as my probable resting height, my summit. I just really, really wanted it to be true.

I was a real primordial soup, you see: Drew telling me to slow down, think of the future. Monica telling me to lean in, be in the moment. Rafty ordering me to screw or be screwed. (When I hadn't even *kissed* anyone yet. Not really. Not a real kiss. Not a *first* kiss.)

And into this soup crashed a comet named Sidney.

Sidney found me a place in the exciting world of mixed-gender intramural volleyball.

"Because you're gonna wanna spike" was Sidney's rationale.

Sidney played varsity volleyball, so she knew some things about the game, and she taught me a few of them. Enough for intramurals, at least. I had some new advantages, of course. For instance, the net? Wasn't as much of a problem for me these days. One hop and I was an arm's length above the tape. And that gave me the spike, which had eluded me the first sixteen years of my life, for obvious reasons. Now I owned it. And thus, I owned mixed-gender intramural volleyball, sport of kings. (And queens.)

"Intramural volleyball?!" Rafty shook his head. "You put Spencer Inskip on his ass, and you're playing . . . *intramural volleyball?!*"

"I thought you'd approve of the 'mixed-gender' part."

"Will, buddy, where's the fire in the belly?"

"Whenever I feel fire in my belly," I said, "I eat. And then it goes away."

Attendance at intramural volleyball games went up, for the sheer curiosity factor. (Some nights, it was Ethan Neville, clicking away for the yearbook, *plus* up to fifteen other people—a tenfold increase.) With me in the rotation, every side-out looked like a gearshift toggling from D to R to N and back. But nobody laughed when a setter gave me a high one and I came flying forward to rain spike after spike on the unfortunate mixed genders across the net.

It was awesome. And stupid. Not punk rock, not cock rock—just dork rock. I felt comfortable there, at the corner of Awesome and Stupid. At the corner of Dork and Rock.

I felt so comfortable that one night after a game, after we'd dropped Ethan at his house, I took Sidney to the Lowlands.

I know, I know.

There were a lot of reasons I shouldn't have done this, starting with the fact that interns aren't allowed in Keeper Access after visiting hours.

And followed by the fact that the Lowlands felt like Monica/Drew territory. Like it belonged to my old life. Not this new one. Hell, I didn't even bring Rafty to Keeper Access. I felt like I was breaking a vow.

That's probably why I did it. I had to break a rule we'd never made. Why? Who knows? Hormones. Enzymes. Biology.

All of this was assuming, of course, that Sidney was interested in anything other than friendship of the strictly intramural variety.

But I had a bit of a hunch. Sidney was relatively direct.

"So," said Sidney as we walked into Keeper Access, "this is where the monkey magic happens."

"*Ape* magic," I said, "technically. And as far as 'magic' goes: most of it comes down to fruit and poop."

"Doesn't everything. What's this?" She was pointing to a collection of sharpened bamboo rods, which the staff had hung on a rack made for pool cues.

"Oh. Um. Murder weapons."

"Funny."

"Not kidding, really: the chimps make those."

"Whoa."

"Yeah. They started doing it a few months ago. Now, every couple of weeks, we have to confiscate a few. They collect 'em here, then send them to the Smithsonian."

We sat in front of the plate glass, watching the nighttime activities of the gorilla troop. (They're diurnal animals, so not a lot to see. Gorillas in nests, gorillas in trees. And somewhere high on his rock, in the dark: Asshole, dreaming of crushed skulls and a gold medal in the fifty-yard poo hurl.) Sid, despite the conspicuous lack of apes, was pretty impressed.

"So the chimps are stabby. How 'bout these guys, the gorillas?" Sid asked. "What are *they* packing?"

"These guys don't go in for shivs. Just crush you to death. Maybe a bite to the carotid if they're feeling ambitious. Gorillas are straightforward."

Unlike a certain zoo intern.

I'd brought Sidney here for *some* reason, but now I wasn't sure what. So I stalled. Ran through my ape patter: the hierarchies, the social structures, the strength comparisons. *Five or six fully grown humanoids, with spears, could* maybe *take down one adult silverback, blah blah blah.*

"You don't go in there anymore, you said, 'cause the big guy thinks you're gonna steal his gorilla ladies?" Sid asked.

"Yep," I joked along. "I was just too irresistible. Maybe it's my opposable thumb—"

And all of a sudden, Sidney Lim was kissing me.

On tiptoes.

Sidney Lim was really good at kissing, turns out.

It was like she was talking to me. A whole conversation, with a rise and fall to it, her arms around my neck. And all my brain came up with was:

Mouths are . . . really detailed. *People are really* detailed. *Inside. Outside. Girls? Girls are* all *detail. And wonderful wonderful wonderful brain flatliiiiiiiiiine . . .*

And after a long, long, long "conversation," during which I didn't feel like I contributed nearly enough, I came up for air, pushed a stray waterfall of hair away from her eyes, tucked it behind her ear. It felt choreographed. Instinct? Or something I'd seen somewhere? Nature or nurture or Netflix? Her face seemed near and far at the same time, and I couldn't choose which eye to focus on, which is something that happens to me only when I'm really, really nervous or really, really close to someone's face or both. Sid, I saw, had faint freckles, little strawberry flecks, reaching from the bridge of her nose in a butterfly pattern. I'd never noticed that before. I was noticing everything, all of a sudden. With my hand on the curve of her hip, I thought the following total nonsense: *I could drive there blindfolded, I could drive there blindfolded, I could—*

Oh, Jesus Christ—

Magic Mike was at the glass, watching us. Sid saw him first.

"Whoa," said Sid, but she didn't jump or freak, which was impressive. (Me? I jumped a little.) She just laughed. "Creepy?"

"Uh. Yes."

"Can you do the sign language for *creepy* to him?"

"These apes don't sign."

Sidney giggled. "You said that like it's . . . like, the badass slogan of this zoo." In an old-time movie-trailer voice, she intoned: "These colors don't run—and these apes don't sign!"

Which sent me right over the giggle falls. Guy needs a certain tension release in a situation like this: first real kiss, first ape voyeurism experience. A Grow-liath's gotta laugh. Also, I was very happily realizing something: Sidney Lim was pretty awesome. And wildly out of my league. And kissing me. Again.

This is my last chance to ruin things with her.

I didn't.

Instead, I kissed her back.

Then I said, "Let's get out of here, because there's a hominid watching us make out, and that offends me, as a biologist."

Sidney saluted. "You're the expert. Lead on."

We went to the parking lot. We got in my sex museum. We set up a very small makeout exhibit for two.

Well, it was *intended* for two.

I'm now fairly sure we still had a hominid watching us that night.

[jack].

TWELVE

6'7"

⟨justjack⟩: how u doin big boy feelin gooooooooood
??????????????????
WillD: you know i send these to the police right
⟨justjack⟩: lol im terrified. sd's finest cybercrime unit = top
shelf! guess ill c u n court! lol j/k hey how's sidney
WillD: ⟨YOU HAVE BEEN BLOCKED⟩
⟨nowwith30percentmorejack⟩: i could do this all day.
can u? whats wrong? u feel okay? is it catching up w u
yet??????

"COACH IS PLAYING me off Forchette," Drew croaked from the back seat. He was crazy dehydrated. Monica tossed him a Vitaminwater, which she called Liquid Fraud and objected to, and Drew absorbed it in two gulps.

"Head games," he gasped. "For no reason. Now Forchette thinks he's acting captain and I'm 'the show'—I mean, it's *all* screwed up."

"That's a drag," I said, in what I thought was a pretty sympathetic tone of voice for someone trying to thread traffic on the inbound I-5.

"Yeah," muttered Drew, in a tone that told me *a drag* didn't begin to cover it.

"Buck up, Spesh," said Monica. "You're killin' it."

Monica was laying it on thick. Maybe because Drew (and I) was (were) taking her to a fancy restaurant for her eighteenth birthday?

Yeah, so this was mid-December, and the Nativity scenes were blooming in San Diego amid the decorative cacti. The Harps, as predicted, were 12–0 so far in regular season play, with Drew hitting a mind-blowing .629 field goal percentage for the season. Meanwhile, I was touching the cusp of six feet, seven inches tall. I'd reached my goal height, and life was good. So far, magical thinking had been a smashing success—even though it couldn't quite delete the distressing image of Monica's sleeping bag stowed at BoB, Drew's duffel nesting right beside it.

There was a lot packed into that image, a lot of questions. Questions cunningly turduckened inside other questions. Okay, just two questions, really, but they were doozies:

Was she sleeping at BoB?

Why?

That last question had an answer that would be weird-making no matter what it was. If the answer was *Because dad*, then the follow-up from Monica would be *And I told you not to ask*. If the answer was *Drew and sex with Drew*, then the follow-up from me might be an embolism. And just asking the first question would mean implying the second question.

Also, asking Drew? Out of the question.

But today's excursion, I hoped, would answer all conspicuously unasked questions (*How are things at home, Monica?*) without asking them at all. Because today was Monica's birthday, and we were going to her house in Barrio Nacional to pick up her party dress.

We were celebrating Monica's eighteenth year of life on earth at a rotating restaurant. Yes: for Monica's eighteenth birthday, we were gonna get *turnt*! But the path to that great turntable in the sky would take us dangerously close to Martin Eddy. I'd get a flyby of Monica's father for the first time in nearly a year.

Martin Eddy was one of those guys who said things like *Nothing gets past this guy,* when, in fact, most of life had. He'd come to Miramar in the mid-'90s to become a fighter pilot; that turned out to be bad timing, since nobody really needed fighter pilots by then. He'd been at TOPGUN a week when they announced they were shutting down the school.

After his navy hitch, he'd entered the exciting world of private security. Meaning: he was a rent-a-cop. Traded his F-14 for a Daihatsu. Somewhere in there, he'd gained a daughter and a drinking problem. Somewhere in there, he'd lost his girlfriend, Monica's mom.

Monica's mom, whose first name Monica never spoke aloud in my presence, had been a lot younger than Martin Eddy when they'd had Monica. ("Apparently, I was not the product of careful planning.") Seven months later, she slipped out one of life's side doors and vanished forever. Until Monica was six, Martin told her the ocean was her mother. Which was kind of beautiful, really, as lies go. It had some poetry to it, enough to get Monica to the water's edge. She and her busted board took it from there.

But since then, Martin Eddy's lies had gotten less charming, less poetic. Now they were lies about *How many pills, Dad? How many beers, Dad?* The lies didn't work, not on Monica, not on his employers. Even the rent-a-cop gig bit the dust, and the Daihatsu was garaged forever. All Martin Eddy piloted today, as we drove up to the curb, was a lawn chair. The alleged lawn on which it rested was a mange of sand and anthills, stubbled with chickweed. The chair sat in the shade of a single teetering cedar, curving precipitously over the swaybacked roof of Chez Eddy-Bailarín like a scythe. Martin warded off this and all omens with a beer, a Lucky, his talisman of Oakland pride. A dry breeze played with what was left of his straw-colored hair. A gut bloomed over his belt buckle, collecting flecks of beer foam in fast-evaporating constellations.

He had no history of violence, but he made up for it with a lot of anger. And he had plenty to be angry about. He couldn't prepare himself a meal. Couldn't even charge his phone without a reminder. Martin Eddy was a life drain who'd been lucky enough to spawn a daughter with life to spare.

"Hey!" called Martin, raising his Lucky Lager. "Hey hey HEY! It's the Snowflakes Karamazov."

Martin Eddy was a reader. He wasn't going to let you forget that, either. Everything about Martin was a dare. *C'mon,* those pink eyes said, *you just try and put this guy in a box! Try! I SAID* TRY, *DAMMIT! Please try? Please put this guy in a box? And then bury that box?*

"Hey, Martin," said Drew, getting out. He used a monotone he'd had plenty of opportunities to hone. Monica gave Drew a quick peck I pretended not to notice (but Martin whistled at), and then she was halfway to the door.

"'Hi, Dad, how was your day?'" Martin prompted.

She didn't take the bait. Just dashed inside for her dress.

I got out of the car. My knees were screaming: growing pains plus plain old spatial limitations. These days, even with the seat at its backmost click, I couldn't spend more than ten minutes folded into the Yacht without needing to unkink.

I realize now: getting out was a mistake. I'd presented Martin Eddy with an opportunity. A big one.

Suddenly it was just us boys in that mangy yard. The wind died.

"Holy hell," said Martin, giving me the once-over. "What happened to Mini-Me over here? Real pituitary case we got here, regular Andre the Giant."

"It's not pituitary," Drew snapped, before I could even issue some kind of inert disengagement. "And don't call him Andre the Giant, it's offensive."

Martin Eddy got up.

This was a bad sign. Martin did not, as a rule, get up.

"Drewy," he said, swaying perceptibly, menacingly in Drew's direction, "your ass is in my yard. That means your mouth does not get to tell me what's 'offensive.'"

Drew went dangerously silent. Just stared into Martin's swimmy pink eyes.

I telegraphed a big ol' *Stand down*.

Finally Drew shrugged. The air unpuckered.

Martin returned his righteous ass to his chaise longue. Drew got back in the car. The situation was returning to equilibrium. Nice, shitty equilibrium. The kind you live with, and live through.

Monica came back out, beelining, her dress on a hanger and a canvas tote of supplies over her shoulder. She clearly wasn't going to stay a second longer than necessary.

That was the moment Martin Eddy took an unfortunate

renewed interest in me. He was weaving his way toward me as I tried to fold myself back into my Fiat.

"Hey. Quick question for you, Dre . . ."

"Dad."

"The other boys . . . they try to . . . sneak a peek? Y'know. At the pisser?"

"Dad!"

"I mean, hell, I'm curious. We're all grown-ups here, cards on the table—"

Monica looked like she'd been stabbed. Humiliation rolled off her in sheets of steam. "Jesus Christ, Dad . . ."

That's when Drew came at Martin like he'd been steam-launched off an aircraft carrier.

Martin threw down his beer. He made an O with his mouth, and it looked like a drain we were all about to vanish down. They were almost chest to chest when Monica got between them. I didn't even see her move, she was so fast. She had her hands around Martin's thick brisket forearms, and she was pushing him back, back, back to his chaise longue.

"We're late," she said, "we're *going*." She drilled her eyes into Drew's. *"Now."*

Drew didn't move.

"Drew? We're *late*," Monica tried again.

Drew was thirty years younger than Martin and in peak physical condition . . . and, I realized suddenly (thrillingly?), *he had backup.*

Me.

Andre.

It didn't come to that. Luckily.

"We're late," Drew said finally. "Yeah."

And got in the damned car, thank God.

"I got a tip for you, Dre!" Martin called to me as we pulled away. "You're the bigger man. And he knows it. So watch out!"

In the car, I just said it.

I'd spent weeks trying to find the right words. Ridiculous. It shouldn't have taken me that long to figure out there weren't any. The time was right, in its total wrongness. Conditions were finally awkward enough. Monica'd just endured the humiliation of breaking up a fight between her father and her boyfriend; now she was staring silently out the window. Drew was deep in his phone, thumbing numbly through game tape and trying to pretend the last fifteen minutes hadn't happened. I gripped my tiny Fiat steering wheel like I was trying to strangle it. Ready to launch.

"Nazis marched in Sacramento," Drew said finally.

"Which kind? Biker kind?"

"No, the other kind. The little Dilberty guys in, like, khakis and shit."

We were talking about Nazis. This moment definitely came preruined so I went for it:

"Mon. Are you sleeping at BoB?"

Monica turned to look at me, her expression souring from Wistful Middle-Distance Stare to Something's Off in the Fridge.

"What?"

"I know you're keeping your stuff there. I saw the . . . sleeping bag, the stove—"

"Oh . . . kay . . ." Monica seemed to be concentrating very hard on the Fiat insignia embossed on the dashboard.

"I just wanna know, is everything okay? Are you . . . are you okay?"

How come it had taken me weeks to ask my best friend: *Are you okay?*

Then Drew got deafeningly quiet, cat-that-got-the-canary quiet. And I remembered: that's why.

I took a deep breath, enough to push out all the wrong words in one big huff: "How bad are things with your dad? And yes, I know: I'm making it weird. I'm making it six kinds of weird. But it'd be weirder if . . . if something . . . ever . . . happened. . . ."

Monica just nodded for a while. The Fiat kept hurtling down the highway, a bubble of silence in a thin fiberglass membrane.

I'd done it. Six kinds of weird. I awaited judgment.

The cement was drying fast on this silence. I almost thought of turning on the radio.

Finally she said:

"So . . . you know how I've always not-talked about my dad and his bullshit?"

"Yeah."

"That hasn't changed."

"Okay."

"You've just got to trust I'm taking care of it." She swiveled to look meaningfully at Drew. "You've *both* got to trust that."

"I know," said Drew, nodding vigorously, looking at his knees. "Just a slip."

Monica didn't have as many rules as Drew did, but this one she'd had on the books for years: nobody laid a glove on Martin Eddy—not physically, not verbally, not symbolically—except Monica.

people seated at that coral lump hadn't been tested as a unit. We were about to test the sustainability of this sustainable dining experience.

"So you, uh, you play volleyball?" Monica ventured.

"Yeah," said Sid. "It's, y'know, it's fun. Might be good for a scholarship somewhere."

"Right," said Mon. "Scholarships are good."

"Monica's getting a scholarship," Drew offered, too quickly. "To Irvine."

The configuration of the coral lump made it impossible for Monica to kick Drew under the table. Otherwise, his shin would've been bloodied to riblets.

"Yeah," said Sid. "I hear you guys have kind of a plan to stick around this area for college. That's cool."

Monica shot me a look.

"Well, yeah, kinda," began Drew.

"It's a pretty loose plan," Monica said quickly, and then retreated into several mouthfuls of responsibly farmed prawns, prawns that had each been humanely suffocated, unlike the conversation at this table, which had just died screaming, in agony.

"So, Drew," Sid tried again, "looks like the Harps are on track to take regionals."

"Well, I mean, we've got a good squad this year. . . ."

"Listen to it, here it comes," I said. "The *SportsCenter* voice. Humility über alles. Guy's breaking local records left and right. . . ."

"Uh, what about *world* records?" Drew came back. "This guy's got *Guinness* sniffing around. . . ."

Oof. I grimaced, and hopefully it wasn't noticeable in the fancy-restaurant near dark. But how irritating: oh, Drew's accomplish-

'Cause Martin was a monster, sure. He was the monster who lasts.

He was also the monster who *stayed*. When the other one ran away. Which entitled him to a certain degree of respect. If he needed dealing with? Monica'd do it herself. Not outsource it to Sir Boyfriend-upon-Testosterone. Or, obviously, to me.

"I'm fine," she said. "Wherever I sleep, I sleep pretty well."

More cement.

"I need more girlfriends," Monica finally said, to no one in particular.

Atoll was "a sustainable dining experience." It was also the only rotating rooftop restaurant in San Diego County. We just wanted something fancy. And to two sixteen-year-olds and a newly minted eighteen-year-old? Atoll seemed fancy.

Well: three sixteen-year-olds, I should say.

Because there, at the bar, sipping Diet Dr. Pepper, was Sidney Lim.

Monica hadn't wanted me to be the third wheel, and if that meant inviting Sidney—someone she barely knew and hadn't really warmed up to—so be it.

We were seated at what appeared to be an enormous lump of peach-colored coral. Outside, San Diego went by, very slowly, very repetitively. Inside, the lighting was half aquarium, half *Star Wars* cantina, and so was the mood: I didn't know if we were just gonna glide along a lazy river of ambient restaurant synth . . . or if somebody was going to light up a saber and lop off an arm. The four

ments of *pure skill* were *absolutely* comparable to my "achievements" of fluke biology.

"Get a room, you two," Monica deadpanned. Drew and I grinned. That almost saved the moment. Almost.

And then everything got worse.

Drew pulled out a box. A ring-size jewelry box.

Wait. Had I misread everything? Had Monica?

Were Sidney and I even supposed to be here?

I could see: Monica was as flummoxed as I was.

Drew grinned. "Happy birthday."

She gave a crooked smile. Took the box. Opened it.

"Oh," she said.

Real surprise in her voice. Plus this mild aftertaste of . . . horror.

Earrings. Very, very nice ones. Emerald clusters to match her eyes, with tiny diamonds nesting in these fairy curls of sterling silver. They must've cost Drew every ounce of allowance and summer job money he'd ever eked out, everything he'd ever earned running endless layup drills at basketball camp.

"Ta-da!" said Drew, and between *ta* and *da* there opened this vast, dark, deep, full-fathom fubar, because everyone at the table who wasn't Drew had just noticed something weird about Drew's gift.

Monica's ears, you see, weren't pierced.

Missing the obvious is pretty par for the course, high-school-boy-wise. Consider, for example, what I did next.

I mean, I've said a lot of stupid shit in my life.

But this one's up there, Hall of Fame:

"Her ears aren't pierced, dude."

Drew laughed.

Then stopped laughing.

Because he was looking at Monica's ears. Really *looking* at them. At how very, very, very *intact* they were.

"I, uh," said Monica, "I've been meaning to get around to it."

She tried chuckling. She wasn't a natural.

And Atoll turned.

The waiter came back and asked, "How are we doing?" and "Would we like anything else?"

We weren't doing well.

We would like almost anything else.

How about some poison? Do you have poison? Guaranteed to kill us all?

I escaped to the Atoll bathroom. The celesta music was deafening in there, loud enough to drown out panic.

Drew came in, went to the sinks, got a handful of water, and tried, unsuccessfully, to drown himself in it. Or maybe he was just washing his face.

"So," I said, "those earrings are really amazing."

"Yeah," said Drew.

"I didn't mean to sound . . . When I said her ears weren't . . . I think that all came out, uh . . . Anyway. They're beautiful."

Drew tore a teal paper towel from the roll. "Thanks, man," he said. "No worries. It was *my* stupid mistake. Not yours."

And he left. Just walked out. Not sure we even made eye contact.

Not yours.

Somehow he made that last bit sound less like *Apology accepted* and more like *Back the hell off.* How'd he do that?

* * *

In the parking lot, we had our weird little goodbyes. Drew and Monica said they'd grab a Lyft. They were off to, I dunno, *pierce?* I didn't ask.

Sidney and I were getting into the Yacht when my phone shook with an incoming notification. I looked, instantly wished I hadn't:

> hope ur havin a fun night. life is short. ull see
>
> ignore me at ur peril

That little valentine capped a glorious day of human folly, the lesson of which, for me, was: Maybe never open your big mouth again? Because your big mouth is a factory that makes weird.

"I shouldn't have come," Sidney said as we sat in the Fiat, outside her house. "I spoiled things."

"Oh, I think the three of us took care of that on our own." I didn't go into Martin Eddy. I was in hot enough water, telling Sid about the Plan . . . and then *not* telling Sid not to tell that I'd told.

"Fine," said Sid. "I didn't ruin things, but I *changed* things."

"Well, sure. But . . . look, the three of us, we're not delicate anemones, we're big boys, and girls, or *girl*, singular. I mean, we're old friends. And things were changing already. With or without you."

Sid let that hang a second.

"So now you're saying . . . I don't *matter?*"

"No, no! That's not what I—!"

But Sid was laughing.

"No wonder trolls love you," she said. "You're so trollable." She giggled, backlit by her house, which was lit up like a luxury ocean liner.

"Your house is . . . blinding. . . ."

"I know," sighed Sid. "Dad made one hell of a carbon footprint just so I can find my way across the lawn."

"He in there with a shotgun?"

Sidney laughed. "How very . . . *Scots-Irish* of you to think so! No. Asian dads don't use shotguns. They kill with sheer, focused disapproval. Also: he's not in there at all. The lights are on a timer. They're both in Singapore."

She looked at me. Raised an eyebrow. I didn't get it. At first.

"*Both* in Singapore?"

"Yeah. They're in imports, remember?"

The word *imports* sounded very exciting all of a sudden, coming out of Sidney Lim.

"Right. Right! *Imports.*" I took a deep breath. I really needed one. "*Both* of them?"

"Both."

"In Singapore."

"Yes."

"And the house is . . ."

"Empty. Little brother's at a sleepover. They're watching *Toy Story. Three.*"

"That's a good one. Dark."

Sidney tilted her head: a question.

Well. More of a suggestion.

Truth is, I couldn't quite believe what was being suggested. What was being suggested was . . . suggestive.

"Singapore," I said again, with my stupid boy mouth.

"Uh-huh. Singapore."

Sid's shirt was off by the time we were halfway up the stairs. There were a lot of stairs.

Stairs take a while when you're making out on every step, losing articles of clothing along the way.

Sid had my shirt unbuttoned down to my navel, and her warm, small hand was inside, a finger tracing the place where my stomach and pelvis came together, that area on Superman nobody knew exactly how to draw or costume. That area, on my old body, was just an area: wouldn't even bother dignifying it with a temporary tattoo. On my new body, though, it looked like a suspension bridge, a ropy Y of strung muscle that was apparently prized by fans of the male physique.

"I guess we could've done this in the Yacht a long time ago," said Sid, in a voice so chill I had trouble matching it with the person in front of me: a shirtless teenage girl, in some kind of lacy bra that said *Summer Plunge* on the inner seam. I read those words over and over: *SUMMER PLUNGE*. "It's just . . . your car's kind of small, no offense."

"No, no, uh, none taken, it's . . . it's small! Crazy small! That car is sure . . . *not a sex museum*! Like, *at all*!"

Ladies and gentlemen, I present: more dumb things that come out of my mouth.

Sidney blinked. "Sex museum?"

"Never mi—"

And she was kissing me again. We were so close to the top of the stairs. I wasn't sure we were going to make it.

Well: I wasn't sure *I* was going to make it.

Sid came up for air. She had something in her hand.

Oh, Jesus.

The old suspension bridge sagged a bit.

What she had in her hand was the One Ring.

"What's this?"

"Well, that," I said, "is the One Ring."

In all previous makeouts, you see, I'd slipped off the One Ring. It had never felt right to have it on, to have it banging against Sidney while we were pawing at each other in a cozy Italian bucket seat.

But I'd worn it that night. Because it'd been Monica's eighteenth. Seemed like a million years ago. Everything before this staircase felt ancient, Paleozoic.

"From . . . *Lord of the Rings?*"

Sidney looked like she had more questions. Then . . . she didn't. She just pushed the One Ring to one side and kissed me again while grabbing a handful of pectoral. Sex is a deep magick, I realized. Sex shows mere talismans for what they are: Toys. Trinkets.

Out of nowhere, Sidney stopped. "Am I going too fast?" She stroked my chest. "It wants what it wants, right?"

I gulped. I think the gulp was even audible, like in old cartoons.

"Um. *What* . . . wants . . . ?"

"The heart. You've really never heard that? Wants what it . . . Wait, what'd you think I meant?" Then she realized what I'd thought she meant. And laughed. "Oh. Well. *That,* too, I guess. Wants. Stuff. I guess. So: what's yours want? *Heart,* that is. The other's not such a huge mystery. Oh, God! Did I actually say that?!"

She'd cracked herself up again.

And while she was laughing at her own dirtyish joke, buying me time, I grabbed for the ring, on instinct, as if it'd answer something.

But it wasn't where it usually was. It'd been pushed to the side.

What an excellent, excellent question she'd asked—

What did my heart want? A question I hadn't asked my heart in months, because maybe I was afraid of the answer. There were a lot of questions I hadn't been asking, I suddenly realized, because I was afraid of the answers.

But the questions also seemed less urgent these days. Events were overtaking them, like they said on the news. Life was overtaking all my questions. Life, for the first time, had even overtaken my heart, had left it behind.

I thought suddenly and painfully of Monica. Off getting pierced, probably. The thought of which slapped me back big-time into the present, set me right back on those stairs, where everything was happening.

"What does my heart want? Well: I'd say . . . this, what's happening here, on these stairs? Ranks up there pretty high. On the list of . . . heart-wanted . . . things."

Sid smiled. "You know one of the things I like about you?"

"This . . . part of my stomach? That you keep touching?"

"No," said Sid. "I mean, yes. That's why I keep touching it. But I also like . . . your friends. And how you are with them. And how they are with you. They're more like family. I mean, I guess one of them *is* family. But . . . well, you know what I mean. You have no idea how lucky you are, Will Daughtry. Can I ask you something?" Sidney was chewing her lip a little. "There's no right or wrong answer here."

"Uh, sure." I think it came out *zure*. My jaw was having a seizure, for some reason.

"You still got your V card?" She drew a V with her finger, on my chest. "The big V." The fulcrum of that big V was my belt buckle, which was apparently hooked up to an electrical transformer, because a thousand joules went through me when she did that. I was so shocked, I had nothing left but brutal honesty.

"Yes. That's correct. No sex. For me. Thus far. I'm so sorry if that's . . . lame?"

Sid was so patient. "No! Not lame at all."

And for some reason, words, honest words, just came Pezzing out of me: "In fact, before last summer . . . I was pretty ready . . . never to? 'Lose it'? I . . . guess?"

This is where Sid could've blown a sweet symphony of bullshit, all about how she knew lots of girls who'd thought I was cute and nice "before." At which point, I'd have to make the distinction for her, between *adorbs* and *doable*.

But she didn't say anything. She just kept tracing the V.

For the first time, I realized she had a square wet wipe packet in her left hand.

And then I realized it wasn't a wet wipe packet.

"That's okay," she said. "As long as *one* person knows what she's doing? We should be fine."

You know what? We were. Just fine. More than fine.

*   *   *

The only problem

and I mean the *only* problem

was that I was thinking of Monica.

Right up to the moment I wasn't.

So yeah, maybe it all did feel just a little like a lie.

But only a little. A lot of it felt true.

Was this how *everything* felt? Past a certain point in life? Like you were always doing a certain amount of damage, just by being in the world and moving through it? Biology Brain flickered on briefly: is it a function of size, how much damage you do?

some people think of baseball

Like the great sauropods, who walked away from their nests

I guess I think of sauropods

so they wouldn't step on their eggs, on their young?

oh my God this is happening

The worst part was also the best part: I felt insanely great

and scared

and stupid

and the king of all possible worlds

and also a little like some awful moral mutant

and I thought—to the extent that I was "thinking," at that point—that maybe feeling all those things is what it feels like to be grown-up. What it means to have "arrived."

Because if I knew one thing beyond a doubt, it's that I'd absolutely

lutely

definitely

most certainly

arrived.

THIRTEEN

6'9"

OR NOT.

Yep. That's right.

I kept growing. Right past my Goldilocks height.

So much for six seven. Bye-bye, Goldilocks, hello, terra incognita.

San Locutus International Baccalaureate had Drew's number. They could double- or even triple-team him, and they'd risk whole possessions just to mess with his head. They were fiendish deployers of infuriating feather fouls that threw off his balance, rerouted his cuts. He couldn't get a rhythm.

What that boiled down to: Drew'd racked up *only* twenty-two points by the fourth quarter, and the Harps were up *only* by four.

"Not good," said Monica as the center from San Lo—the

freakin' *center*—somehow nailed a three, and their side of the gym went absolutely bananas.

"How goes the Irvine application?" I asked Monica.

"Don't you start," she said, and then, *"Hey! What the hell, ref?"*

The ref had just called a crap foul on Drew. Reaching in. Monica delivered a counternarrative the official didn't quite hear and wouldn't have appreciated.

"See, this is the problem with being a basketball widow," Monica muttered in my ear. "You start to care about this stuff, in spite of yoursel— OH, COME THE HELL ON, REF!"

Something in her voice sounded ... brittle. Un-Monica. "Basketball widow"? But I'd recently learned a lot about my big mouth and its consequences, so I stayed quiet.

San Lo had drawn a foul from Eric Forchette, his third, that dumb hothead. Their forward sank the free throw and tied things up.

Naturally, that's when Drew ignited the turbines. It happened in a series of steps. A "plan," if you will.

First he pretended to lose control of the ball, way upcourt. That sent two giddy, overconfident San Lo guards lurching in the wrong direction. Drew recovered the ball and bounced it hard to Embry as he ran downcourt. Embry pump-faked, then lofted it over the center lane, where it was met in midair by Drew, who escorted it—

GUH-DONG! Right in for the slam. The buzzer exploded just as Drew's feet reconnected with terra firma.

Somewhere in there, I was on my feet, and so was Monica, and we were screaming so hard, sincerely and with no subtext whatsoever, in praise of this thing of beauty Drew'd just pulled off that

Monica jumped into my arms and I was swinging her around and around—

That's when I noticed: we fit.

I had a great view of her earlobes.

Still unpierced.

Seeing that sent the worst, the wrongest thrill through me.

I could smell her.

My head was full of her, in a way my head had not been full of her since, I realized, BoB. Since last spring, my birthdaypocalypse. The night I'd been so painfully conscious of how *uneven* we were.

Yet here we were, her face in the crook of my neck. My arms holding her. She weighed nothing to me now, I realized. And yet the mass of her felt meaningful and right. This term from chemistry came swimming up out of my head. *Specific gravity.*

Monica's gravity felt so specific.

Specific to me.

I looked down at the court and saw Drew, mobbed by teammates, but staring up at us with a crooked smile. He was doing his pointing thing, his *For you guys!*

But I saw his victory smile wobble when he saw us.

It was like he'd just seen what I'd just felt:

The *fitting* thing.

I felt like I'd just gotten away with something, like I'd robbed the Mob or something. I didn't want to feel like I'd robbed the Mob. I had so many perfectly *licit* things to feel good about—like Sidney, like not being dead, like finally feeling strong—why would I want something illicit on my books?

Monica saw it, too, when I set her down. She gave Drew a plain wave. He waved back. And we didn't talk about any of it. How I could still feel the outline of Monica on my body a day later, for example—I had no plans to talk about that with anyone.

But not too long after, the whispers changed.

I was used to the looks in the hall. They'd started in the fall: *Is that the same guy? The little guy? No! Him? What happened?*

They evolved: *There goes That Guy. He's even bigger! Swear he was shorter yesterday. . . .*

And now: *You know what I heard about Big Guy? Drew's stepbro? Bigger than Drew is now? Hangs out with Drew's girl. Well: this is gonna come as, like, zero surprise . . .*

⟨jacksquatch⟩: hey! hey there! u heard?

WillD: . . .

⟨jacksquatch⟩: this is big

WillD: . . .

⟨jacksquatch⟩: this is . . . will daughtry big

WillD: . . .

⟨jacksquatch⟩: i hear . . . will daughtry . . . is a damn DOG yo

WillD: . . .

⟨jacksquatch⟩: EPIC dog

WillD: . . .

⟨jacksquatch⟩: didnt know he had it in him

WillD: . . .

⟨jacksquatch⟩: not only is he putting wood to sidney lim . . . him gots him a SIDE piece . . .

WillD: Hey asshole?

⟨jacksquatch⟩: and its his BROTHERS GIRL!

WillD: When they catch you

(jacksquatch): drew tannenger hoop hero gettin all CUCKED by his BIIIIIIIG bruvver PUT THAT ON NEWS 8 & SMOKE IT!

WillD: you're going to jail.

(jacksquatch): hahahahaha . . . u funny . . . anyway crazy rumor huh bruh?

WillD: Or we could just meet, the two of us.

(jacksquatch): why? r u flirting w me big boy? dont u have enough going on?

WillD: Blind date. Let's meet and I can beat the shit out of you and dump your dickless troll corpse in the ocean BRUH. Name a place.

(jacksquatch): look at us. we r finally having a real conversation. proud of us!

WillD: Name a place. I'm serious. Let's finish it.

(jacksquatch): all that blocking was hurtful big man

WillD: Name it goddamn coawrd

(jacksquatch): aw. u mad. dont b mad. thats how u make misteaks . . .

Suddenly I wasn't just a curiosity, I wasn't fascinating, I wasn't even a freak. It was worse:

I was a *character*. In a *drama*.

And I was a villain. An orc. And I had an arc. I was an orc with an arc.

And my orc arc was: Will's Gone Dark.

My story was about Power Gone Wrong. An unnatural gift—

"Great," I said. "So I wait. For what?"

"Menopause." She clapped me on the shoulder. "Relax." She smirked. "At least you're not 'Yoko.' That's what they're calling me. We've all got our trolls, right? Modern life. 'And a thousand thousand slimy things lived on; and so did I.'"

"Hell's that from?"

"Hamilton."

But for once, I wasn't in the mood for banter. I didn't have Monica's surfer chill, I guess. I wanted to throw her phone into the ocean. I wanted to throw the whole internet *attached* to her phone into the ocean, let the slimy things thrash and drown down there, caught in their own drift net.

Slimy things don't drown, though.

Slimy things, as a rule, float.

The Lims were in Singapore again, and Sid and I were in bed again.

We were getting better.

And I was getting bigger. Sid seemed okay with that. Truthfully? I felt a little like a piece of gym equipment.

That wasn't such a terrible feeling. I wasn't, after all, a *neglected* piece of gym equipment, with laundry draped on it. No, I was very much in use when the Lims were in Singapore, "importing" or whatever.

One afternoon, we were in Sid's bed, and she reached over me for her water on the nightstand—and what feels more grown-up than a girl reaching across you in bed for a glass of water?—and her fingers grazed it there, on the nightstand.

The ring.

abused! A family—torn apart! Good stuff. Compelling. Now everybody was waiting for the steroidal hobbit's inevitable comeuppance.

Where was all this coming from?

Well, from [jack], of course. And from video. Irrefutable GIFage. The evidence that keeps on evidencing, in four-second cycles.

There was this smidge of News 8 footage, a cut from Drew's buzzer beater to Monica and me, celebrating: I was hoisting Monica, all very innocent on the surface. But somebody ([jack]) had trimmed it to GIF length and given it to the winds of douchery that blow ceaselessly across this great internet of ours. Arrows had been inserted, thoughtfully, to interpret our body language. Where my hands were. How her legs wrapped around me for a second.

The trial was swift, the jury back with a *guilty* before the GIF even fully unspooled.

The assumption was that justice would come at the hands of Spesh, who got his own story line: the great warrior, the Harps' record-breaking small forward, betrayed . . . backstabbed . . . cuckolded . . . by his own brother! An epic, Bible-y tale! What a world!

And then there was Monica, the femme fatale, turning brother against brother. Classic character, never gets old.

Finally there was Sidney: the wronged girlfriend.

"I have the shittiest role" was Sid's only comment. "Worst lines. All the crying." She didn't believe the rumor, having been on the receiving end of many rumors over the years. Her advice was: *Just wait it out, do nothing, say nothing, don't feed it, let it pass.*

Monica's take was similar.

"Enjoy being Every Girl Ever," she told me. "Your changing body is the object of fascination. Then disgust. And finally: furious anger. Just gotta wait it out."

I was usually pretty good about getting it off discreetly, but I'd gotten sloppy, comfy. I'd plunked it in plain view.

Sid wove the leather thong around her fingers. "I've got an idea," she said. "Maybe I can wear it? Like, I'm your nerd bride?" She laughed. "You know I'm a total dork, right? I've even been to a Ren fest. I won Ethan a fried pickle at the dagger throw. Oh yeah, this damsel? Yaaas, queen! Bull's-eye. I've worn a goddamned *ear cuff*. Daughtry, c'mon! I'm bona fide."

She thought this was hilarious. I wasn't sure.

No "total dork" says or needs to say, *You know I'm a total dork, right?*

And Sidney Lim was nobody's nerd bride. This whole conversation felt, in my innermost gut, wrong.

I found myself with nothing to say, except: "Uh . . ."

Sid frowned. Untangled herself from the thong. "Or not," she said.

She handed the ring to me, got out of bed, and went to the bathroom.

None of this had anything to do with Monica, not really. Definitely not.

This was just irrefutable fact: Sidney Lim and the One Ring went together like chocolate and ball bearings. All relationships have limits, have boundaries. I'd read that somewhere.

I listened to her peeing for a solid minute.

I thought, *This is the most grown-up I've ever felt.*

⟨dayofdajackal⟩: r we having fun yet

WillD: we will be soon

⟨dayofdajackal⟩: oooh

"Maybe we just start beating the shit out of people?"

"Yeah?" said Drew, contemplating his subpar turkey sub, then setting it down on its wax-paper wrapper. (Mine, of course, had been consumed in three bites.) "Which people?"

"Thinking we could start with Spencer Inskip."

"Huh."

"He's my top pick. For [jack]."

"Logical," said Drew. We were decompressing at the Lowlands. Drew was enjoying some rare downtime.

But *enjoying* might've been the wrong word. This whole topic annoyed him. And I knew it. And I kept on going with it. I just wanted to say some things I was ashamed to feel out loud, and I wanted to say them to another guy. To see if that other guy'd ever felt the same shameful way. Was that so wrong?

"I mean, there's Spencer's whole Sidney history," I rattled on. "Plus, I flipped him at football tryouts. Hey, think we could take him and a couple of his meat-cube pals?"

Drew was staring at the apes. Like he was trying to pretend I wasn't there, and succeeding.

"I'm kidding. Of course."

"I know," said Drew. "But . . . you're still talking to this [jack] guy? This troll?"

"*Talking* is dignifying it a little—"

"You know what I mean: you . . . respond?"

"I block him like crazy, he respawns, comes back. But some-times, yeah, I try to draw him out a little—"

"Will."

"Just, y'know, keep him talking, so he'll make a mistake."

"You're making the mistake. This isn't a movie, and it's not your job to 'draw him out.' You know what your job is? Don't feed the troll."

"I know, but . . ."

"Let's stick to the Plan, huh, buddy?" said Drew, tossing his lunch wrappers. "Beating up sad little men, or even big ones—that's not the Plan."

Son.

Then he just floated off, back to practice.

He left something behind, though. A scent. Detectable.

Not the plan, Will.

Irritation?

Anger?

Hell, I was irritated, too. I was angry.

And, as long as we're being honest, not just at [jack].

At Drew. Drew and his practice, Drew and his Plan. Drew and his Dad Voice.

At Monica. For dropping all these hints about friction with Drew, friction with Martin, friction with the world—but never wanting to talk about any of it. For keeping me at arm's length while making it harder and harder for me to stay at arm's length and still be her friend.

At Rafty. For filming everything. *Everything.* Like I was this caged freak he was trucking from town to town.

Even at Sidney. For being so goddamned *understanding.* For not being (at least not obviously) jealous of the other girl I spent a shit ton of my time with. For not asking more of me. For being 1,000 percent out of my league and still so . . . *indulgent*. Did that mean she didn't really care? Did it mean she cared *too* much?

At Brian and Laura. For being concerned. For pretending *not* to be concerned.

Brian, in particular, had become deeply annoying. He'd gotten (how can I put this?) *keepery* around me. I was starting to feel a little overkept.

"Last week, I was in the commissary, talking to Duning about his saltwater crocs," he said "casually" one day, over turkey subs at Keeper Access, "and it hit me how wrong observational data can be."

Most people wouldn't hear parental meddling in a statement that nerdy and dense. But I did. I knew where Brian was going with this. I squirmed.

"I mean, for years, people just assumed indeterminate growth in crocodilians, and most other large reptiles, and it's not until 2011 that you get—"

"Thanks, Dad, but I'm kinda . . . all biologied out for the day."

Fact is, now that I was busier, now that Sidney and volleyball and doctor appointments took up so much of my life, Brian and I saw each other less. When we did cross paths, it was usually at the zoo.

The zoo used to be where I went to observe other animals, to try to feel better about myself. Now it's where I went to *be* observed by primate keeper Brian Daughtry.

Being classified, taxonomized, observed by your own father— well, it's probably unavoidable, even under the best of circumstances. Which these weren't. Worse, Brian was starved for data.

That was my fault. I wouldn't let him take me to HUGE for my sessions with Dr. Helman. He was never thrilled about that. Lately he'd been saying so.

"I think I really ought to be at those appointments, Will, don't you?"

I remained pretty convinced that Brian in that waiting room would make me unbelievably nervous.

"I'm fine. Really. I like it this way."

I really, really didn't want to feel Brian Daughtry on-site, classifying and reclassifying my problems, or nonproblems, or future problems, or whatever. I always felt like he was fitting me for a habitat anyway. I couldn't be Brian Daughtry's kept behemoth.

Speaking of: *Guinness* had sent a letter of introduction and a packet of info on requirements for world record verification. I'd handed it all to Rafty. Honestly, that whole idea—of being a record in somebody else's collection, somebody else's *taxonomy*—made me feel queasy. Like I was already in a jar, on display. Pickled. Mummified. One more weird, dead thing awaiting a theory.

FOURTEEN

6'10"

ONE DAY, AFTER a typically inconclusive appointment at HUGE, Monica smelled my fear. So she did what she generally did: took me to BoB.

For the usual hydrotherapy, I assumed.

I assumed wrong. I was off by 150 feet or so.

"Okay, ready?"

Acrotherapy. We were standing on the cliffs. Instead of descending to the cove, we'd climbed up, and now we stared down the barrel of a killer drop, with waves gnawing rock at the bottom. No, I was not "ready."

"That depends. Does pissing myself mean I'm ready?"

"Hold out just a little longer," said Monica, eyeballing the chasm. "We'll be at the top soon. Then you can piss off the edge of the world."

And before I knew it, I was spread-eagled between two giant

boulders at the far end of BoB's southern jetty, my sneakers providing just enough friction to keep me there. I couldn't have done this even two weeks ago; I wouldn't have had the span. Monica knew that, of course. *That's why she brought me,* I thought. *Another lesson in fear, and how to shank it.*

"Make me a stirrup," said Monica. "You're my way over."

So I made a stirrup with my hands, and Monica put her foot in it to spring across and grab a high handhold at the top of the rock.

She then turned, braced herself, and offered me her hand. I shook my head.

"What if I don't make it? I'd take you with me." The wind screamed, underlining my point.

Monica smiled, shook her head. "I don't see it going down that way."

"Nice," I muttered, adjusting my footholds, "choice of . . . words . . ."

"Will?"

I looked up. "Yes?"

And there she was. The ocean behind her. The sun starting its long slide. Green eyes, copper on fire. "Take my hand."

I did. Monica had a steadier grip on the rock than I'd thought. When my back foot left its safe perch, I had a moment of panic—

—I'm falling, she's falling, we're falling, and it's my fault—

—followed by the absolute thrill of being still alive, and higher on this goddamned rock than I'd ever climbed.

The view was cloudless and 100 percent bug-nuts, eye-crossingly insane: angles that didn't seem processable in three-dimensional human vision, an endless sky forced into this fish-eye parabola, and down below, far, far below, the hungry Sawtooth, noshing on sandstone. It was another planet up here, another dimension. A cormorant sailed past at eye level. I thought of a picture I'd seen in a history book of a workman with a hammer, strapped to a church steeple above some black-and-white city that'd been bombed down to the subcellars, everything flattened except this one stubborn spire, sticking up above the rubble like a flag or a middle finger or both.

As the sun dripped yolk slowly off the edge of that long parabola, Monica said, "Not bad, huh?"

"Not . . . bad," I answered. Then I noticed: Monica wasn't looking at the sky, wasn't looking west. Wasn't looking east, either, back at bad old civilization.

No, Monica was looking down. Straight down.

At the Sawtooth. Eating the cliffs. It did not chew with its mouth closed, the Sawtooth.

"You don't ever feel sorry for the rocks?"

Monica wrinkled her nose. Didn't appreciate my weak-sauce joke. "Dude, that wave? Made BoB. And BoB made us. That wave is a goddamn *miracle*. Fuck the rocks."

I laughed. But she was serious. Something pulled taut in her voice.

"From the beach, it's just a big wave. Fine. But up here—look, follow my finger," and she pointed at the chaos. "See, it's really *three* waves coming together. Look, there's the main one, coming straight off the ocean. But with a southern swell, you get that reflection off this jetty, *and* you get rebound from the reef. And every few minutes . . ."

She watched the chaos that was, to her, all pattern, beautiful pattern. "No," she said. "No." She let a few more pass.

"There." She grabbed my arm, a rough whisper, as if she didn't want to scare some wild animal. "That's it."

And I saw it. I saw the barrel form. The perfect pocket. Monica's mystic fold.

Jesus. It *was* beautiful.

The shape that haunts the wet dreams of surfers the world over: I'd seen tubes before, live and on video, but never anything like this.

That day, I saw it the way Monica saw it: as a kind of holy thing, this perfect architecture of converging violences, so beautiful it was indistinguishable from a miracle.

For a moment.

And then . . .

. . . that gorgeous blue cathedral just tore itself apart on the reef between the jetties and was gone, as if it had never existed.

Trying to mirror Monica's mood, I said solemnly, "Death of a perfect wave."

Monica was peering at me now, mouth screwed over to one side. Like I'd missed the point.

"*Near* death," she corrected. And pointed. "See? The tube takes you around the rocks. If you trust it. If you find the fold."

I squinted. She was right. But she was *barely* right. It was a narrow margin, and I said so.

"'Nor so wide as a church door,'" Monica mumbled, "'but 'tis enough, 'twill serve.'"

"Huh?"

"Hamilton." She was screwing with me, but I decided it wasn't

the right moment to screw back. She was sighing one of her end-of-the-world sighs. "Nature made something *exceptional*. Is the point. Maybe we should just be grateful."

Was this her way of cheering me up? I wasn't sure I wanted to be cheered up. I wasn't sure I wanted to be compared to a monster wave.

I assumed that's what she'd meant. I assumed that's why we were up there: To buck me up. To assure me *I* was the exceptional thing.

I think it was either Charles Darwin or Shakespeare who said, "Boys: they're not so smart, y'know?"

Something about that little day trip stuck with me, a pebble in my brain shoe, grit in the oyster of my gray matter. Something about it, about Monica, bothered me. Couldn't quite form that niggling bother into a pearl, though.

Maybe I just didn't have the bandwidth. There was so much Me to deal with. I had bigger fish to fry and/or hormonally brake. A week later, I was back at HUGE. Action was being taken.

"So what we're doing here," Dr. Helman said as she gave me the injection, "is tapping the brakes. Just tapping. A little hormonal nudge-nudge."

"And if . . . my body doesn't take the hint?"

Dr. Helman smiled her cartoon-pig smile. "Then we'll try something else."

By then, I didn't want to "tap the brakes."

I wanted to *stop*.

On the other hand: I still felt incredible. I felt like I could handle anything, anyone.

It was a perfect time for a fresh interview with our local network affiliate.

News 8 was now checking in with Drew *and* me after every game: half sports segment, half "human interest" (i.e., freak show).

I don't think Drew loved that.

"The two towers . . . the basketball star and his brother, a growing wonder of the world . . ."

He didn't like the freak show for me. He didn't like it for him, either.

Was I in Drew's spotlight? Maybe a little. Did I like it there? I wasn't ready to say. Certainly not to myself. Obviously not to Drew. Definitely not to the cameras.

To the cameras, I said: "The best part about being up here is it gives me better views of Drew's games."

And I'd pass him the mic.

"Dude," said Rafty. "Let's take it to twelve."

"Dude," I said, lounging on the grass next to the Royalls' driveway. "Let's not."

Rafty was perched on the trampoline, fiddling with his phone.

"Aw, c'mon, you could dunk on a twelve-footer now."

"Let's just play. At regulation."

"No, man," said Rafty, "it's no fun playing against you now. I mean, no offense, it's just, y'know, no contest."

Looking straight up, I watched a cloud divide, then divide again.

No contest. The words made me suddenly, viciously depressed.

"Fine," I said. "Take it to twelve."

Rafty eagerly went to work. Then he rolled the trampoline over.

"What's that for?"

"Let's make it bonkers," said Rafty.

So we made it bonkers. I'd run. I'd leap. I'd ricochet off the trampoline and hurl my whole ridiculous fuselage through the air to the rim, taking care to release at the last possible moment—otherwise, I was afraid I'd tear the hoop right off.

And then I saw Rafty, filming me.

"Raf, dude, what the hell? Can we not?"

"This is great shit, man. Great shit. C'mon, don't be a nozzle, we're moving into the, like, X-Man stage of your fame, and people want to see *powers*."

Powers, huh?

Great shit?

"Hey, Raf," I said. "Here's some great shit."

I took a flying leap. Bounced off the tramp, heard a *RIP!* Made it airborne and came down, ball palmed. *GUH-DONG!*

And then:

CRASH!

I'd shattered the glass of Rafty's stupid basketball camp backboard into roughly nine billion pieces.

When I came to earth, Rafty was still filming. But he wasn't looking at his phone. He was looking at me. He didn't speak for a while.

I'd scared him.

I was glad.

"I'll be honest, dude," he said, and his lip was quivering. "I'm not sure what that's gonna do for your image."

"Yeah," I said. "Me neither."

And I walked off. Like the badass I thought I was.

A block later, I realized my car was still at Rafty's.

I walked back. Then I waited in the woods a half hour for Raf to go in. Feeling increasingly creepy, like some kind of fairy-tale monster lurking. It seemed like Rafty'd never leave. He just sat there on the trampoline, looking at his broken goal.

Q: Who takes Lennie to the river?

A: Geo—

THUMP!

Did you know . . . even when you're almost six feet, ten inches tall, you *still* jump out of your skin when a large, hairy, fleshy mass connects with the window not five inches from your face while you're trying to finish your English homework?

Magic Mike was plastered on the observation window. Looking stunned. He hadn't been moving under his own steam. He'd been *thrown*.

Jollof.

I guessed the Blue-grooming had done it. Mike had been getting bolder. Big problem. Ape hierarchies don't change overnight—not without a catastrophe.

I picked up the Aggression Log and was starting to add yet another sad entry to our primate crime blotter when—

Bloodcurdling screech.

Different from the usual bloodcurdling screeches. A catastrophe in the making.

I looked up, and there, next to the viewing window, Jollof had Magic Mike pinned down in the dirt, and he was—

Holy shit, he was *biting his neck*. Going for what looked like the jugular. I'd seen him *display* his teeth before, but this—

Yes, there's a protocol for situations like this. But that protocol's not really intended for interns. Even six-tenners. Especially not ones who'd been expressly prohibited from entering the habitat. Unfortunately, at that terrible moment, an intern was the only person in Keeper Access. I hit the alarm, but I knew precisely how long it'd take for the cavalry to arrive.

I knew it'd take precisely one beta male ape life.

I was through the air lock before I even knew what I was doing.

Jollof looked up from what *he* was doing—which was murdering Magic Mike—

—and saw Will Daughtry, all 210 pounds of him, coming out of the air lock, waving the flag of the California Republic. (Which was the first large item grabbable as I plummeted into the air lock.)

Jollof had never seen a flag. Had no idea what it was, and could only conclude that it was Large and Unpredictable and Not Good for Jollof. With a snarl that must've translated to some truly fragrant gorilla profanity, he retreated, and Magic Mike rolled away and hid in the bushes.

I'm not sure any of this counted as deconfliction. Or was legal.

Quickly, very quickly, I ducked back into the air lock, sealed everything.

By the time the cavalry came, the situation was defused, and we were all clear.

After it was over, after everyone cleared out and Brian debriefed me, I sat on the floor a good long time, just breathing, filling my huge lungs and emptying them. Filling, emptying. Listening to the air I was displacing just by being here.

Then I thought of Monica.

How, if I'd been mortally wounded fighting a gorilla, she'd be my first last call, hands down.

What did that mean? That *Sid* wasn't my first last call? My first instinct?

I'll be honest: all that crazy, furtive, dangerous-feeling teenage sex may have blurred things a bit. My blood felt like lit kerosene in my veins, fiery little trails, a map to further adventures, absolutely terrifying, completely amazing. So improbable, given where I'd been, given *what* I'd been.

Maybe it all even *meant* something.

I was too afraid to ask. Maybe I wasn't the only one.

Maybe that's why we didn't say *love*, Sid and I. After. Or before. Or ever.

Maybe it wasn't because Sid was "cool." Maybe it was because Sid was scared. And so was I.

I realized I wasn't breathing.

When I got my breath back, all of it, all forty gallons or whatever it was I held now, I went the hell home, in a car that felt way too small for me, with a full choir of crazy things gibbering in my head.

That was probably the beginning of it, my devolution, my long slide down the ol' descent-of-man chart. All because I acted on instinct, to save a life, to aid the weak. All because I felt strong enough. Big enough.

I wasn't.

Look, I was just minding my business.

Just walking through a high school gymnasium to fetch my

girlfriend from volleyball practice. Me, a mild-mannered six-ten intramural volleyball semi-celebrity with a talent for AP biology, just going about my day. Trying to tune out the *smack-smack-smack* of basketball on polyurethane, trying to let Drew and his Harps stay in their zone, practicing for the Sweet Sixteen against Kearny Science & Math. When I heard . . .

"Daughtry! C'mere!"

Coach Guthridge's voice. Never heard it directed at *me* before.

I hope I didn't jog over too eagerly, like a benchwarmer, or a Weimaraner.

But I think I might've.

Coach Gut was standing with Drew, who wore an expression that suggested he was fighting off a fatal liver fluke. Coach Gut, I saw instantly, was screwing with Drew.

Coach Gut liked mind games. Drew knew this, but he was still susceptible. Coach must've thought he was irritating his star player into releasing energies said star player never even knew he had. He was that kind of coach. The kind who enjoyed the result of all that goading, but also the process; the kind of guy who loved his work, especially when it was a little evil. He'd have made a great troll, Coach Gut, if he'd been born a little later.

"Daughtry," said Coach Gut, "let's borrow you. Spare a minute for your school?"

I answered, too puppyishly, too avidly by half: "Sure, whatcha need?"

Yeah. *That* tone. *Put me in, Coach!*

Drew rolled his eyes. And was justified in doing so.

I don't know what I was expecting Coach Gut to say. *Fetch the Gatorade vat, big man?* But no:

"Kearny Science has a center 'bout your height, Daughtry," said Coach Gut. "You wanna stand in, let us get a feel for it? We're a running team, we don't have a tower."

Drew's eyes pleaded with me: *Please have somewhere else to be.* But Drew's mouth said, "Yeah, Will, it'd be a big help. Just two or three possessions."

"Uh, yeah, sure. Lemme just change."

I played it cool.

I wasn't cool.

I was thrilled.

I donned my intramural volleyball sweats to play varsity basketball.

I like the pick-and-roll, I like the give-and-go. So shoot me.

And the whistle screamed.

For the first two possessions, I took my stand-in role very literally: I just stood. Played minimal D. I received incoming passes and dutifully chucked them toward the hoop, but made no special effort to deliver the mail. I played in mannequin mode, which is what I thought Coach wanted and Drew preferred.

I was half-right.

"Goddamn, Daughtry, what's wrong with you?" Coach moaned. "Little bit of hustle wouldn't kill you, would it?"

I flushed. Something ignited in my gut. Then spread to my hands.

Well then. Okay, Coach. One little bit of hustle, coming up.

I could feel the adrenaline, could almost hear the high whine of my cellular centrifuges spinning up as the rocket fuel hit my bloodstream. Boy, oh boy, it did *not* take much poking to unlock beast mode. What the hell had I been damming up?

Drew and I were about to find out.

Next time the ball came in, I really posted up, really pivoted. Really faked.

Launched. And stuffed it.

I'd had months of practice, after all, on Rafty's now-humbled hoop.

By this time, Sid had shown up. I remembered: she was going to grab a ride with Ethan that day; they were supposed to see a movie or something. Now Drew and I were our own movie, and that movie was *Godzilla vs. Mothra*. Sidney sat in the bleachers in her sweats, grinning through the postpractice-sugar-crash granola bar she was eating. "C'maw, Harpsh!" she hooted, mouth full. "C'maw, Will Dawtshee!"

Maybe that's why I did the next thing I did, which I really shouldn't have done.

Or maybe it's because I caught a *look* on Drew's face I didn't like much. This weird curl to his lip. This expression that said, *Stop being a clown, son.*

That said, *Slow down, son.*

It came home to roost in that moment, this pigeon of revelation:

That *every* look from Drew these days was *Slow down, son. Stop being a clown, son.*

P.S. You look ridiculous! SON!

And so, on defense, with Drew on a drive, I waited till he was airborne—

—and then hooked the ball, right out of his paw.

And took off. Breakaway.

Unlike the typical big man, I was quick, see. Thank you, proportional growth. Thank you, weight training, proprioception, *biology*.

Drew was still quicker, of course, and he had better stamina. But he also had a lot of ground to make up on that play, since he'd started this possession going in what turned out to be the wrong direction. He arrived under the basket just in time for me to stuff the ball more or less down his throat.

I even hung on the goal for a second, let the hoop groooooooan with the weight of me. Then returned to earth. *BLAM!*

Voltron is formed, motherfuckers.

"Wooooot!" Sidney applauded.

Drew tucked his tongue under his top lip, the way he did when he was absolutely stubbed-toe, jammed-finger, dick-in-zipper furious. Then he launched a midrange jumper on the next possession—

—and I batted it down, Kong-like.

I could see his anger flip into a whole new gear.

"Hoo doggy!" barked Coach Gut. "If it's gonna be like that, let's go one on one!" His cracked leather saddle of a face split into six different grins. He was enjoying himself, that old turkey buzzard. And, I'm sorry to say, so was I.

So Drew and I played to fifteen. I released some lovely field goals, but did most of the work in the paint, posting and pushing.

Against me, his jumper was garbage. Not because I was great at blocking it (though I did block a couple), but because I was in his head now, and he took wilder shots. Tied at fourteen, he muscled in hard, and I instinctively planted my feet to draw the charge. Drew hit me full force, missed his layup, and I flopped dramatically, Duke-like. (By the way, when a six-tenner goes down like that—it's never *not* dramatic.)

Fweeeet! Whistle.

Coach was on the court. "That was some ugly ball." It was

unclear whom he was addressing. He saw me draw the charge, right? He saw my feet were planted? Coach looked from one of us to the other. Like he was deciding who'd inherit. He was enjoying this.

Maybe not a great human being, Coach Gut.

But look who's talking: the guy who just made shaming his brother into performance art.

"No basket." Gut pointed at me. My ball.

Drew turned away. I couldn't see his face. I didn't need to.

Fweeeet!

I faked. Drew lurched.

I saw it: I could win.

And I went the other way.

Put up a skyhook. My dumbest, least reliable shot.

GUH-DONG! Brick-a-lickin' . . .

Drew rebounded, and I couldn't flank him.

Well. Put it this way: I *didn't* flank him.

Anyway, he stuffed it. And then . . . he pointed at me.

Hoots. Boos. The peanut gallery had been on my side.

Drew turned his back on the peanut gallery and walked off the court.

Later, in the shower, I thought a lot about what had just happened.

The way he'd *pointed* at me.

Once upon a time, when I'd been safely in the stands, tiny and bendable and beta, pointing at me had meant, *That was for you, blood brother.*

That day, on the court, it meant, *That was* at *you, blood brother. Right at your head.*

Dominance display.

Drew believed the rumor.

Maybe not in his forebrain, with all his higher-function gear, but in his back brain, his subbrain, his lizard brain—and maybe even lower, in his heart, in his guts—he believed it.

FIFTEEN

⟨jacksonpolyp⟩: nice job skooling ur bro. go team. should put that nasty cuck rumor to rest

WillD: Anytime, buddy. Name a place, name a time.

⟨jacksonpolyp⟩: naw u seem 2 busy. family is important!

IT WAS DARK already, winter-dark, and I was coming out of the Lowlands, turkey sub under one arm, when she just sort of materialized, all in black.

"Hey."

"Holy shit, Mon!" My sub shot up like a Trident missile, disintegrated in midair. Debris rained.

Monica had her wet suit under one arm, the new, patchless one Drew'd gotten her after he'd returned the stupid earrings.

"Sorry about your sandwich. I'll buy you a new one." She was fidgety, jittery. "I want to do something a little crazy," she said. "But only a little crazy."

"Where's Drew?"

Monica sighed a long sigh. "I was blown off. Night practice." She studied my face, which probably betrayed some fault lines. "What. Did something happen?"

One-on-one. Drew pointing at my head, with murderous intent. Sure. Lots had happened.

"Uh. No?"

"Anyway," said Monica. "You're plan B."

There are men who'd have been insulted being plan B, even if the people who plan B'd them didn't mean it as an insult.

I was not one of those men. Was I a man at all? TBD.

She wanted to go to Black's Beach, surfer central, a popular destination. McDonald's, Monica called it. Nice, steady corduroy waves, very predictable. Big, though. Very big, heavy, hollow waves. Ten-footers that night, according to the report. And, of course, it was night. But Monica—I think with her earring money—had acquired waterproof LEDs. And a plan.

The sand was white under the moon. The sky was clear. We each got into our wet suits, on our separate sides of the car, the old Orthodox wedding. We hadn't had to use that trick in years. Usually when we surfed, we were at BoB, where one person could duck into the cave for a quick change.

I had my suit pulled on to the waist when I thought I heard the knock on the roof that meant Monica was ready to roll, chop-chop, get the lead out, time and tide wait for nobody, etc., etc.

Instead, I walked around the car and found Monica half-naked.

Her back was turned as she tugged the squeak-tight neoprene over her hips.

Did I look?

I looked. Okay: yes. It happened so fast. Boy eyes—they're like cockroaches, fast little shits, skittering everywhere and hard to grab back once let loose. So yes, before I could unlook, I looked. But what I was looking at was . . .

Jesus. What *was* I looking at?

A claw mark.

Three deep scars, thick and ropy, white with time and imperfect healing. Slashed in parallel on Monica's back. The scars began near her left shoulder blade and arced over her spine, reached all the way to her starboard rib cage.

From an animal?

From a human animal?

She felt my eyes on her then. Turned.

"Can I help you?"

"Your . . . back," I said. "Monica, what . . ."

"Old news," she said, shrugging the suit over her left shoulder, zipping herself. It took some doing, some stretching. "Seriously, it's nothing."

"Doesn't look like nothing." I tried to make this sound lighthearted.

She wasn't buying it. She came closer, an ember of warning in her eyes. "William? If it's on my body, and I say it's nothing? It's nothing."

She grabbed her board and started toward the beach. I just stood there with my weather vane spinning. Then she added over her shoulder, "Dude, zip up. You're not decent. And we only have all night."

We hit the goat path down to the water. Out past the silver strand, the ocean was muttering, grinding its molars.

Why didn't Drew tell me? He had to have seen those scars.

I hated thinking about how he'd seen them, in what context, but the scientist in me had to admit: he'd seen them. And he'd said nothing.

Because that would've made it weird?

I wondered what the New Plan had to say about night-surfing Black's? Just the two of us? Dressing in a parking lot? And no Drew in sight for miles?

"Why are we doing this?" I called over the breakers, which were getting louder.

"It's a thing," she assured me. "People do it. I've got a light."

"But . . . why?"

"There's no shore breeze at night."

Like this was a perfectly sufficient answer.

She started heading down. I followed.

"It sounds kinda rough for winter."

"It is," said Monica. "Crazy out of season. Climate change: the surfer's friend!"

They were coming into focus: waves at high tide, under the moon.

"Chaos, right? But no: it's a particular kind of chaos. The kind I need to practice on."

I stopped. Planted my feet. "I can't surf that."

"Oh, I know." She kept heading into the water, pancaked onto her board, began paddling.

"So what did you need me for?" I yelled.

"Witnesses!" she screamed over the breakers. "Gotta have witnesses!"

She cut the cleanest lines out there, on the far spit, bright blue whorls in a red tide. The big breakers weren't all that distant cyclone had washed up on our shores: bioluminescent dinoflagellates were cookin' tonight, and every little disturbance in the water spawned Dopplers of unearthly light, like an oil fire. She almost didn't need the LEDs she'd studded her board with.

Watching Monica surf always made me feel like life wasn't just a mindless killing machine I'd been studying from a safe distance since I was eight.

Which isn't the same as saying it made me feel safe.

Watching her do things I couldn't do and didn't quite understand made me want to fit into the universe the way she did when she surfed. Monica had a niche. It was a moving niche, and hard to pin down. But it was there. To watch her surf was to see how a person, however tiny, could fit into those great, grinding gears, if only for a few perfect moments. It made me want to find my own fold. And a few good friends to share it with.

Monica wasn't so content. Not that night.

I saw her pick a victim. A big one.

She waited a beat.

Paddled five strokes fast. Crested, rose on the board.

And then down she went, and in.

Pitted. In the tube.

It was beautiful.

What I saw of it.

Watching her, I let my guard down in the dark, and a dinky little four-footer broke over me. I went crashing over backward, 225 pounds of chaos. It didn't hurt a bit.

Monica's next few rides were uglier.

At first I thought the waves were getting nastier. Then I realized that it wasn't the waves, it was the rider.

She'd delay and delay, then launch a deep takeoff way too late—even a dragger like me could see it—and go straight into the barrel, choosing too high a line . . . and getting sucked over the falls and pounded into a shallow sandbar.

The shit-eating wipeout that resulted looked so bad, I started paddling out.

But up she popped, gave me a game-show smile and the *All's well*. I stood down.

The next wave she shanked exactly the same way. And the one after that.

Finally I realized: *She's practicing wipeouts.*

She's making *chaos that isn't here.*

That's when I realized what she was practicing wipeouts for.

The parking lot was basically empty by the time we got back. The usual ghost car, somebody sleeping one off, maybe, and beyond that, a world empty of everything but us and the chew we'd just walked out of.

"You're gonna hit the Sawtooth. Aren't you?"

Monica stopped. Studied me. "You gonna stop me?"

I hadn't gotten that far in my thinking. So I went with: "If I have to." The words came from a place in my testicles so deep and strange, I couldn't even draw you a map. Not that you'd want a map of my testicles.

Monica ... smiled. Like she'd *seen* the map of my testicles, and had found it amusing. "And how do you plan to do that?"

"Seriously? Are you really going to make me call someone?"

"'Call someone'? Who are you going to call, Will?"

"I don't know. Someone you'll actually listen to? Drew? Your dad? A suicide hotline?"

"Oh, God. Are we really having *this* talk?"

"Monica, *promise me* you aren't going to do anything stupid."

"Sure. Easy. I promise."

"Promise me you aren't going to try the Sawtooth."

"William," she said, coming closer until she was just five inches away. So close I could smell the salt on her. "Here's what I'll promise you. I promise that if I do it, when I do it, it's because I know what I'm doing. It's because I've figured it out."

"Monica—"

"No, listen, I'm serious: I've spent years picturing it, and you want to know something about that picture?" She paused and looked away from me. "You're always in it. *You* are the person who's there when I do it, because *you* are *the only* person in my life who'll understand." She peered into me. "I'm right about that. Right?"

Then she went and sat in the car.

I stood there for a while. Listening to the ocean mutter.

No. Not muttering now. Laughing.

SIXTEEN

"CAN WE HIT those brakes a little harder?"

Dr. Helman's nose was in my lab results. I sat across from her, slumped in a chair that used to engulf me but now felt comically undersized, like we were in a clown act.

"It doesn't really work that way," Dr. Helman said absently as she read over my endocrines. On the chart, I clocked: *TACE inhibition. GHBP imbalance. Epiphyseal hypertrophy.* Jargon that sounded eerily familiar.

"It doesn't work *at all*, as far as I can tell," I said, in a hopefully not too obnoxious way. "I'm still going strong here."

Dr. Helman looked up. Fixed me with her sweet, infuriating cartoon-pig eyes. "Will, two things. One, this isn't a bar. You can't just order another shot of hormones."

"I was under the impression that's *exactly* what people can do these days."

"No. It isn't. Certainly not for *this*, which is . . . well, we still don't know. And two, you're a minor. Remember? We've bent the rules a little, let your friend pick you up from these appointments, because they've been so frequent. We know that's hard."

"It's not hard. I feel fine. You keep telling me everything's normal, except for, y'know, the obvious. So it's not *hard*—"

"Psychologically," said Dr. Helman.

"Isn't that a little outside your job description?"

"I'd like your father here," said Dr. Helman, "for your next appointment."

"See, now, *that's* hard," I said. "On *him*. This stuff stresses him out. And you know my dad's whole . . . *history* with this place—"

"I know," said Dr. Helman. "And that's *why* I'd like him here for these checkups. Especially if we're looking at getting more aggressive with hormone therapy. Will?" She leaned across her desk and was suddenly a very serious cartoon pig. "You've got to let me do my job—Are you all right?"

I wasn't. I was sweating. Breathing felt thick. The air was suddenly sticky, syrupy—how does anyone get this stuff into and out of their lungs?

I was hot. So hot.

I'm in the wrong body. Running hot. Melting down.

Mouse metabolism. Elephant body.

I was gonna burst into flame.

I remember Dr. Helman saying, *Lie down, just roll. There we go. Now. Feet up. Don't worry about the wall, scuff it up, it's fine.*

A few minutes later, I was on my back, my massive legs pointed straight up the wall. Dr. Helman and a nurse were standing over me.

"'S okay, I'm fine." I started to get up. Dr. Helman knelt, put a hand on my chest.

"Not yet. Stay still a little longer."

I laughed. "I'm gonna die, right?" I felt rivers of hot salt passing my temples. The ceiling was coming down, acoustic tile by acoustic tile. "I'm gonna die, let's just say it. I'm gonna die of the same thing that killed my mom."

"No," said Dr. Helman. But I saw a bulb flicker behind her eyes.

"Something about it, though, reminds you of her thing. Right?"

Dr. Helman took a deep breath. "You don't have cancer. This isn't . . . that. You have . . . you *had,* I think, an insensitivity to growth hormone before this . . . spurt."

"Can we . . . not call it that?"

"Before this *phenomenon.* Near as we can tell—and, Will, we're working with specialists from all over—near as anyone can tell, your body . . . *compensated* for your innate insensitivity to growth hormone. And then all of a sudden, those factors blocking the hormone? The binding proteins that stopped you from growing? Just fell away. For reasons we don't really understand. So you got both barrels from your pituitary gland. And . . . here we are."

"And you're saying this has *nothing* to do with my mom's cancer? They've got nothing in common? Nothing at all? Not the GHBP? That's growth hormone–binding protein, right? I see it on my labs, just like I saw it on hers. Not the TACE inhibition, either? C'mon, Doctor."

Dr. Helman sighed. "You pose an interesting question, Dr. Daughtry."

Don't mess with Biology Boy.

Dr. Helman spoke slowly, chose her words carefully. "Your mother's cancer," she said, "involved a very rare interplay of hormonal and enzymatic factors regulating cell growth generally, and musculoskeletal growth and regeneration, chondrogenesis, and ossification in particular. And yes, some of those same factors are in play here, too. But we're talking about the most basic mechanisms of growth, on a biomolecular level. So saying they're related is like saying basketball is related to rock-paper-scissors. The answer is *Sure!* and also *Not at all!* The fact is, it's still early days, and these therapies—it isn't like stomping the brakes on a sports car. It's *pumping* the brakes . . . on an *aircraft carrier.* You have to give it some room, Will."

I thought about that, the room I'd given "it," given myself. I thought about that all the way home in the car with Monica. I thought about how all games were feeling more and more like games of chance, not tests of strength or skill. Which made me feel all seasick and loopy again. I didn't want to feel that way. I wanted to feel more like I felt when I spiked over the net, or when I moved Jaylen Teixiera off his stance, or when I broke Rafty's backboard, even.

(Better scary than scared, right?)

So I just decided to feel that way. Just like that. And I felt better.

Maybe, I figured, *I can just hold that thought.*

I can't even remember what we were having for dinner, the night it happened. My memory has it down as Sad Bowl of Corn and Tragic Lump of Mashed Potatoes, though that seems unlikely, given where Laura was with carbs.

This much is crystal: the Daughtry-Tannengers were engaged in what I'd classify as the Bitter Family Dinner, a classic of the genre. Kids' eyes trained on their plates, parents' eyes cutting to each other, signaling furiously, concerned. Brows furrowed, frowny faces over food that looked like plastic props in a local commercial, perfectly fine food made depressing and doomed by the grumpy people eating it. Dinners like that make the basic act of eating seem disgusting: you hear the chewing because there's nothing to drown it out, and the business of placing organic matter in a mouth hole and dissolving it with enzymes in order to stay alive becomes hard to avoid, harder to dress up as anything other than what it is.

I still ate a lot. I mean: it was still *food*.

Anyway, the assembled mouth holes ate, and didn't do much talking. When they tried, results were sketchy.

"How was everybody's day?" Brian actually said, out loud and for real.

"Nothing," Drew returned. Then he pushed away, got up. "Going to bed, g'night."

"Uh. Good . . . night?" Laura said, watching him go.

Brian leaned over. "What's going on?"

"Y'know. Stress. Sweet Sixteen's coming up. . . ."

Brian peered at me with diagnostic eyes. "Did something . . . happen?"

"Huh?"

"Between you two?"

Hahahahahahaha . . . Oh, Brian! Where to begin? I thought of Drew's pointing finger: *Right at your head, brother.*

"No. Just, I dunno, a stressful time, I guess."

"That word again," said Brian. *"Stress."*

"Puts it on himself," I sniffed. "He doesn't really have anything to worry about. Sixteen's a dance, it's just Portola again, and the Eight'll be either Salazar or West Mira Mesa, and they're both weak sauce—"

"I'm not talking about Drew." Brian put down his fork. "I mean: I'm not *just* talking about Drew. I'm talking about everything that's been going on."

"Uh-oh. What are the chimps up to now? Are they running numbers?"

But Brian was really staring me down, giving me the ol' *Recess is over.* Now I saw: he was going to use this awkwardness to pile on *overdue* awkwardness. Parenting deferred is never parenting denied.

"Will. I'm going to your appointments from now on. It's not a request."

I put down my fork. Gently. I didn't want to look bratty. Even though I felt bratty. But nobody likes a bratty giant. Only the gentle kind, the low-talking, no-sudden-moves kind. "So . . . you called Dr. Helman?"

"She called me."

"What'd she tell you? That something's wrong? Because she keeps telling me everything's fine."

"She told me the same thing," said Brian. "Look, Will, I've been pretty relaxed about all this, because at first I . . . I didn't want to add to any . . . general hysteria—"

"Hey, don't side-eye me," Laura warned him, "when you say *general hysteria.*"

"I didn't! I wasn't!"

"We give you guys a lot of leash," Laura said to me, "we know that. But this is a pretty . . . *unique* time. . . ."

Brian put his hands together, as if saying grace. "If we're continuing these hormone treatments—"

"Oh, we're continuing them," I almost snapped. So much for brat suppression. "I mean, unless you want to put a vaulted ceiling on this place."

"Will? Hear me out. I should be there, and I want to be there."

"You already *know* everything, you know everything I know, which is nothing, and you know everything they know, which is also nothing, but with data to back it up."

"I want to *be* there. I want to be ..."

He trailed off.

Because he heard it then. The sound. The cry. The call of the wild. I heard it, too. So did Laura.

"*... Monica? ... Monica!*"

There are certain sounds that'll stop you in your tracks. One of those is that of a largish-sounding human male in your front yard, at night, calling your friend's name. A largish-sounding human male you did not invite.

"*... Monica!*"

I recognized the voice. It sounded like a death rattle in a crushed beer can.

Laura—who didn't know that voice the way I did—was at the door before I could stop her. "Laura, wait—"

But the door was open already, and there he was, in a mist of Beam: Martin Eddy, navy pilot, retired. Looking drunk and defeated and nonspecifically at war with his surroundings, and that wasn't strange. Looking that way on our front stoop, after dark? *Was* strange. Martin had on his old Miramar flight jacket and, for some reason, aviator shades. They were crooked, or maybe bent, like he'd put them on by falling face-first into an open box of aviator shades.

Martin Eddy (6′2″) was not a small man.

"Quick question: where'n the good goddamn is my daughter?"

"Martin," said Brian, stepping into the doorway, "you don't seem well, buddy, let's get you—"

Martin shook his head vigorously, like a horse with a brain parasite.

"You think I can't tail a *city bus*?" Martin called into the house. His voice was still calm, but there was something swollen under it. "I was a *fighter pilot*, honey."

"Martin," said Brian, in the voice he used to calm big cats, "I think there may be a misunderstanding. Monica isn't here."

"See, *that's* a misunderstanding. 'Cause I just saw her climb in your boy's window." He jerked his head at me. "Not this one, the other. Your little one."

"Go home, Dad."

Her voice was muffled by Drew's bedroom door, but audible.

Ah. So Monica *was* in Drew's room. This surprising yet also not surprising fact sent a sour thrill through my GI tract.

"Send my daughter out, would you, good buddy? She left before I could explain. . . ."

"Sleep it off!"

I heard the door to Drew's room open, and I knew this was about to get a lot worse.

I could see Brian knew it, too. Monica was eighteen. She could do what she pleased. Martin was drunk. He could do what *he* pleased.

So Brian Daughtry made a keeper move.

He walked through the open front door, turned to me briefly, and said—

"Lock the door, Will."

And because he'd said it to me in keeper voice, I did exactly what he told me. I shot the dead bolt.

I could hear them talking on the lawn.

Laura got out her phone. By then, Monica was standing in the dining room, hoodie and jeans pulled over pajamas. The clothes she'd fled her house in, clearly.

"Don't call 911," said Monica. "Please. He's . . . he just needs to sleep it off."

But Laura just shook her head and stepped over toward the kitchen, keeping the phone clapped to her ear. I heard her speaking in a low voice to someone on the other end.

Drew appeared behind her. "Where's Brian?"

"Outside. Talking to him."

"I'm going out there."

"No, you're *not*," Laura said, in a voice that actually sat Drew down at the kitchen serving bar.

We heard murmurs outside. Male voices transacting something, it wasn't clear what.

Then sirens. Distant, but nearing.

"I wish you hadn't done that," Monica said to Laura, through her hand.

Laura looked confused. "They told me someone had already called. Maybe the neighbors . . ."

Monica looked at Drew. Drew looked away.

"No," Monica said. "It wasn't the neighbors." Her voice was several degrees below zero. For the first time since one-on-one, I actually felt bad for Drew. He'd done the right thing. But he'd done it on the sly, because he was afraid of Monica. The 911 call she'd forgive him for, eventually. But the fear? I wasn't so sure.

"It's okay!" Brian called from outside. "We're okay."

There was another sound. Coughing. The vanquished-sounding kind, the kind you associated with a fine mist of blood and bad news from the doc. It was Martin.

Monica'd already turned and headed back down the hall. She picked a room that wasn't Drew's—the old computer room—went into it, and shut the door.

Drew put his head in his hands.

"Just give her a minute," Laura said to Drew.

She went to the door of the computer room. Knocked gently, announced herself, and entered.

I wasn't sure what the New Plan and its many vague rules said about this situation. What was I supposed to do? Which room did I belong in? I was standing in the foyer like some gigantic useless weather vane on a windless day. Which friend was I allowed to comfort?

Maybe no plan can withstand impact from a Martin Eddy, from an object of such size and sadness.

Drew sucked on his teeth. I sent up a flare: "Hey, man, I think—"

Drew went into the bathroom, and *SLAM!* went the door.

He was in there awhile.

Red and blue lights painted the foyer, made the wallpaper dance epileptically. San Diego's finest had arrived. The Crisis was ov—

THUMP!

The front door rattled in its frame. A hard impact. Body-hard. Had Martin—

"Dad?"

I was alone in the foyer, studying the hallway chandelier I was now basically at eye level with. My father was out there, protecting us from a scary drunk. But I was bigger than my father, bigger and stronger. And I was doing nothing.

So I flipped the dead bolt, jerked open the door, and saw . . . nothing.

Then: Brian. Safe. Over by the curb, leaning into the window of a police cruiser, saying, "He's a family friend. . . ."

And then, right next to me, in the portico, I saw Martin. At first I thought: *Has he been shot? Tased?*

No. He'd just fallen against the door, and was now trying to right himself against a portico column. He looked deflated under his lumpy flight jacket, bald spot lolling like a haywire satellite dish. A little kid wearing his dad's clothes—maybe that's how all grown men look when they can't stand up straight anymore and keep the illusion going. Martin's dopey aviators were sprawled on the bricks a few inches from his hand, like a crushed insect. Without them, his unguarded eyes were the pink of an albino lab rabbit.

"Hey. Big guy."

I wondered if I should help him up. Decided he seemed comfortable how he was.

"Before I grab a ride," said Martin Eddy, "with those fine gentlemen in uniform . . . I wanna have a talk with you. Who knows? We might not get a chance to conversate again." He fixed those pink eyes on me. "I want you to know something. About your friend. Story of my birthday."

"Uh. You lost me, Martin." I was in full humoring mode. I'd decided to treat him like a concussion victim. *Keep 'em talking!*

Martin didn't need prompting. He was on autopilot. "My

birthday ... few years back ... she took me to the beach. Beautiful day. Sweet gesture. Picnic, barbacoa from my favorite truck, cupcakes with my name on 'em—very nice celebration, all the trimmings. Well. Not quite *all* the trimmings, and that's why I brought ... just this *one* little sixer, that's it, slipped it in the cooler under the ice, big deal. But she sees it? And it's freakin' *Armageddon*. She's screaming mad, *You promised! You said you wouldn't! This is why Mom left!* Blah blah blah ..."

Martin was knocking a little rhythm against the doorjamb as he spoke.

"And she gets so mad ... she picks up her board ... and she runs into the water. Now ... this is Black's, and there's a warning that day, everybody out of the pond, 'cause the waves are, I dunno, thirty-five feet if they're an inch. And here she is, fourteen years old, hundred pounds soaking wet, and just to spite me, see, she grabs her board, *throws herself* on one of these pro-grade waves, like she's saddling a freakin' dinosaur. *WHAM!* Bastard stomps her into the sand, then gives her a wallop with her own board. Had three fins on it, and those things, they're carbon fiber, they're like knives. ..."

Martin made a claw with his shaky hand. Raked imaginary ribs. *Slashes. Like a bear had taken a swipe ...*

Fourteen? At Black's? In thirty-five-foot swells? Why hadn't I heard this story?

"We go to a clinic, they patch her up—one of those fins was a quarter inch from nicking a lung. 'Nother one coulda severed her spine if things had wiggled a little different. Terrible accident. 'Cept it wasn't, was it? An accident? She ran in there *on purpose*. She even *ate it* on purpose. *I watched her flip her board.* It wasn't the wave! She had that thing handled. My girl's a prodigy. But she kicked out on top, let that thing take her apart. Now . . . what would you call that?"

I'm not saying a drunken Martin Eddy was the most reliable source.

But something about this story rang a whole carillon of bells right down my damned spine.

"Boy, does that girl get mad when people let her down," he went on. "You notice that? When our Monica gets mad . . . well, she takes it out on the closest soul in striking distance. And that always turns out to be . . . the same . . . person. . . ."

Martin coughed, loudly. The sound of a car that wouldn't start but kept cranking.

Brian was walking toward us with an officer who didn't look much older than me and was a foot shorter. "Will, get back inside," he said.

Martin was still coughing. Some kind of attack.

The cop gave me a once-over—*Holy shit, is Lurch here gonna be a problem?*—then crouched beside Martin and said, "Mr. Eddy? We'll give you a ride home."

Now I saw: Martin wasn't coughing. He was crying. That's just what crying sounded like when it came out of the broken thing that was Martin Eddy, fighter pilot.

That's how Monica Bailarín became our housemate, for a brief and not very sitcommish time.

She wasn't into the idea, at first. But she'd never experienced the full-court press from Brian and Laura combined. Unlike Drew and me, they weren't so easily denied. I mean, she *could* have, if she wanted to. She was eighteen. But there are forces of nature stronger than legal/technical adulthood, forces stronger even than Monica Bailarín's tungsten stubbornness.

Martin Eddy was under house arrest, judge's orders. He could only come out for treatment and group therapy. A nursing service checked on him three times a week. He was in the system now. That's what happens when you call the police.

Monica couldn't live there anymore, of course.

At first she'd said, "I'll camp at BoB." Because she was still mad at Drew.

To which Laura answered, "No." And this was a different kind of no, a no that Monica—raised by Martin Eddy—had never encountered.

Three days later, we're all brushing our teeth in the same bathroom.

Brushing your teeth in proximity to someone is very different from being best friends with that same someone. Brushing your teeth in proximity to someone you once considered your one true love, but who's now confirmed to be just a best friend—that's just *strange*.

Her smell was everywhere. Every time I sat down on a couch or got an extra pillow from the linen closet, this plume of *Monica* would rise and wash over me. I started having flashbacks: I was back at BoB on Birthday Night, and we were pitching my lifts off the cliff, into the ocean. . . .

Here it was. The Plan, writ large, writ now: the three of us never had to say goodbye, good night, see you tomorrow.

Hooray?

Monica slept in the computer room. I assumed she snuck out after everyone had gone to bed, slipped into Drew's room—at least on the nights when they weren't fighting. *Were* they still fighting? I didn't actually know. Also, I didn't like thinking about scenarios that involved Monica slipping into Drew's room.

Every morning, I'd come downstairs, and she'd be in our breakfast nook, reading *Leviathan* and not eating the oatmeal she'd made. She'd do this until 7:42, then eat *all* her oatmeal in three feral bites and jump into the Yacht with us.

Every morning, I'd not-ask about the story Martin told. About Black's. And the bear swipe on Monica's back.

There was less and less talking in the Yacht. Was it because we all saw each other all the time now? Is it what they said about old married couples? The mystery's gone? On the contrary: everything felt like a mystery, everything and everybody. Two surly mysteries, and one massive, puzzling medical mystery.

"When are you gonna be done with *Leviathan?*" I asked, "You've been reading it, like, forever."

"I'm never gonna be done with it." She was looking out the window. "It's a *reference* book."

That's all she said, the rest of the morning.

And then, Tuesday night of the second week of this bad sitcom, I came down for my midnight snack (this was not a bad habit, it was a metabolic necessity) and found Monica at the kitchen table, eating yogurt in one of Drew's old basketball camp T-shirts.

I was wearing just boxers and a shirt with a cartoon vole on it.

The vole was wearing a helmet and carrying a popgun, over a banner that read *Vole Patrol*. I have no idea what it meant, or was meant to have meant. It was just the kind of shirt you sleep in.

"Chobani?" Monica asked.

"Nothankee." I got out a tub of heavy, gory Bolognese sauce instead. Went at it cold, with a serving spoon. I know: sexy, right?

Monica watched me eat. I expected a joke. No joke was forthcoming. She just watched me eat meat sauce. She meant nothing by it, but something about the way I was being studied, in my natural habitat, annoyed me enough to ask a question I'd been suppressing.

"What happened? With your dad?"

It wasn't a story Monica had volunteered. I didn't necessarily expect her to spill now.

But she did. A little. "I gave an ultimatum. He made a promise. Then he broke it. So I said I was leaving, and he started breaking things. Most of the stuff in my room, to start with. I said, *Fine, break everything.* And I left. And then he followed me." She spooned out a dollop of yogurt, let it drop back into her cup again. "Keeps forgetting I'm eighteen."

"Well. You can stay here. With us. For however long. Until, I dunno, Irvine."

Monica laughed, like that was *hilarious*.

"Right," she said. "The Plan."

Was the Plan hilarious now? Had it become a joke, without my knowledge or consent? Wasn't there something in the Plan about not changing the Plan without my input?

My inner monologue was coming to a boil. The outer one stayed glassy.

"You know you're always welcome here. You're basically famil—"

"Uh, don't. Say that." Monica got up, dropped her spoon into her yogurt cup with a *thunk*. She didn't meet my eyes as she spoke, which was highly un-Monica of her. "I mean, it's beautiful, I'm flattered, I . . . I don't deserve it. But that . . . particular combination of words . . . it's just not what I—"

"I get it," I said. "I get it." But I didn't, not entirely.

The reaction Monica'd just had—I recognized that reaction. It was the reaction of the friend-zoned. The head-patted. The sexually decommissioned. Except, obviously, for a billion reasons, it wasn't that. Obviously.

Obviously.

"You've got . . . enough blankets and stuff?" I always know the stupidest thing to say, and I always say it.

"Yeah," said Mon, "Laura keeps me in blankets, thanks."

We just stood there. The half-eaten Chobani between us. Staring up at us, lidless.

We were about eight inches apart.

I had this whole speech in my head: Calling her on the carpet about the Sawtooth. Telling her I knew where the scars came from. I was going to find out what it all meant: Had she wiped out? Or busted on purpose? To hurt herself? Or worse?

Was she going to do it again?

At the Sawtooth?

I was going to tell her I couldn't let her, and wouldn't let her, and if that sounded overtestosterous, well, shit, maybe it was.

Instead of all that, I was suddenly just kissing her.

It didn't even feel like a decision.

Good thing, too, because if it had been? It would've been a terrible decision. Warning lights were flashing all over my brain console. It didn't matter. More elemental forces were at work.

Like gravity. Monica's very specific gravity. Which I could feel now.

[WARNING: DREW]

And how about "trusting the water," the way she'd always told me to?

[WARNING: SIDNEY]

Plus, we fit. I could feel that, too. Our bodies met perfectly now. How bad could it be? After all, she was kissing me back.

[WARNING: MONICA]

Until she wasn't.

She jumped back like I'd bitten her. Put her hand on her mouth. Choked. Not on Chobani. On the acid of complete and total disappointment in the human race.

And my first awful thought was, *Hey, as long as you're equally disappointed in both of us, then we're fine, we're in this together, let's keep going*—

Then her tears came, and exterminated all my awful thoughts, and all my nonawful thoughts, too. When tears came out of her, they didn't come in little spring-rain spritzes, either—they came all at once, a rogue wave.

"Mon . . ."

She turned and walked into the computer room. Shut the door so quietly, it felt worse than a slam.

I stood there, waiting for her to come back so we could talk. Waiting for me to come back, too. I needed to find out who I was now, and if I'd ever be okay again, after I'd done what I'd done.

It was a long wait, and in the end, neither of us came back.

At 12:58 p.m., I gave up and went to bed.

Two hours later, I woke up starving, went to the kitchen, and ate half a chicken.

For lack of a better idea, I dug the tape measure out of the drawer. Measured myself.

Yep.

It was next month already. I'd gotten there early.

Two days later, I was at the Lowlands, and fruit was being served to a dyspeptic monarch. Jollof'd been under the weather. He was in a mood. He also had idiopathic diarrhea, which probably explained his mood. It was nothing but superficial colitis—not uncommon in a gorilla Jollof's age, and very treatable, Brian said. He'd live. He'd be a little woozy on his meds, but he'd live. In the meantime, he'd make everyone around him want to die.

Generally, Jollof was sweet with the female handler (5′3″) who now brought him his chow, but that day, from Keeper Access, I watched him snarl at her.

"Not a good look on our boy," she said as she came in.

"Tell me about it."

Magic Mike just watched from a safe distance. Which made sense, given what Jollof'd done to him a few weeks before. (Back when Asshole had been in a *good* mood.)

I was doing inventory: bamboo pallets, protein supplements. Riveting stuff. I was watching the gorillas make their usual rounds in the habitat, just out of the corner of my eye. And I noticed, after a while, that Mike wasn't on his typical pig path.

That pig path was a rangy one, giving the main troop a wide

berth. But today he was closer in, closer to town center. Testing the troop, maybe. Testing Jollof.

Every time I looked up, he was closer.

And then he was just ... gone. Vanished.

I got up, went to the glass, tried every possible angle. No Mike. Maybe, I figured, he was at the waterfall, in one of those little nooks that can only be seen from the concourse. I was about to go upstairs to check when—

A roar. Like a giant tree being pulled apart. The kind of sound that stops a conversation, or maybe a civilization.

Jollof.

Bellowing. Furious. Actually *beating his chest.* It wasn't the superficial colitis.

It was Magic Mike. And what he'd done wasn't superficial.

Magic Mike was sitting on Jollof's rock. He was in the throne room.

Eating a mango. Casually. Like this was something he did on the reg.

And he was up there with Blue.

Suicide by silverback was my first thought. *He's finally snapped. No, Mike, no.*

Jollof seemed to grow three sizes. It was mostly hair, but damn, was it effective. It looked like he'd been inflated. He tore up the path to the rock, scaled the boulder face in a matter of seconds. Blue'd already run screaming. Mike retreated, and my heart stopped.

Because Mike had moved farther *into* Jollof's lair, which was a blind alley, a stone wall. The worst move he could've possibly made. Now there was no way out. No backing down. No way to show deference and restore the status quo.

This is how wars start, and how they end. This is the vanishingly rare situation in which you might actually lose a captive gorilla.

Silverbacks don't usually kill. It's incredibly uncommon. Even assholes like Jollof—they're just not *killers* by nature. But when there's an imbalance in the leadership, a change in troop social structure—yes, very occasionally, bad things can happen. It's the exception, though, not the rule.

Magic Mike had backed himself into the perfect exception.

Jollof charged into the throne room, bellowing, pounding his chest, reaching for Mike's head to crush it like an overripe melon. And Mike backed up, backed up, kept backing up—backing up when he should've been backing down. I couldn't see what he was doing anymore; he'd retreated past the lip of the rock, where my sight line stopped. What the hell was he—

SCREECH! SCREECH! SCREECH!

Now I saw them: Mike had *catapulted* himself at Jollof. Bounced off the back wall and gone right at him, at a dead run, screaming. This scrawny, neurotic little gorilla—I say *little,* he still weighed almost three hundred pounds—gambled it all on a kamikaze dive, and this completely unexpected, out-of-character move so freaked out Jollof—hell, it freaked *me* out—that he reacted with a traditional gorilla defensive tactic: he broke left.

Except there was no left.

There was just air. A drop. A long one.

Which Jollof, in his surprise and colitis and medication, had apparently forgotten.

And so down he came,

this monster, this victim,

falling backward from throne room to forest floor—

SHUK!

A very bad sound when he hit the ridge of rock at the base of the throne.

Jollof didn't move much after that.

There were twitches. Awful twitches. Meat, short-circuiting. Strange whistling noises that were not what the general public would think of as gorillaesque.

Whimpers.

Up above, on the throne, Magic Mike looked down at Jollof, his tormentor and king, shaking in the dirt, the life leaving him.

I hit the alarm.

In came the cavalry.

Out went Jollof, in traction, on a gurney.

Broken backs aren't easy to treat in higher primates, even in state-of-the-art veterinary facilities. Jollof was gone by dinnertime. Just like that. Almost twenty years in charge, almost twenty-nine on earth. An endangered species, a little more endangered than it had been that morning.

One wrong turn. Broke left when he shoulda broke right.

And then: just *broke.*

All of us hominids, gorilla and human, we just sort of stood around for a while. Stunned. At sea. Wondering what came next.

I didn't know.

Magic Mike, though, he sat on his throne, sat on it like a champ, and didn't fidget. He sat there like he knew something. Like he was waiting for someone to come ask. Eventually, someone did. It was Blue.

We locked eyes at one point, Magic Mike and I. And my blood went cold.

Because he gave me a nod.

More than likely, it was just a twitch, a fleabite. But to my biased and unscientific eyes, he gave me a nod, and what—if you're inclined to anthropomorphize gorillas, which I would never do, oh no, not I, because that way madness lies—you might even call a smile.

Who'd have thought? said the smile. *Couple of nice guys like us. Look at us now, brother man. Look at us now.*

PART THREE

LEVIATHAN

SEVENTEEN

6'11"

⟨jackofclubs⟩: this could get worse u know

WillD: ⟨YOU HAVE BEEN BLOCKED⟩

⟨clubofjacks⟩: want 2 know how?

WillD: ⟨YOU HAVE BEEN BLOCKED⟩

⟨bjscuckloaf⟩: okay maybe ill just show u

GAME DAY. FEBRUARY 27.

A day that shall live in infamy. A day that should've died in infancy.

So many portents and omens ignored: Martin Eddy's visit. Jollof's dethroning and death. The awful Unkiss in the kitchen. All leading up to this Very Much Not Good Day.

The night before, I'd had a dream.

It was just a cell, at first.

One cell became two. Then four. Eight. And so forth, until there was a clump, which bloated into a bumpy sphere. A blastula: the gloppy primordial basketball of life.

A dent formed in the basketball. Rotten crater opening on a ripe peach, just a pimple at first, then a sucking wound, and the first feature to form was the blastopore. Which was and is a mystery. Was it a mouth?

Or was it an asshole?

Biologists disagree on which came first, asshole or mouth, evolution-wise. On my happier days, I tilt mouthward. Not sure that really makes me an *optimist*, though.

Mouths are far worse than assholes. Mouths bite. Mouths devour. Mouths are ambitious. Assholes are . . . humble. They're just doing their jobs. Anyway, let's call the thing in my dream a mouth. (Because I feel gross enough already.) A mouth forms, the ball deflates, folds in on itself: a blind gut. That's what they call it. *Congratulations, Life-Form, on your blind gut! You're now a sac.*

I tumbled *up*, ass over blastopore, up through evolution, hitting every rung on my way . . . coming to a stop, mercifully, at the Age of Fish.

A great age, the Age of Fish.

Long before the big, farting, dumbass dinosaurs and all their bumbling, stompy bullshit, the oceans were high and twitching with chilled-out ectotherms of great size and variety and (I like to think) total self-control. They looked manga-sleek, and they moved like music through rippling forests of green. These creatures—they bled no heat, they risked no flameouts. They lived and loved and ate and eventually died, and it was all very relaxed, very casual. Even predation, murder—no one took it personally. Carnivorousness was just bodies sliding easily over other bodies, enveloping them. Not some big screamy deal.

They had only one problem, these fish. They never stopped growing. But even that wasn't really a problem. They didn't measure. They didn't categorize; they gave not a single fish shit about taxonomies. They just grew and grew and grew, totally unselfconscious, until something ate them. That was all there was to it. Simple.

I woke up feeling just like them, one with the current at a nice room temperature. Took just a minute or two before I ran aground and remembered what I was. Remembered my desperate mouse metabolism scurrying furiously on its doomed treadmill in every groping, gasping cell of my giant and now-unbeautiful body, a body that had already betrayed one best friend and fallen in a big creepy heap on the other, hungry blastopore gaping, trying to swallow her up into its blind gut.

It's not like I hadn't tried to talk to Monica. I had. Since the Unkiss.

There'd been many flavors of evasion. She'd ducked me at breakfast. She hadn't been at BoB. She'd ridden the bus in. Drew didn't know where she was, either. Not that Drew was really talking to me much. Our ride to school was pure NPR, Drew's nose in his phone, watching game tape.

I'd finally found Monica at the library, after lunch. "Should we talk about it?"

Monica didn't take her eyes off *Leviathan*. She just said: "No."

"I want to make this right," I said.

"I think you should stop wanting that," said Monica. Then she'd closed her book and walked away.

I *did* want to make things right, though. I needed to re-Jekyll and de-Hyde. I wanted to get clean. I wanted to be good again, nice again. Because I *was* nice. Right?

So I did the right thing. The nice thing.

I broke up with Sidney after school.

There are many ways to have a bad meal at Carl's Jr., but this one's up there. Top five, I'd say.

I called Sid and told her we needed to talk.

"Well," Sidney said, after the words *need to talk* came out of my mouth, "see you at fucking Carl's Jr., then." She wanted a hand-crafted biscuit that wasn't actually handcrafted and maybe wasn't even a biscuit. She loved Carl's Jr. Normally she'd never take Carl's Jr.'s name in vain. But she had good reason.

"I'm about to be dumped, right?" she said as we sat down at one of Carl's Jr.'s plastic tables. "That's the great thing about *We need to talk*. You already know what you're gonna talk about. So I figure let's just skip to where I medicate with junk food."

Her handcrafted biscuit was bleeding grease, squirting cheese out the sides, and she ate it while I explained what had happened, why I was doing what I was doing, without precisely saying, *I need to feel like less of a monster, so I'm dumping you.*

I had no food in front of me as I did this. I couldn't eat a biscuit, no matter how alluring, no matter how industrially handcrafted, in front of someone I was dumping. I wasn't that much of a monster.

But I was getting there.

I did, however, *want* her biscuit. I coveted it. It looked amazing. My stomach generated horrifying wild Serengeti sound effects while I was breaking up with Sidney, this amazing person I'd never deserved in the first place.

Life is chaos, y'know? Hungry, lip-smacking, earth-eating chaos.

Here's the thing: I didn't really want to break up with Sid. I liked Sid. A lot. I may have even loved her, under different circumstances. I'd have been lucky to have loved her, if events and brain chemistry had taken me in another direction, if life had broken right instead of left. As I may have mentioned, Sid was someone I didn't deserve, and as I also may have mentioned, Sid was beautiful. Out of my league at any height.

And we had to end. Right away.

I was the guy having sex with someone I'd never said *I love you* to, while ambush-kissing someone else, someone I'd loved from the moment I'd seen her, and also betrayed and repelled, maybe permanently.

I couldn't be sure of anything anymore, so I confessed everything.

Sid listened, then offered the following:

"Well, Daughtry, obviously you can burn in hell. I like you a lot. You're fun. You're my favorite kind of fun: a sweet dork in a body I wanna swallow. But I'm going to hate you for a while, I'm going to keep talking instead of crying, do you mind?"

I said I didn't, and tried to absorb the barrage of utterly incompatible feelings all of this sent through me, but Sid didn't slow down, Sid plowed right on: "Even sweet dorks screw up, though, and you screwed up real bad, not knowing how you felt, and I screwed up, not listening to what everybody was saying—"

"The rumor was bullshit—"

"And then it came true. Right?"

I clammed up. Sid just nodded.

"Course it did. Warning signs were there all along. I saw them, and I didn't do shit about it, because we were having so much fun. So I'm mad, yeah, mad at you, mad at me, too, and I might cry about this later, but not until I'm by myself, because, frankly, *you don't get to see that.*"

She took a big bite of her biscuit.

"A little advice. You, Will Daughtry, need to get over yourself."

Now, that didn't seem fair.

Sure, I'd made mistakes. I'd been selfish, maybe. But I *was* a good guy. A nice guy. Who suddenly, through no fault of his own, had a lot of self to get over. Whole mounds of self I never asked for. Way more self than most people had to deal with.

Her biscuit looked *so good.*

I think she saw me eyeing it. She put it down. Like her intestinal fortitude had deserted her. Or maybe just because I wasn't talking and responding like a human.

"I'm gonna go now," she told me, rising. "We'll be friends later, maybe. Maybe. You're not one hundred percent a bad guy, I don't think." She picked up her purse and turned to go. Then turned back. "But also: who gives a shit?"

Then she put that beautiful biscuit in the trash and walked out. Against every animal instinct, I left it there. I got out of that Carl's Jr. I was off to do more damage.

Game Day. I was just getting started.

My self-loathing was definitely on the upswing. But it was [jack]'s loathing of me that put Game Day over the top, sent it into the record books of Epic Awfulness.

The picture started making its infectious rounds a little under an hour before tip-off, when the Harps would face puny West Mira Mesa and presumably waltz to the semifinals.

[jack] was a master of his trade. Knew his high school news cycles.

I was headed to the gym when I heard about it. Rafty met me ten steps from the door.

"Don't go in there."

"Huh?"

Rafty took a deep breath. "First off, I forgive you. For the back-board. I see now: it was a demonstration. Powerful messaging, really. I only wish the camera'd been on."

"Raf, I'm sorry about the backboard. I'll pay for it. But I gotta get—"

"Not yet. Lemme brief you first. Fact is: we're in crisis mode."

"What? What are you talking—"

"Don't worry, it's nothing the team can't handle."

"Don't say *team*. There's no team. Also: WHAT?"

Finally Rafty showed me his phone.

And I saw why he hadn't been eager to.

It was a new image. [jack's] handiwork, obviously. Lots of help-ful arrows and things, annotations, etc. It had been taken at night, and the image was wreathed in the porny greenish glow of infrared. Technology is wonderful.

The image showed the parking lot at Black's. And two people who—stupidly, I realize—thought they were alone: Monica and yours truly, Grow-liath, stripped to the waist. You couldn't see Monica's face; her back was to the camera. But her shirt was off. And Grow-liath was staring at her. Grow-liath was *rapt*.

(What Grow-liath was looking at, of course, were the old scars on Monica's ribs, the ones that looked like a bear mauling. The ones I'd thought were from Martin. The ones Martin said were from Monica, trying to destroy herself.)

At first the image didn't seem to add much to the existing rumor: Will Daughtry was hooking up with his stepbrother's girl-friend, their mutual pal. Everybody knew that. *I mean, did you hear? She* lives *with them now!* All salacious enough on its own.

Ah, but there was more.

The headline for this photo was a bit farther south.

Around Grow-liath's fabled midsection. At the corner of Pelvis and Rumor.

In the night vision, there could be discerned . . . by the discern-ing . . . or by the just plain old pervy . . . *a shape.* "Fusiform" is what the sea cucumber researchers might've called this shape.

The shape in the photo was—to use a ninety-dollar Monica word—*tumescent.* A dopey cartoon bomb of a thing, pointed more or less straight at Monica.

You could almost hear the cartoon bomb whistle sound that went with it.

It was just my rolled-down wet suit, of course, but that didn't matter. If the shape fits, share it. And lies don't need much traction if they're based on a true story.

"We can spin this," said Rafty. "There's precedent. In fact, it could be our friend. Our little friend. Our not-so-little friend, right?"

"Rafty . . ."

"Kidding! Sorry! Look, two pieces of advice: Don't go to the game. And . . . if you would just . . . say the *Scarface* line into my phone?"

"What?"

" 'Say hello to my little friend!' Just say it into my phone, let me record it? I could attach it to the picture, and we can get in front of the story with a little irony, a little self-parody—"

"Rafty."

"Totally kidding. But . . . not kidding. This could add! To your mystique! Will! Where're you going? Come back! *We can leverage this!*"

I went into the gym. Against managerial advice.

I wasn't sure if Drew had seen the picture, or if Monica had. I only knew I needed to see them. To talk this through. To make a plan. Or change the Plan. Or replan. Something. Anything.

I ended up sitting right behind the Harps' pep band as C+C Music Factory's whatever-that-one-song-is assaulted my eardrums. The bleachers shook with chaos and brassy blatting, because the Harps were one quarter into completing their ceremonial annual pummeling of West Mira Mesa, an annual Feast of Beatdownery that even WMM's long-suffering fans seemed to enjoy. News 8 had its spidery viscera, wires and such, spattered all over one end of the gym. Tonight, local media was here for Drew and Drew alone.

I searched the stands and found Monica next to Laura and Brian. She gave me zero direct eye contact. It was still more than I deserved.

And yet.

She'd kissed back.

Fweeeet!

Game on.

Drew was in the zone. And the zone was sealed off, air-locked, quarantined. In the zone, Drew breathed only the canned air of Purpose, Mission, GAME.

It'd been a waltz for West Mira Mesa so far. An accident of bracketing had pushed this team, a mediocre-to-bad squad, right into the slaughterhouse chute that was Keseberg. They were poised for a hard Harping.

But they were about to get an assist from a remarkable player.

Andrew Michael Tannenger.

He hung on a good long time before it all came down, like a casino on fire.

Third quarter, and the Harps were up by twenty. No surprise.

Then West Mira started fouling. Fouling Drew. Fouling like crazy.

Pretty soon, the whole game was just Drew at the line.

Which should've been the end of it. Because Drew was great at the line.

Like, 78 percent for the season.

That night? He hit two of thirteen.

They weren't even respectable misses. Drew was bricklaying. And every time he did, he'd shake his head, like there was something in there he was trying to shake loose.

I knew what it was. So did everyone else.

Except Brian and Laura, who didn't understand.

Across the bleachers, I lip-read Laura asking, "Is he sick?"

I lip-read Monica saying nothing.

Drew ponged one off the back of the rim. His seventh miss in a row, and I watched the zone collapse. *Implode*, like a nuclear sub sinking to depths it wasn't designed to tolerate, crushed by pressures no one ever imagined it would have to cope with. Trying to recover the rebound, he fouled. His fourth. With eight minutes left.

And that's when Drew . . . *laughed*.

I couldn't hear it over the noise, but I saw him laughing. I saw his teammates look at him like he'd sprouted a tail. And I knew just from looking: it was a crazy laugh. An all-done laugh. An O.K. Corral, hail-of-bullets kind of laugh.

His eyes met mine.

I shook my head at him: *No. Don't do whatever it is you're thinking of doing.*

Drew was still laughing as he was setting up for the inbound. The Mira center passed him on his way to the key, said something to him.

I could guess what. But it didn't matter, because—

—Drew punched the guy right in the face.

The geyser of blood that came shooting from the big man's nose was truly impressive, and showed up really well, from multiple angles, on the literally hundreds of videos made of that moment.

Here's the other thing you can see on the video: Drew, blood on his hand, wheeling . . . and pointing to me.

That was for you. . . .

Oh, I had no doubt.

Whistles blew. Refs converged. Madness reigned.

I looked over at Brian and Laura, clambering down the bleachers to get to Drew, who was being escorted off the court by Coach Gut and Eric Forchette.

Monica was gone.

You don't need a play-by-play from here, I don't think.

Drew was ejected, with the possibility of suspension for the remainder of the postseason. But that wasn't necessary, because four minutes later, the Harps' postseason was over. Without Drew—and totally blindsided, completely demoralized—they just fell apart. Crummy old West Mira Mesa, on the other hand, saw a nice fat corpse to feast on. They were avenging their big man and his big, squirty broken nose. The slaughter was vast and epic. (By which I mean: the Harps lost by seven. Against West Mira Mesa, that's like losing by fifty.)

A program, a legacy, and a Plan with a capital *P*—this whole starry constellation of possibilities—sank into the ocean. Just like that.

I couldn't go to Drew, couldn't comfort him. What was I supposed to say? *I wish you'd punched me?*

I couldn't explain to Brian and Laura why I couldn't go to Drew.

I couldn't go to Monica, because chances were, Monica was somewhere waiting for Drew. I even hoped she was. He needed her.

So I went to the woods.

Not just any woods.

The woods.

But first I sent a message.

* * *

The message I sent was addressed to two recipients: Spencer Inskip and his thinly veiled troll persona, [jack]. Copied 'em both. Why beat around the bush?

When you can *burn* the bush?

Isn't that a thing? Like, in the Bible? "We'll burn that bush when we come to it"?

> **WillD:** hey buddy! let's do that thing we keep putting off.
> let's do it tonight. you and me. the woods next to the party
> toilet. bring all your bones so i can break them. one by one.

And then I headed for the Party Toilet, my Fiat reaching speeds Fiats rarely reach when they're not being pushed off cliffs.

I sat on the stump of the fallen tree, the place where I'd had the misfortune to cross paths with Spencer Inskip last spring, putting me back on his sociopathic radar for the first time since middle school.

Now it was his turn to have a misfortune. If he showed.

He had to. He just *had* to. I needed this *so badly*. A monster needed slaying tonight.

"Daughtry, what the hell?"

Spencer. He'd come. He'd actually come.

"Oh, thank God," I actually said, mostly to myself.

I wanted to squeeze his head off like a childproof bottle top, empty his contents all over the pine needles. I was so happy he'd showed. I was so grateful.

"Hi, [jack]."

Spencer sauntered into the light. "What's *jack*? Your safe word?"

He was a head shorter and eighty pounds lighter than I was now.

This seemed almost cruel. It nearly gave me pause.

Luckily, he kept talking. And sauntering. Right into twisting/squeezing range.

"Heard you dumped my ex," said Spencer, inspecting the clearing like he was thinking of moving in. "Well done. Power move. I can confirm: she gets more irritating over time."

I cocked a fist back, with every intention of sending it right through Spencer's skull—

—and was surprised to find myself suddenly on the ground.

Something of substantial mass had collided with me from behind, sent me tumbling down like the towering rage inferno I was.

Something . . . rhomboid.

Of course he hadn't come alone. Parallelogram and Quadrilateral were there, too.

Four against one.

Weirdest part was, this little wrinkle kinda made me happy. I wasn't the least bit worried now. Not because I was sure I'd win a one-on-four against beefed-up, daily-deadlifting football players. No, I was happy because all of this seemed fair—everybody, including me, seemed to be getting just what they deserved, and I was sure I'd like the outcome, no matter which way the wave broke.

I started to get up. Parallelogram and Quadrilateral sat on me. Actually sat on me.

"Damn, Daughtry, you are a weird freakin' beast," Spencer was saying. He was seated on the log, kinda prim, straight-backed, great posture, Jane goddamned Austen.

"You troll the hell out of me for months, show up at football tryouts for one damned day, just to make me look like shit. Bang my ex. Run me down to all your new friends, 'cause you have all these new friends, 'cause all of a sudden, people think you're an X-Man kinda freak instead of a special-ed kinda freak, and then, after I've almost forgotten I even gave a shit about you and your bullshit— you *challenge* me! To a *fight*! And since I'm such a nice guy, I'll give you one." He flicked his eyes at his boys. "Just had to even the odds a little. You understand."

"I do understand," I said.

And then I got up.

Upending two meaty polygons.

Spencer got up, too. He hadn't realized quite how strong I'd gotten. I hadn't realized it, either.

Suddenly the odds didn't feel so even.

I enjoyed the look on his face so much. Too much. I'd actually made him afraid. I'd shown him a bigger monster.

Now I wanted to do more than show. I wanted him to feel it.

His henchshapes were thrown, literally and figuratively. But they were recovering. And arming themselves with tree limbs. *Welp,* I thought, *here it is. Somebody's going to the hospital, somebody's going to jail. Either way: change will come.*

Lucky for me, at that precise and fatal moment, when I was all too ready to throw everything away, two bright lights cut through the darkness.

Tires squealed. A car hopped the curb, pulled up grumbling over Jazzy's wide green lawn.

Mutual *What the hells* united me with my enemies for a hot sec.

Drew? Monica? Rafty? None of them knew I was here.

A figure emerged from the car, backlit by halogens.

It took me a very, very, very long time to realize it was Ethan Neville.

The yearbook photographer. Returning to the scene of his forced intoxication last spring, when I'd found him draped over this very stump, barfing his guts out, with these very meatheads standing over him, laughing. Right before Sidney saved us both.

Ethan Neville had just driven his battered Hyundai Sonata across Jazzy's lawn.

That was weird enough.

Then Ethan said, "Kill me."

Spencer shrugged. "Okay."

"No," said Ethan. "Not you. Him."

He pointed to me.

"I," said Ethan Neville, in a Gandalfian voice I did not know he had, "am [jack]."

I just stared at him. Nothing was connecting.

Ethan clarified. Dropped the voice-of-God thing. "I'm . . . y'know, I'm [jack]. Your troll? I sent out the photos? I humiliated you? Hi."

"You? What?" My head was full of Legos that didn't quite fit. "Wh-why?"

Spencer started laughing. "Oh, my God. Is . . . *this*"—he pointed at Ethan—"why you're here? Because you let this little shit stain wind you up?"

There came rumbling, hooting polygonal laughter. And suddenly it was all just one giant *joke*. All that fear and rage, balled up in anticipation of good old-fashioned male violence . . . just released itself. All over us. In a (I'm *so* sorry, but it's true) *spurt*. It was like we'd been sprayed by baboons, and also *we* were the baboons doing the spraying.

I wasn't angry. I was too confused to be angry. The adrenaline was draining fast.

I think Spencer sensed the derision wasn't having quite the effect he'd hoped. So he got back in my face. Game move for a small man who'd, just a second ago, looked pretty terrified of me. So terrified, in fact, that he'd made *me* a little terrified of me.

"Hey, Will. You still want us to fuck you up?"

I made a thoughtful sound. "Um. No? I . . . I just don't think that's necessary now. Unless you do?"

I was very close to Spencer now. His backup boy band was too spread out in the confusion. There was nothing stopping me from a first strike. Strategic incompetence, inability to read a changing field of play: this is why Keseberg football sucked so hard.

Spencer digested all that. He was looking for an exit now, I could feel it. So I gave him one. Stepped aside. He hesitated a second, then started to go, with a dismissive *hmf!*

I have no idea why I couldn't just leave it there.

"Spencer?"

He looked at me. Those empty eyes, those caves.

"I'm sorry," I said.

One species peered into the face of another and saw no kinship. No common ancestor. And yet, just a few minutes before, we'd been the same animal. We could've died of each other's diseases. *That* kind of closeness.

"Let's go," Spencer said to his polygons. "Give these two a moment alone. They deserve each other." He walked back up the drive, bumping Ethan hard as he passed.

"He's right," said Ethan. "I deserve . . . whatever you're gonna do to me."

My high-metabolism inner lava mouse screamed for his blood.
He squeezed his eyes shut. Waiting to be pummeled.

The *drama*. I was so tired of *mammals*. All their heat and fuss.

I asked myself, *What would a Great Creature from the Age of Fish do?*

"Ethan? I'm taking you to fuckin' Carl's Jr."

So I took him to fuckin' Carl's Jr.

I took my tormentor, the garbage troll who'd ruined my life, to Carl's Jr.

For a long time, I just watched Ethan Neville eat a chicken sandwich. He had salt crusts on his cheeks, like slug trails, where his tears had dried. They wiggled when he chewed.

Finally I asked the natural question:

"Why?"

"At first?" said Ethan. "Because I'm in love with Sidney Lim. I have been since eighth grade. Didn't you notice? Let me answer for you: no. You didn't. No one did. Not even Sidney. My point is, I'm in love with her, and you're not. You never were."

"How do you know that?"

"Because I studied your whole life like it was that film of Kennedy getting shot. Because I was this nothing thing, and you were this nothing thing, and then . . . off you went! And at first . . . I just wanted to know why . . . and then wanting to know why became . . . wanting to do something about it. . . ."

I nodded. This made a lot of sense. It was bonkers, it was creepy, but it made a lot of sense. Hell, it almost gave Ethan Neville a kind of . . . I wanted to say nobility? And insanity, of course.

"You know, we broke up. Sid and I."

"Uh, you make it sound mutual. *You* broke up with *her*, bro. Really messed her up. I drove her home, she was a wreck. That's why I dropped the atom bomb with that photo, before the tip. I was on the fence about it. Then you broke my girl's heart. On Game Day! On Game Day, man! You don't get away with that, no matter how big you get."

The buzz in my hands again, and the blood in my ears. "Hey, Ethan? You still want me to kill you? 'Cause that's definitely still on the table, especially when you talk like that."

Ethan thought about it. "I'm gonna finish this sandwich first."

He started eating again. I held on to the table very tightly, until civility returned to my extremities. Which were feeling pretty extreme.

"You said, *At first*. What changed? Why are we here?"

Ethan chewed thoughtfully. "It seemed evil."

"Yeah? Which part?"

"Serving you up to Spencer."

"Oh, THAT seemed evil."

"I mean, *did* I save you? I think you would've taken those guys. You're a freakin' dreadnought, man. This is weird, but I swear it's true: I'm a troll, but I'm also a *fan*."

I got up. The rage electricity was tickling my hands again.

"Where you going?"

"Home."

"You're blowing it, man. I gotta tell you, as a fan, you're blowing it."

I stopped. Ethan didn't.

"You're living the life people like me dream about, and you're blowing it. You throw away things other people think are precious. You even threw *Sidney* away—"

I got into Ethan's face. I had to stoop. A long way. Because he was sitting. And I was me. He smelled like chicken.

"Of all the shit you said to me . . . all the shit about Monica and Drew . . . the shit about my *mom,* man, my *dead mom*—"

"I know. I know! I'm a piece of—"

"I didn't throw anybody away. First off. Second, you don't get to decide *what* I am. How I *should* be. You don't get to study me from a safe distance. *There is no safe distance,* you shitty little—"

I caught our reflection then, in the fun-house mirror of the Coca-Cola Freestyle machine. I saw a broken person, and there was a *creature* towering over him, a tall, rangy thing, all long, grasping limbs, half gorilla, half spider. This thing, this menace, this monster was leaning into Ethan's small, crumpled face, roaring, showing how big his gullet was and how easily a broken thing could go down it—

I sat down. I diminished myself.

"Hey. Hey. Ethan? I'm . . . I'm sorry. I'm . . . I'm trying to figure some shit out myself."

"Do you know . . . ," Ethan sobbed, ". . . do you know the worst part of all this?"

I didn't. I really didn't. There was so much to choose from, right here in this Carl's Jr., where people were starting to stare.

"We used to be friends."

I blinked.

"At basketball camp? You, me, Drew, Rafty. We were Blue Squad?"

I had no memory of this. I mean, I remembered Blue Squad. I

remembered Drew and Rafty, back when we were all little boys, and the stakes seemed high but weren't. The stakes were Red Squad. I remembered Red Squad. But I didn't remember Ethan.

"See?" sputtered Ethan. "*That's* the worst part. You never saw me coming. Because you didn't see me *at all.*"

And that? I understood. All too well.

"You used to *be* me," said Ethan. "And you *still* never saw me coming."

EIGHTEEN

7' 1"

ETHAN WENT INTO therapy. He had a great LCSW. Talked my ear off about him.

I could probably have used some therapy myself. Ethan was the closest thing I had to a sympathetic ear. Sad to say.

I was suddenly [jack]less. And without [jack], without my fellow monster, my mirror monster, my failures as a person became impossible to hide.

"I don't want you to take this the wrong way," Rafty began.

We were sitting on my car, the two of us. Sitting on my car had recently become much easier than sitting *in* my car. At least for one of us. I lay back with my head on the roof, scalp grazing the rear window, my body draped down the windshield and hood. My feet were planted firmly on the pavement. Rafty perched on the rear bumper, looking the other way.

"I can't keep you on as a client."

"Okay."

"Your case . . . the image management issues here . . . they're beyond my powers. That's . . . that's tough for me to admit. But now that you're in *Guinness* . . . well, you might want to explore more . . . professional options." I heard a little gulp. Real emotion in Rafty's voice. "I hope we can stay friends, though."

"Rafty?"

"Yeah, Will?"

"I don't know if I was ever your client. Since I never signed anything or paid you or agreed to be your client."

"Well, that was because of our preexisting friendship."

"Can we just stick with *that*? Our preexisting friendship?"

A pause. Then Rafty said, "Yeah. That'd be good, I think."

We watched a small plane fly over.

"I'm sorry I made the dunking video. I . . . I should've asked."

"It's okay. I'm sorry I got scary and broke your backboard."

"It's okay." Another long pause. This one was warmer. Felt less like a void, more like a cushion. Then Rafty said, "How's everything with Monica and Drew?"

"Bad."

We'd all managed to avoid each other for almost a week. Granted, it was a busy time. Drew had juvie-mandated anger management classes to attend. Monica was, presumably, finishing up college applications and prepping for interviews.

My seventeenth birthday came and went without a single candle lit, without a single song screeched. I'd asked Brian and Laura not to make a big deal of it this year, not to make anything of it, and definitely not to make a cake. In a measure of how bad things were, they agreed to those terms.

The good news just kept rolling in. My last appointment with Dr. Helman was . . . well, I don't want to say *informative*. Those appointments rarely were. But it was *terrifying*. Terrifying and clarifying.

I'd already bled for Nurseferatu and was heading back to the waiting room to find Brian when Dr. Helman appeared. "Would you like to sit?"

No. I would not. Chairs were back to being uncomfortable. Also: I didn't like it when doctors invited me to sit. Nobody's invited to sit for good news, not in real life.

"What's going on?"

"I wanted to talk to you before I talked to your parents."

Oh, Christ. Oh no. Not now.

"It's not bad news."

Okay? "So it's good news."

"It's what science usually is: it's ambiguous."

I sat.

"Those extra brakes we applied," Dr. Helman began. "They aren't really . . . applying themselves. At all."

That much I'd figured out on my own. "Okay."

"You're healthy. You're not presenting with musculoskeletal imbalances or joint problems or any pathologies related to the growth trend. And you're still feeling *good*. . . ."

I was getting tired of these relative measurements. What was "feeling good" to a guy who'd spent the last year ruining his life?

"Dr. Helman," I said. "I am over seven feet tall. I weigh three hundred pounds. I can't keep going like this. Right?"

Dr. Helman took off her glasses. I'd never seen her without her glasses. She looked younger. Less like she knew everything. More like me, like someone who tried to get his head around scary things by reaching for the biggest idea, and when that effort came up short, reaching for the next-biggest. Someone who'd gotten to the top of a mountain after a hard climb, a real slog, and looked out from the peak to see . . . not the ocean, not the promised land, but . . . more mountains, and mountains behind those mountains, and all higher than the one he just climbed.

"Will," said Dr. Helman, "why we grow to a certain size and stop, how those genetic switches work—it's still pretty mysterious. Plenty of animals never stop growing. The dinosaurs didn't."

(Ah, Dr. Helman. Tone-deaf as ever. Of all the examples to choose from, in the vast smorgasbord of biology, she *would* go with an extinct one.)

"The point is, it's not as simple as *off* or *on*. It's not as simple as *you're growing* or *you've stopped*. This growth, what's causing it, this hormonal-enzymatic feedback loop: it's *stable*, it's not changing, and your bone density is keeping pace with—"

"Are you saying I could just . . . keep growing? Like this? Forever?"

"I'm saying," said Dr. Helman, laying a tiny hand on my enormous forepaw, "that we'll just have to see."

We all react to bad news in different ways.

I, for instance, react to bad news badly.

First, I slept on it. As much as I *could* sleep, which wasn't much.

Then at five a.m., I texted Monica. I said it was an emergency.

It *was* an emergency.

I told her to meet me at the Lowlands. Then I texted Drew and told him the same thing. Actually, I'd pulled my old trick: I told Drew to be there an hour later. I needed to talk to Monica alone.

Something had to give. Nice Guy Will had failed completely. Time for Grow-liath to take the wheel.

The Aggression Log needed updating, because the Aggression Log always needed updating. Things had been especially rocky since Magic Mike took over. There were questions among the keepers—and, apparently, among the apes—about whether he was up to the job he'd lucked (*murdered?*) his way into.

(No one else thought it was murder, of course; that was my interpretation, and mine alone. But then, nobody knew Magic Mike quite the way I did.)

I was in my apron. It looked like a miniskirt on me these days. All my clothes looked ridiculous again, now that I'd been swallowed by one end of the bell curve and shat out the other. I was a freak again, just a different-size freak. My brief intermission of normality was over: my clothes were rags, my bed was too short for my legs, too narrow to turn over in, my car was too small for me, wasn't even drivable by me anymore, my whole life felt like a toothpaste tube I'd been squeezed out of, and the villagers with pitchforks and torches were probably right around the corner. So I sifted protein kibble for mealworms and waited for destiny to arrive.

Monica came in.

Her hoodie looked even more beat to shit than usual, like she'd slept in it. Her hair was longer, wilder, her anime spikes drooping.

I looked at her and thought, in defiance of a whole year of monstrosity:

Nothing's changed.

It can all be like it was, back when it was good.

I love you. I've always loved you. I'll always love you. That'll never change.

That was my plan. Basically, to say that.

In case you were wondering.

"Whatever your plan is," said Monica, setting down her backpack, "do me a favor and . . . don't."

"Mon," I said, "I texted Drew. He's coming over. We're gonna work this out."

I love you. I've always loved you. Nothing else matters.

Monica gave the long sigh of a thousand-year-old kung fu master.

"No," said Monica. "Just no."

"We made a wrong turn back there somewhere. Somewhere between the Old Plan and the New Plan, we just . . . we just broke the wrong way!"

Monica was shaking her head. "Will, listen to me—"

"I love you."

Monica pitched forward, like she'd been stabbed or poisoned. Her hair fell in front of her face protectively.

We'd finally arrived, I thought, at the untakebackable thing.

She mumbled something into the hand she'd slapped over her own mouth.

Now, I'll admit: this body language was discouraging. I'd been hoping for body language that was more *Yes, everything you say is true, let's find a sunset and drive off into it.* I decided to spin again, hope for a winner.

"Look. We survived you and Drew. We'll survive this."

Monica looked up. "We? 'Survived' me and Drew?"

Whoops! Maybe that phrasing wasn't top-notch. "You know what I mean."

"I don't think I do, Will."

"We can get back to where we were. When it went wrong."

Now Monica was downright curious. Or downright furious. Her expression was parked somewhere between those two. "And where was *that*?"

I sucked in two zeppelin lungfuls of air and began. "Mon . . . last year, at BoB . . . night of my birthday . . . I told you eight-fifteen. . . ."

"What?"

"I told you to come at eight-fifteen. But I told Drew nine. Because . . . because I needed the time . . . to tell you . . ."

Monica just nodded. Utterly befuddled.

"And then . . . ," I said, and my momentum deserted me. "Well, and then you . . ."

"I what?" Monica's eyes focused on me again.

"You gave me the ring." I pulled it out of my shirt.

Monica stared. "You've still got it?"

"Of course I do."

"But . . . you were such a dick about it. When I gave it to you."

"I know! I was! *Such* a dick! Because I thought you were friend-zoning me. Frodo-zoning me."

" 'Frodo-zoning'? Will, Jesus . . ."

"And then you . . . you patted me. On the head. And I couldn't believe it. You, of all people. That's when I figured it was never gonna happen. And then, that same night, you and Drew . . . well, you guys kinda *confirmed* that."

Monica stared at me. "Patted? Your head?"

"Wait. So. Hang on. You *weren't* patting my—"

"I was trying to kiss you, you total goddamned mental case!"

A hush fell over Keeper Access.

"I was . . . reaching . . . Look, I'm a . . . tall girl, okay?" She regarded my massiveness and revised that: "I mean, I am tall, for a girl. Look, I've got my own hang-ups, maybe? Can I have those?"

I wasn't processing any of this fast enough. "Slow down, slow down—"

But she was on a tear now. "And then I tried to take some initiative, since nobody else was, and you . . . you freaked out! So I, uh, y'know, determined that consent was neither clear nor enthusiastic, and I backed the hell off. But who do you think I dressed up for? Christ, Daughtry, I climbed down a cliff in that absurd lacy top. . . ."

My mouth felt slow. It made a word, slowly: "Drew. You dressed up for Drew."

"No, dummy," she said.

While I was trying to figure out what that meant, Monica lifted her eyes. And stared . . .

. . . at the observation window.

Blue stared back. A hairy hand on the glass. Solidarity?

We had an audience. High drama for high primates.

Was it my line? My brain was a dial tone. It didn't make sense, what she was saying.

But she kept saying it: "I needed . . . *something* . . . to change. Maybe needed it more than you did, even." Then she said: "I was . . . awkward."

Before that moment, I hadn't thought Monica was capable of awkward. I hadn't thought she was capable of anything less than . . .

capability. Supernatural, paranormal capability. God-mode capability.

As my blinking brain tried to catch up, she went on: "I tried to play it off, and I . . . I touched your hair. And then you went *bananas.* So that was that. And I guess the ring was the wrong present, or I *said* something, or I *did* something—"

"Monica," I blurted. "It wasn't! Wrong! The ring. Monica. I loved it! I love it! Look! I've had it on since you gave it to me! And it was me: I made everything weird. Not you. All me. Just my insecure little-man shit. And—I'm past that now. I mean, ha! Obviously!"

Monica was shaking her head, though. I wasn't getting through. I needed to make her see: I had all the answers now. Or at least all the data. No more theories, no more rules, no more Plan. Not necessary. This was it: biology in motion. Planless, reckless biology in motion.

"We can get it right," I said. "Now."

She took the ring from my hand and ran her fingers over it.

"No," said Monica. She put the ring in her pocket.

"No? You mean because of Drew."

"Yes. Because of Drew. But also because of me. And because of you."

"If it's about what happened . . . in the kitchen . . ."

"It is. You should've asked."

"I know. But you . . ."

"I know I did! And I shouldn't have! Jesus!" Monica paced to the coffee maker, then paced back to the chimp spears. "Stop looking at me like that!"

"Like what?"

"Like I've got answers! Why do you do that?!"

"You don't have answers, you *are* the answer. For me."

I watched a single tear well in Monica's eye, break, and rill down her cheek.

"I'm NOT. Okay? I'm not even *my* answer, how'm I supposed to be yours, Will? There are things about me, things you don't know—"

"Like those marks. On your back. Your dad told me . . ."

Whoops.

"What," Monica said slowly, "did my dad say I did? The day I got those?"

Say it.

"He said you . . . hurt yourself. On purpose. That maybe you were trying to . . . send a message or . . . a cry for . . . something . . . or . . ."

A cold front moved through the room, brittled my stammers into teensy icicles.

"Surf?" said Monica, steel in her voice. "I was trying to surf? Actually? Surfing. It's a thing that I do? To take me away from everything? Even people I love? Even myself? *Especially* myself? My *friends* know this. But *you* . . ."

She laughed. It was a strange laugh, more like a cry. The first of many, it turned out.

" . . . *you* talked to my dad. My *utterly reliable* dad. And you *concluded* . . . that I'm suicidal. Hooboy. Hoooooooboy." She was pacing again now, fiddling with a chimp spear.

"Monica, I'm not saying . . . *that*. Obviously."

"Oh, *obviously.*"

What *was* I saying? Before I started saying it, I'd known, I could've sworn. "Look, I wasn't *there*, but I do know . . . I *know* there was more to it. . . ."

"Oh!" said Monica. "And how do you 'know'?"

"Because I know YOU! Because I love YOU!" I reached for her, a hand on each shoulder, hoping a touch might do more than my gasping, gaping dead-fish mouth. "And because we are *right*! Right? For each other. You know it. You knew it a year ago, it's why you dressed up. I was too stupid and small to see it. I had to grow up, but . . . I did!"

I laughed. I hoped it didn't sound unhinged.

"Like, a lot! And now I know why! For this! Monica, Drew knows. And I think he gets it. On some level. Because, let's face it, you two—you two *didn't work*, okay?"

Monica whipped away a tear like a samurai flicking blood off a sword.

"How do you know?" she said. "You never asked if it was working!"

Because I didn't want to know.

"Because I didn't want it to get weird! *Because I was sticking to the Plan!*"

"Well, that's a fuckin' relief."

Drew.

A little early.

There he was, in the door. Practice sweats. Looking exhausted. Like he'd spent the morning running drills, even though the season was over, even though he was technically suspended. Like he'd been running laps, just out of habit. That's probably exactly what he'd been doing.

I didn't know how much he'd heard. It didn't really matter.

But in an ideal world? I'd really, really meant to be further along with the Monica portion of my argument by the time Drew showed up.

"I'm so glad you stuck to the Plan, Will. Otherwise, something terrible could've happened to our friendship."

At the sound of Drew's voice, the planet's sweaty poles refroze.

"I'm glad you're here," I said, for the save.

"*I'm* not," said Drew. He had an expression on his face I couldn't quite classify. It might've been *fratricide*.

I ignored that. "You guys, even before all that goddamn trolling started—which was all just bullshit, nothing happened—you have to admit that it wasn't exactly clicking, right? You two? As a thing? You guys just . . . fell into each other. It was random."

"Random, okay," said Drew. "Keep telling me about me and Monica, I find it fascinating. First, though, quick question. What happened? Between you two?"

Monica face-palmed. There are people on this earth who enjoy being fought over. Monica was the opposite of those people. This was absolute torment.

"I kissed her," I said, and I really meant it to sound like a confession, I did, but it came out like an end zone spike, like a goddamned triumph, because too much had been dammed up for too long.

I watched it hit Drew in the chest, I watched the ripples pass through him in a meat wave, and I'll admit, shittily, it was a little satisfying.

"Me. I did it. Because I'm in love with her, okay? Because I've been in love with her since we were ten."

"I knew it," said Drew. "I *knew* it."

And then I felt this balled-up anger rise, like hot vomit.

"Oh, you did?" I couldn't help myself. *No attacks,* I'd told myself. *Defenses and explanations only.* But diplomacy's a fragile thing. "You knew? How I felt about her? That night? And you just thought, *Ah, screw it,* and grabbed her anyway—"

"Seriously? Boys? The third-personing? Is starting to piss 'her' off," said Monica, voice rising. "I did some grabbing, too, okay? *I* did some fucking up. *Me.*" Monica was the last person in the world you wanted to third-person.

Drew was still standing in the door, but he suddenly seemed to be *filling* it.

"Listen . . . ," I started—

—and out of the corner of my eye, I saw something that half filled the observation window.

Him.

The others had cleared to the edges. He had his own skybox.

My other blood brother from a distant mother. My fellow beta, the maybe murderer.

He sat back on his hairy haunch, arms crossed. Watching the show.

We gave him one.

"Here's what happened," I said, summoning my science voice. (No anger, no fuss. Just facts. An evolutionary progression.) "You two blew us up, for something that didn't even *work.* Okay? And look, I don't blame you. I tried to do the same thing. And so did she."

Drew looked at Monica. Monica sat on the couch. Dropped her head into her hands like a bowling ball on a car hood.

"Yep," she said. "At BoB. That night, before we came to get you at Jazzy's."

Drew sagged. "What?"

"I..." Monica laughed. The strangest laugh, kind of indistinguishable from some night creature's death rattle. "I made a pass!" She laughed again. "Guess that makes me the original piece of shit, huh, guys? Garden of Eden?"

Drew hadn't reached the ironic detachment portion of the discussion yet. He was scratching his scalp, hard and fast. Processing. "And?"

"And..." Monica stopped laughing. "He didn't get it."

Now *I* felt a little third-personed. But Monica was on a roll.

"And I didn't get that he didn't get it." Monica ground the heels of her hands into her eyes. "I don't know why I...needed...I don't know! Can I just be a moron? Is that okay? It seems to be okay for you two...."

Drew was still thumbing through these new cards. "A moron because you wanted him...or because you wanted me?"

Monica sighed a sigh of great weariness. "I just know...you're both so special to me." Which, let's face it, wasn't a great line, and wasn't a very Monica thing to say, and maybe that's why her voice kinked like a cheap garden hose when she said it.

"Special," said Drew. "Meaning: swappable?"

"No," snapped Monica. "*Not* meaning that."

Now Drew was looking me in the eye. But to do that, he had to look *up*. (And I'll admit, part of me really loved that.) "I tried to fix this, I did. I tried to make a new Plan, and you two just laughed it off—"

"Because," I said, not nicely, "it was laughable."

Drew's mouth pulled piano-wire tight. "Okay. Sorry for *caring*—"

"Caring?" I said, looming. "Try *controlling*. Try trying to be everybody's dad, just because *your* dad—"

"Oh, buddy," Drew said, and his voice had this dangerous teeter to it, "you better watch that."

"Watch what?"

"Your fucking mouth."

I heard Magic Mike hooting, muted, on the other side of the glass. Drama. In wide-screen. He was loving this.

The humans, on their side of the glass, less so.

"No," I said, "I don't think I will, Drew. I think I'm going to say something I should've said a long time ago: you need to let go. *Let go.* Stop trying to be a cop or a dad or a team captain or whatever the hell it is you think you're trying to be—"

"Jesus," said Drew. "You're so goddamned selfish, it's insane." He took a step in my direction, and I felt the hair rise on my neck and arms.

"Selfish? Me? I'm selfish? Says the guy who takes what he wants, no regard for consequences?"

"Guys?" Monica said, rising. "I'm not a fan of this . . . whole thing we're doing here. Nobody got 'taken,' okay?"

"I'm not a fan, either!" I barked, and I heard my voice bouncing off the glass, louder than I'd intended, and I'd intended it to be pretty loud. Blue actually took a step back. "You think I want to be here? Saying this shit out loud? I haven't been a fan of *anything* that's happened to us, the three of us, as a unit, ever since the night you two decided You Two were more important than . . . Us!"

"Why's that, Will?" asked Drew, taking another step toward me. "Because suddenly it wasn't about you anymore? From that point on? That's it, isn't it? Oh, but you fixed that: *freakish growth spurt!*"

"Wait wait wait wait: go back to the part, *Spesh*, where everything's about me?" I said, closing the distance. "In what possible universe was *anything ever* about me—"

"Are you kidding? Are you fucking kidding?" Drew's voice broke like a fifth grader's. "It's *always* about you! Since forever! Look, here's a brand-new car for Will, 'cause we feel sorry for him! No car money in the budget for Drew, though, oh no. Drew's gotta ride with Will! In Will's new car! Which Will . . . resents! 'Cause it makes him feel small! Well . . . maybe that's cause he IS!"

The bombs were falling thick and fast. And Drew wasn't finished.

"We all walk on eggshells around you! First 'cause of your mom! Then 'cause you stopped growing! And now? Because we're all afraid you're gonna fucking DIE!"

Monica said, "Okay, that's enough."

But it wasn't enough for Drew. "Remember, Will, when you were worried you weren't in the right body? Well, guess what, buddy? You're *not*. Can't fool me. I *know* you. And to me, you're still a needy little shit in a big, baggy T-shirt, and you can't handl—"

The decision to hit Drew wasn't really a decision, any more than you *decide* to chew a tough steak you've already shoveled into your mouth.

It's not *exactly* like breathing.

It's not exactly like *deciding*, either.

Anyway, my fist was halfway there, halfway to the bridge of Drew's nose.

Magic Mike was hooting again.

And around three-quarters of the way there, three-quarters of the way to the point where Monstrosity hit Humanity, because they SO deserve each other, was when Monica got there . . .

. . . got between us.

I didn't hit her, exactly.

Not exactly.

She hooked my swinging arm with her arm, at the elbow. The force lifted her off the floor, and threw my equilibrium off-kilter . . . and we fell . . . together. . . .

I landed

more or less on her

and her head

hit the concrete

with this terrible wet and heavy sound

I'll never stop hearing, as long as I live.

Then Drew was grabbing me. Rolling me off her. And there was blood on the floor.

And Magic Mike was hooting.

And everything was untakebackable.

And nothing mattered.

Whatever old scores I'd tried to settle.

Whatever gleaming future Drew had been planning for.

Whatever perfect moment Monica had been trying to live in.

All gone.

Untakebackable.

NINETEEN

WE SAT IN blue plastic chairs in the waiting room of the ER, Drew and I. Man and monster. Waiting. To see what was left of the world.

They worried she'd been concussed, the first responders at the zoo. They worried about the blood.

Some of it was on me. Some of it was on Drew.

The EMTs had just stared at me as they loaded her into the ambulance.

I'd told them I'd fallen.

True.

Drew and I didn't talk on the ride to the hospital. Now we huddled under a chunky old tube TV hanging perilously from the drop ceiling. On the screen, one of those awful daytime court shows gibbered and snarled. It was still morning, and the place was deadish. But there was one kid, about ten, with a phone, sitting across from us, couple of rows away. He kept stealing looks. *Grow-liath, in the wild*. I'd been sighted. Great.

Finally I just came out and said what I assumed Drew was thinking, too.

"I wish it *had* been cancer."

Drew didn't answer.

On TV: Applause. Hoots.

"Should I . . . expand on that?"

"Well," said Drew finally. "If you want to compete in the Wish I Were Dead Olympics, sure, let's go."

"Okay," I said, preparing a case for my immediate elimination from the human gene pool. "So you were right: I am . . . wildly . . . insanely . . . selfish. And I thought . . . you two owed me something. I thought the world owed me something. Because I'd been . . . nice. But I hadn't been nice. Not really. I was just . . . hiding?"

Drew nodded. Then he said:

"You want to talk about hiding? I've been hiding for a year, Will. I came out and showed myself when I punched that kid in the face. Oh, and you want to know where I was hiding? I think you know already. The Plan."

I snorted. "Well, there was room in there for all of us to hide, I think."

"I don't even know," Drew said, "if I remember exactly what the Plan was supposed to do. Except keep everything the same. Keep us the same. *You're heading for Scripps! She's going to Irvine! We'll always be together!* But, man, in case this wasn't obvious? I don't know the rules, I never did. I just hoped other people would follow along. Because . . . because I'm scared shitless I'm going to lose. And lose and lose and lose." He put the heels of his hands on his temples, rubbed hard. "I've been on a crusade up my own ass for so long, I've forgotten what I was trying to do up there."

"Well, you seemed busy up there. And I was busy up mine."

"Look at us. Couple of . . . what's the word? For, like, cave explorers?"

"Spelunkers."

"Spelunkers." Drew nodded. Like that solved everything. "I guess I haven't been the best fake brother to you."

"I haven't been the best fake brother to you."

"I just felt . . . I felt like I always worked, you know. Like, really hard," said Drew. "I practiced and practiced, even if I didn't totally know what I was practicing for or why. And while I was practicing, while I was working and working and working . . . you . . . just . . . happened. You didn't even try. You just, like, arrived. And everybody went bananas. And that made me . . . that made me really, really mad."

Okay. The unmistakable odor of rubber meeting road.

"I wanted you to lose," I said.

Drew was quiet. Waiting for the rest. I gave it to him.

"Over and over—and this is before you and Monica—I just . . . I wanted you to lose. Games. Life. Just a little. I wanted you to come back to me. To where I was. So I sat in the stands and I . . . *prayed* for you to lose. So we could be closer again. I mean: how crazy is that?"

There was a moment of silence. The waiting room took a breath of alcohol-smelling air and held it.

"Well, I wanted you to stop fucking growing," Drew said. "You had to keep going, you little asshole."

"You know, I never really thought of us this way," I said, "but we *are* a couple of only children. And they're the *worst.*"

He laughed. I laughed.

"But we weren't the ones who got hurt."

Drew stopped laughing. "No. We weren't."

We stared at the blue galley doors to the ER. They didn't so much as flutter. They kept their secrets.

Back there, behind those doors, our best friend was getting sewn back together, all because she'd come between a couple of monkeys, a couple of monsters, all because she'd tried to hold together a civilization she didn't even believe in, a civilization that hadn't been particularly good to her in the first place.

Applause. On TV, somebody was guilty.

My stomach was making science-fiction noises, so I went foraging among the vending machines in the vestibule off the lobby.

I thumbed in my quarters and made a play for that Grandma's cookie. Still just hanging there, tormenting the miserable denizens of the waiting room, as it had for millennia. The corkscrew turned, the bag started to fall—and then got stuck again. Of course.

You're never going to eat that cookie, my dead mom told me. *You get that, right?*

I gave the machine a light bang with my caveman forearm, and it turned out to be not so light a bang. A nurse at the desk turned toward the sound, saw me looming there, over my kill. Looked away.

And the bag fell.

I got what I needed: that soft cookie was mine. Then I noticed, spidering the plexiglass of the machine: a tiny crack. Hairline.

This was my new world. A world that broke when I touched it.

I looked at the cookie in my hand. It was very small.

I thought about what Dr. Helman had said. About how there was no telling. How I could go on like this. And on. And on.

I held that soft, soft cookie in my huge, huge hands.

Then I left it on the waiting room table, on top of a dirty old *National Geographic*. For the first time in months, I didn't feel the least bit hungry.

When I got back, Brian and Laura were standing with Drew and a doctor in green scrubs.

"You're the other brother?" asked the doctor, whose name tag said *Bhalotra* and whose eyelids were varnished with purple sparkles. "She said you fell."

"I'm Will," I said. "I fell."

The doctor looked us over: the Addams Family, featuring Teen Lurch. I realized how the whole thing looked.

Fell. Come *on.*

"Luckily, it wasn't bad," said Dr. Bhalotra. "Just three stitches. Head wounds bleed like crazy."

"And are there any special instructions," Brian asked, "for, y'know, wound care—"

"You're a family member?"

"She's staying with us," Laura said. "She's a family friend. There was trouble at home—"

"But this apparently happened at, uh, my place of business," Brian interjected. "I work at the zoo? Will here, he interns there, and he's been under a tremendous amount of stress, physically and . . . otherwise. I don't know if you heard, we had a very upsetting incident—"

"The gorilla who died," Dr. Bhalotra said. "Yes, very sad."

Brian was *presiding*. He was being careful. He seemed to think he was filling out a police report.

I couldn't hold it in: "Can we see her?"

Dr. Bhalotra and her purple sparkles looked puzzled. "What do you mean?"

"I mean, can you take us to her room, or . . ."

"She's not admitted," said Dr. Bhalotra. "She left. I assumed she'd meet you here."

"What?" I asked, in a voice that came out louder and more demanding than Dr. Bhalotra liked, or so it seemed from the subtle half step backward she took.

"She's eighteen. She checked herself out."

She wasn't at the house, either.

Her stuff was gone. The computer room was what it had been before she'd arrived: just a pullout couch and an obsolete desktop cinder block nobody could bring themselves to responsibly discard.

Monica never traveled with more stuff than would fit in a duffel. Ghosting on us probably hadn't taken her five minutes.

Her phone was on the bed. Dead.

Monica, as she'd long predicted, had come ungridded. And that was ominous.

Drew was in the process of freaking out, pacing, turning over pillows he'd already turned over twice. "She left a note somewhere. She wouldn't bug out without leaving a note."

So we combed the place again. No note. Nothing.

Well. Not *nothing*.

On the highest shelf in the computer room, the shelf only I could see the top of, there was a thick manila envelope, unsealed. Monica's college application. On paper. In longhand. Of course.

The first thing Drew noticed was that the application wasn't to Irvine. Or even UCSD. It was to the Polytechnic Institute of Leiria in Portugal, and it was only half-finished. The deadline printed at the top was two weeks gone.

Drew just blinked.

"What," asked Drew, "the hell?"

So *that* was Monica's plan.

"And why leave it here?"

"Because she's not going." I was reading her personal statement, which was full of wavy Monican language and wavy Monican philosophy. And us. Her boys. How to build a civilization out of chaos, with a couple of lost kids you found at the end of the world. Nothing, though, about how to build a new civilization when the old one betrays you. Or just collapses into the ocean under its own weight.

"Look at this," I said, but Drew was already grabbing the Yacht keys.

"Let's go get her," he said.

We knew where she'd be, after all.

In the passenger seat, Drew's leg bounced like a fidgety grade schooler's. He rolled down the window, let the wind dry the tear I pretended not to see.

Then Drew said: "Tell me the truth. Our game. Did you let me win?"

"Only a little."

We ate a few more miles of asphalt not saying anything. Two little guys in a tin egg flying along at speeds hominids were never meant to reach. Two little guys who'd lost things, lost people. Who probably weren't done losing people.

The road seams kept time.

Chuh-TUP.

Chuh-TUP.

"She's okay, right?"

"Course she is. She's Monica." Even though I wasn't sure what those words meant now. "We just gotta find her."

We saw it from the cliff as we clawed our way down.

And we heard it before we saw it. Dull, crushing booms. Something chewing on the edge of the world.

The Sawtooth. Jesus. The lips were thick as anchor chains that day, and there were *teeth* behind them: this was the kind of boiling churn they warn you about, the kind that holds you down. The waves were coming in a steady corduroy, the offshore wind making them perk up straight. They walked in all stately, all elegant, but when they met the Sawtooth, they broke nasty, splitting every which way, left, right, no pattern—it was just *energy,* ricocheting off the jetties. I remembered, vaguely, some stray radio burble: something about a storm. A cyclone, half a world away. Waves coming our way, throwing themselves at our cliffs, heading to BoB to die.

And there, on the shore, at high tide, where those waves touched her feet, was their undertaker: Monica, knees up in her old motley wet suit, watching the water, waiting for something to rise. The Leviathan, maybe. Like it'd pop up and roar, in a monstersplaining voice, *You were right all along, Monica: people are garbage.* And then eat her. Or maybe us. Probably us?

She'd clearly been waiting for us, while just as clearly pretending that we'd ceased to exist, that the Big Wave had carried us off along with the rest of the world's disappointments.

Drew hit the sand first. "Hey! Where'd you go?"

"And here they come," yelled Monica, over the din. She didn't look back. The wind plastered down her hair, and the blue butterfly suture at her hairline looked like a barrette on a first grader. "Can't a girl have some peace?"

"Hi," I said. "I'm a monster."

"Don't," said Monica, not looking at either of us. "Don't be a boring monster. You already apologized."

"Are you okay?"

"Don't, Daughtry," she said. "Just *don't.*"

Drew waved the application.

"It's fine that you don't wanna go to Irvine. That you wanna get out. It's fine. You could've told me."

"Oh, but it would've gotten *weird*," mumbled Monica, eyes on the Sawtooth. "And I didn't want to hear you say, *It's fine,* and give me your permission."

"That's not what I was— I'm not giving perm— ARRRGGH." Drew slapped himself in the head with the manila envelope. "The point is," he said, "you're still applying *somewhere*, right? This"—he shook the envelope—"is a copy, right? You got the real one in?"

"Maybe." Monica shrugged.

"Look," said Drew, sitting heavily next to her, cratering the sand around him. "You can't sabotage yourself to spite us."

Monica just stared at him.

I tried to be funny: "Just because *we* suck doesn't mean *you* have to. You don't need to prove—"

"You think *that's* what I'm doing?" Flashing green eyes bull-whipped between us, from one boy-man to the other. "I'm proving something? To . . . *you?* Wow! I had ZERO idea that's what was up! Thank you SO much! For explaining *me*! *To me!*"

She stomped up the beach, into the BoB cave.

Drew was doing what Drew could: trying to make a new plan. "Okay. When she comes back—"

But she was already back. Carrying her primal eldest board, the one that was all wear and tear and repair, slashes over slashes, this crazy plaid of damage. Damn thing looked like it'd fallen from the sky with an alien alphabet scrawled on it. Like it was trying to tell me something, warn me. I'd been looking at that board since practically the first week we met. How had I never seen what was written there?

She walked right past us, not even a pause.

"You really shouldn't . . . Mon?"

She walked into the ocean.

She paddled out.

And I had the funniest feeling . . . that I'd seen this before . . . this particular chaos. *Déjà chaos* . . .

"Great," said Drew. "Now we've gotta babysit for an hour of ankle biters while she practices her footwork."

I watched her paddle out. I watched her pass on a couple of four-footers. I watched her pass the jetty. But I think I *knew* even before she stepped into the water.

"She's not . . . ," Drew said.

She was.

"Shit. She's not . . . she's . . . she'll kill herself." Drew clutched my arm. "Go get her."

I took a step toward the ocean, toward Monica. Then I stopped.

"Will, what the . . . *Go get her!*"

I *could* get her.

My lungs, my arms, my legs. I could get her. I could pull her right out of there.

Or I could trust her.

if I do it

And there was Monica, paddling to the wrinkle of the Sawtooth, south jetty side.

when I do it

And she was too close to the jetty. And on the other side of her: the thumb-meets-forefinger swell of the wave itself. Tearing itself to pieces every forty-five seconds. Jetty and Sawtooth. Monica between Scylla and Charybdis, like in her monster books—

it's because I know what I'm doing

Drew had given up on me. He was kicking off his shoes.

because I've figured it out

Drew was running toward the water.

you *are* the only *person in my life who'll understand*

I ran toward the water, too. In two strides—

—I got Drew in a bear hug.

And lifted.

His bare feet came off the sand, kicked the free air.

All kinds of insane curses came out of him. I didn't squeeze. I didn't need to.

I held.

I saw her paddle over the first of the three waves.

Then the second.

Then the last.

And then she was ready.

Drew fought so hard, I was shocked at how easily I could hold him to me. How natural it felt. To hold. To just hold.

Love. And restraint. That's civilization enough, probably.

Monica dug deep, hurled herself up and over the lip—

—onto the face of the Sawtooth.

It writhed. Bucked. Didn't want her there. I saw her on the knife's edge, trying to make the single decision that would either deliver her safe to shore or kill her dead.

And I thought, *I'm wrong. I blew it. I let her go. It's on me, it's on me, I've lost her*—

Drew was screaming.

And then I saw her . . . let go. Watched her knees bend. Watched her body relax into a perfect moment.

I watched her trust the water. Search her way inside.

Find the fold.

I knew she'd done it.

This was between her and the water. Always had been.

Drew was saying, *No no no no no no no Monica no no no . . .*

I held harder.

And Monica came down off the crest.

A red streak on the black curtain, a tear in the fabric of the universe, and the universe was howling for blood. The wave broke left. She vanished.

Pitted. In the tube. Inside the sea monster.

Drew went limp in my arms.

"It's okay," I told him. "It's okay."

And that's how the Big Wave came. And the world ended.

And then behind that wave...

the tip of a board

... there's always another one...

through the rocks, not so wide as a church door

... and another world.

Monica

Laughing. Crying. Upright. *Alive.* And riding it in.

Then we were all in the water, waist-deep, three people, holding each other like always. And like never before.

Because we were three different people now.

Maybe a new civilization. Maybe a new species.

We held each other for a long time, the three of us. Just to feel what it was like, being the new thing we were. Knowing the new thing wouldn't last forever, either; maybe it wouldn't even last the summer.

Knowing there were other ways we'd love each other and hurt each other that none of us had dreamed up yet.

Knowing those people, the people we'd love and hurt in the near or distant future, in those other not-yet-dreamed-up worlds—*those* new people wouldn't be the new people we were now. They'd be *entirely* different people.

And then they'd be different again. Somehow they'd find a way to hold on to each other anyway, despite the slippery shedding of skin after skin.

Because we were going to grow forever, like the Great Creatures of the Age of Fish, whether we liked it or not.

Finally Monica peeled herself away. Said something. Barely audible over the Sawtooth—

which was furious with us,
which, like all monsters,
even the ones inside, *especially* the ones inside,
is never beaten, but can be cheated, can be fooled.
What Monica said was:
"I'm hungry. Let's eat."

ACKNOWLEDGMENTS

This book didn't begin with me.

(If I have one key talent, it's showing up at the right moment, like Super Grover or penicillin. I highly recommend *showing up*. It works. Over time, it really works.)

This book began when two remarkably sharp, remarkably busy authors I know—Dustin Thomason and Michael Olson—started cracking a modern fairy tale about a runty kid who suddenly starts growing, growing, *growing*. Then didn't have time to write it.

I had time.

And then: I had help.

XL wouldn't have amounted to much had it not been for a whole Middle-earth's-worth of gracious humanoids. Here they are, the small nation who made this book with me:

Jennifer Joel, agent and sorceress. Who suggested I jump aboard in the first place. Who took an airy notion and sold it into existence. Who makes things real, then makes them better.

Erin Clarke, editor and alchemist. Who took a chance on a weird little guy with no books to his name. Who made this story deeper with every judicious, whip-smart note. Erin, Biology Boy bends the knee.

I'd like to talk about the people who taught me how to write.

The ferocious voice-in-the-darkness known as Gillian Flynn, famed author and less-famed co-paddleboat-helmsman and appreciator of the lost art of pig-imatronics, who has read me since we were cubbies, who has generously come to my aid, in the wilds of Alabama and the mean streets of Kips Bay, and who has taught me, directly and by example, how to get out of my own damned way. She is, quite simply, the bravest and best there is.

Anthony King (also a reader and noter and deepener of this book), my best and oldest friend in the world, the funniest guy in the room, and the bar I've tried fruitlessly to clear since we were fifteen in Durham, North Carolina, writing sketches about guys who think they're awesome because they listen to Chicago. [For the record? *We* listened to Billy Joel. And *didn't* think we were (all that) awesome.]

Mark Harris. I wish every aspiring writer a Mark Harris. Great wit, great understanding, great clarity, and great kindness, miraculously gathered in one human, and that miraculous human actually takes the time to tell you the one thing you need to hear, in that moment, to unclutter your mind, your soul, and your writing.

Adrienne Kennedy, oneirist and thaumaturge, who shed some of her considerable light on me. She taught me to live in a dream of my own design and not apologize.

Tom Bailey, author and educator, my first real writing teacher. Who made me feel like it was worth it, like *I* was worth it. Who plays the music beautifully, and shares it. Elizabeth Clark, Doug

Torrington, Scott Price, Rita Goebel, Isabel Samfield, Richard Marius—I don't know where I'd be without you.

Brian Raftery, whose hyperfunnysmart voice is always in my head, making connections and cracking wise, and Jennifer Williams Raftery, a gifted storyteller and storylover in her own right, who read this book when it was nothing but pages, and had brilliant suggestions that made it more-than-pages.

There are two unforgivably brilliant Davids I don't deserve, both of whom read my first few pages and gave me notes that made the opener infinitely better: David Stuart MacLean (*The Answer to the Riddle Is Me*) and David Auerbach (*Bitwise: A Life in Code*). You can walk into a bookstore and buy their unforgivable brilliance, and you absolutely should.

Thanks to artist Kelly Chilton, searcher and surfer and dreamer, for the surfing research and associated soulfulness; to Cheryl Blount, for making my wavy blatherings sound a little more real; to Michael Fisher, for straightening out my tangled basketball plays.

If you enjoy a mostly typo- and fragment- and continuity-error-free book-reading experience, you can thank my fastidious copy editors, Stephanie Engel, Artie Bennett, Amy Schroeder, and Dawn Ryan. Kelly Delaney, you shepherded this thing through the summer storms, and we all survived! *Salute!*

David Levine and Anne Heltzel both saw something in this book early on, and made things possible that would not otherwise have been possible.

Many, many thanks to the magic eyes and mage-like judgment calls of Elisabeth Gehrlein Marsham and Zack Rosenberg, who advised me on the cover art.

I wrote this book in a series of cafes and restaurants—Cafe Evolution, Roost, and Riff's Joint, mostly. Thank you for being patient with me when I turned your coffee bars into standing desks. And thanks to Daniel Bullen (*Shays' Rebellion: The True Story of America's First Resistance*), my office roomie, for finding a space that was both dog- and standing-desk-friendly.

Finally, I'd like to talk about the people without whom I would not exist, in this or any form: my extraordinary sister and brother, Holland and Robert, hearts like steam locomotives and minds to match. We share a soul that knows no distances.

To my wife, Katie, whose patience and love and strength and towering talent for life I somehow lucked into, in some cosmic lottery.

To Pat, for all the support, for opening a new town to us, and a new existence.

To my kids, Zoe and Harry. I hope they'll read this someday. I hope it'll make sense. Don't let anyone tell you you are who you are. You're *more*. You decide. And then you decide again. That's okay.

To my parents, Robbie and Roger Brown, for their boundless love, for building me up from minute one with blood and treasure, for pushing back on the things that mattered, and for giving in on the things that mattered more. For letting me be who I wanted to be, even when that didn't make a lot of sense, even when I was scribblingly inconsistent, even when I was short with you. At one point or another, I was short with everybody.

That's a little joke.

Very little.

Thanks for sticking around anyway. The road goes ever on. . . .